GUILE

GUILE

Constance Cooper

CLARION BOOKS   HOUGHTON MIFFLIN HARCOURT

BOSTON   NEW YORK

Clarion Books
3 Park Avenue
New York, New York 10016

Clarion Books is an imprint of Houghton Mifflin Harcourt Publishing Company.

www.hmhco.com
The text was set in 12-pt. Garamond Number 3.
Map illustration by Jennifer Black Reinhardt

LIBRARY OF CONGRESS CATALOGING-IN-PUBLICATION DATA
Names: Cooper, Constance.
Title: Guile / Constance Cooper.

Description: Boston ; New York : Clarion Books, Houghton Mifflin Harcourt, [2016] |
Summary: "In the Bad Bayous, guile—a power in the water that changes people and objects,
sometimes for the worse—sets Yonie Watereye, 16, on a path that puts her own life in danger
as she traces her family tree and finds a murderer"—Provided by publisher.

Identifiers: LCCN 2015020438 | ISBN 9780544451711 (hardback)

Subjects: | CYAC: Fantasy. | Families—Fiction. | Adventure and adventurers—Fiction. | BISAC:
JUVENILE FICTION / Fantasy & Magic. | JUVENILE FICTION / Action & Adventure /
General. | JUVENILE FICTION / Girls & Women.

Classification: LCC PZ7.1.C648 Gu 2016 | DDC [Fic]—dc23

LC record available at http://lccn.loc.gov/2015020438

Manufactured in the United States of America
DOC 10 9 8 7 6 5 4 3 2 1
4500578243

To my husband,
for helping make this dream
(and so many others) come true.

CHAPTER ONE

YONIE WATEREYE lived under false pretenses in a
stuffy garret overhanging the Petty Canal, in one of the
cheaper districts of Wicked Ford. Dry land never showed
there, even in the midst of summer, and the rickety buildings roosted up on wooden stilts that would have long since
rotted away if not for the water's high concentration of guile.

Yonie's garret was a narrow, slope-shouldered room
in which anyone of adult height could stand only immediately below the spine of the roof. As of late, that had
included Yonie. In one of its two vertical walls, the garret
had a stingy window that might once have been a vent. It

provided a view of the canal through gum tree leaves and, on hot days, a swampy canal odor like an army's dirty laundry. The opposite wall held another window-vent and a door that opened to a tacked-on balcony barely strong enough to hold the weight of the rain barrel at one end. Shaky steps led down through several switchbacks to the boat slips and floating trash behind the building.

Unlike most lodgings in that neighborhood, Yonie's had a collection of books. She stood them in the space where the roof angled into the floor, and in her two years there had filled almost one long side of the room. They ranged from treatises about ancient history (mainly dull, with a few useful nuggets) from the cut-price boxes at the water market, to collections of travelers' tales (mostly lurid) splurged on when business was good, to *The Unlucky Prince* (the only one of her childhood favorites to survive, since she had had it with her in the canoe that night).

Other than that, Yonie's furnishings were ordinary — a small table, two mismatched chairs, a meager stove, a bed of reed matting behind a curtain. Cheap pans and crockery stood at attention on homemade shelves, and a chamber pot crouched discreetly out of sight. The only thing a visitor might remark upon would be the profusion of pillows, and perhaps the way a shingle had been loosened and propped open, like a miniature trapdoor, in the roof above.

On that particular July afternoon, the air was humid and still, caged in by the closed door and shuttered windows.

Yonie's hair was crawling with sweat underneath her kerchief. She imagined it soaking all the way down her long brown braid, past the wooden luck-beads tied at the end, and dripping off the point like paint off a wet brush. She longed to strip off the kerchief and throw open the windows and the door to catch what breeze there was.

But instead she sat sedately in her chair, sweltering, because she had a customer. The kerchief made her look older, according to LaRue, and she needed every bit of age she could claim. Although at sixteen she'd already grown to a remarkable height, it still took the right clothing and dim lighting and her most imperious High Town accent for her to successfully impersonate a grown woman.

Even then she might not pass as a pearly. Not all pearlies had really been pearl divers, true, but most were old. Normally it took a lifetime of soaking in swamp water to acquire that much guile. But there were exceptions, and most of her customers came to her by referral, already assured of her competence. Certainly the man across the table was showing her due respect.

He'd given his name as Andry Gerard from Damnable Swamp, an outlying fishing village Yonie had heard of but never needed to visit. Gerard had an angular, stubbled face and hunched shoulders under his faded shirt. He kept his fingers pinched tight around the drawstring of a canvas carry-bag.

"It came to me in a fish," he said. His eyes flicked away

from hers as he set the bag down on the table. "A Fish o' Fate, ma'am — you know?"

"Indeed?" Around Wicked Ford, finding an odd object inside a fish's belly was normally no fairy-tale event. As in most parts of the Bad Bayous, cemeteries flooded often. Finds ranged from the prosaic (turtle-shell buttons, clay bottle stoppers) to the faintly interesting (old pennies, keys) to the downright disgusting (finger bones, yellowed human teeth). The local fish weren't fussy.

There were always stories, of course, about fish who swallowed richer fare — rings for the finger or the ear, gold coins, ivory combs, jeweled silver belt buckles. These Fish of Fate then sacrificed their treasure to the gutting knife of a deserving fisherman or on the dinner plate of a poor widow. Yonie enjoyed such tales, although LaRue always pointed out that firsthand accounts were rarer than dry feet in Deadfish Marsh.

"It must have been quite a large fish, sir," she said in what she hoped was a cool, professional voice. "Did you catch it yourself?"

"Aye, ma'am."

Yonie tried not to stare too obviously at the carry-bag on the table. It was heavy canvas, too stiff to reveal the shape of its contents, with a little blue-glass wily charm at the end of the drawstring. Yonie's father had had one like it, to keep his lunch dry when he took the fishing boat out on rainy days.

Yonie hated handling business by herself, but LaRue had gone out hunting, and there was no knowing when she'd be back. It was too bad — Yonie felt much more confident with her there, even though LaRue couldn't take part in the conversation. Also, LaRue had promised to bring her something, and Yonie hadn't eaten since dinner last night.

"Have you had a Seeing done before, sir? No? Well, I charge one gallon to examine an object. I can tell you if it's guileful, and in most cases I can determine the nature of its wiles. Or, er, half a gallon for an especially interesting object," she backpedaled, seeing Gerard's stricken look. "I also take payment in kind. A chicken, for instance, or a string of trout."

"Got a couple o' sand crabs we been feeding up on the kitchen scraps. My wife'll cook 'em up for you if she's feeling better. She's been 'ere nine years now, but she still knows 'er Northern spices."

Yonie's stomach scraped loudly. She moved her chair to cover the noise.

Gerard pulled the bag open and lifted out a bulky item shrouded in a cloth. He flipped back the covering to reveal the ugliest ornament Yonie had ever seen. Two black and white steer horns had been varnished and inset in a platform of polished bone. They curved up and together to form a steep arch not found on any cattle skull in nature. Suspended from their points by corroded chains was a disc of tarnished brassy metal the size of a dinner plate, indented in a spiral pattern like the cinnamon buns they sold at the Blackmire Inn.

"I'll need some time alone to look at this, M'sir Gerard. Could I ask you to return at, say, the eighth hour tonight?" LaRue should be back by then. She would have to be.

Gerard looked up in alarm. "Eighth? I was 'oping for sooner, ma'am." His big callused hands kneaded the edge of the carry-bag. "It's my wife, see. When I brought this 'ome today, I thought she'd be pleased, but instead she took all over queer."

"She's not ill, is she?"

"Nay, ma'am, not ill, but not 'appy with me, either, seems like. Well, never you mind. I'm going 'ome to 'er now, but I'll be back tonight with those sand crabs, and 'oping you can tell me what this thing's about."

Yonie watched out the window as Gerard unhitched his boat at the canal side below and rowed hastily away. Most pearlies would have done the Seeing while the customer watched, or at least while he waited, but she could not offer that service. Yonie frowned, then turned and lifted the brown jug off the shelf. LaRue would need water for the Seeing.

Skirting the rain barrel on the balcony, Yonie headed down the stairs. The canal inlet that served as a docking area between her building and the one behind was stagnant with floating green scum and, like every body of water in the Bad Bayous, thick with guile.

Some argued that Wicked Ford proper was less wily than its outlying areas, but these were mostly city innkeepers eager for trade. The truth was that guile was widespread throughout the whole region that the High Town folk called the Delta and the villagers called the Devil's Foot.

In the far north, the rushing waters of the River Stride were pure. Even after they joined with the dubious River Skulk, which trickled from the Shunned Lands, the waters upstream of the Delta contained only trace amounts of guile. But where the Skulk started to slow and wander, where it widened and divided into the maze of marshes and shallow passages known as the Bad Bayous, the water was clotted with it.

The dock behind Yonie's building reared high out of the water, its legs dark with crackly dead algae. Yonie gathered up her skirt with her free hand and stepped down into the bow of the *Dragonfly*. From inside her canoe, she leaned down to scoop up the greenest, murkiest water she could find.

Back in her attic room, Yonie stood Gerard's knickknack in a dented tin dish. The movement set the round of brass swinging between the horns, and now she saw that it was a sort of gong, like the one outside the Palace of Justice, except small and ugly. Carefully she poured the cloudy water around its base.

By the time LaRue came in, Yonie had already shut the door and fastened the mosquito cloths over the windows.

She had lit a candle and was sitting at the table paging through *Everyday Life in the Old Delta*. It was a fat, water-stained volume with only a few torn-out pages, and since those were in the chapter about hats, this had not been a serious inconvenience.

LaRue nosed through under the loose shingle and dropped lightly to the top of the shelf. It always amazed Yonie that the cat could fit through such a small space, but her body was far smaller than her fur implied. LaRue was carrying something brown and furry in her mouth, which she set down on a plate as elegantly as a waitress in a Grand Canal café.

"Oh, LaRue, not another rat?"

"Not at all, my dear — it's a bat! My first. I know you asked for a bird, but this seemed much the same."

Yonie eyed the bony, folded shape lying limp on the plate. "Thank you, LaRue. It was very kind."

LaRue swept her fluffy tail around herself like a full orange skirt. "Every bit of it's for you, Yonie. I've already eaten."

"Well, I hope you saved room for more. A man's coming back later with a sand crab for each of us. He left us this thing to do a Seeing on — isn't it funny? He said he found it in a fish he caught."

LaRue sprang up to the tabletop and settled down to study the gong, ginger fur lapping around her like petticoats.

"Hmf. I must say I'm skeptical. To fit that thing in its

belly, a fish would have to be as big around as a hunting dog. Did this man boast about his catch, or even hold up his hands to show the length?"

"Er — no."

"That doesn't sound like any fisherman I've known."

Yonie stared at the varnished horns and the dangling dish of brass. "But people do find treasures in fish sometimes, don't they? There's talk about that brooch of M'dam Orley's —"

"My dear sweet Yonie, what an innocent you are! M'dam Orley's husband may need to believe she got that from a fish, but you do not."

"So M'sir Gerard was lying?"

"Oh, I doubt he expected you to really believe that story. It was a courtesy, no more. Doubtless this is stolen goods, or grave plunder, or something else unsavory, and this Gerard needs to know its properties before he sells it."

LaRue leapt down into Yonie's lap. "Now, now, don't wrinkle up your face like that. If he's honest enough to pay us, that's all I care about. Even thieves and fences sometimes need a Seeing done." She stroked Yonie's arm with one furry cheek. "I'm sure you did a fine job. He wouldn't have left his treasure here, such as it is, if he didn't think you were wily. Word is getting round. Soon we'll have customers coming in from all over the Delta. We'll have chicken and cream and silk pillows."

"I just hate lying to them."

"I know you do, but what choice do we have? I can't exactly set up in business for myself. Every fool in the Bayous would be after me with a hatchet."

Guileful animals, or slybeasts as they were called, were far from common even in the Delta. There were tales of water-dwelling creatures that, upon attaining a sufficient age, gained unusual abilities: alligators that could counterfeit a floating log down to the leafy twigs sprouting from its back, and swamp turtles that could stay underwater for days at a time, withdraw into an invulnerable rock-hard shell, or bite clean through a steel-sheathed oar. But as with humans, it normally took prolonged exposure to the water before the body accumulated a noticeable amount of guile. Animals with shorter lifespans seldom became cunning — and if they did, they risked extermination unless they could keep it to themselves.

Even pearlies — less politely known as slyfolk — were not exactly popular. Veteran divers or canal dredgers who developed webs between their fingers and toes tended to wear shoes and keep their hands closed in public to avoid cold looks. Those who grew gills or scales wore high collars and avoided daylight when they could. Members of uppercrust society, who generally received their guile concentrated in shellfish or caviar, ignored such differences with punctilious silence. Even folk who showed no outward signs of wiliness, but possessed a sensitivity to guile, didn't talk about their skills in polite society.

LaRue put her paws up on Yonie's shoulder. "Don't fret, love. So long as the work gets done, our customers have nothing to complain about."

The queenly orange cat settled herself on the table before the dish of water, nose almost touching the surface, and peered at the swirls of silt and grains of swamp life that stirred under her breath. She sat sphinx-like long after Yonie had returned to her book, while the candle burned down and insects bumped angrily against the window-cloths.

"It has wiles and to spare," LaRue said finally, rising and stretching each leg in turn. "It may not have come from a fish, but it's been steeping in swamp juice for years over years. I couldn't quite see the direction of its guile, but I know now what it is. It's a boat-gong."

"Yes, I just found that out myself." Yonie held up her book. "It says people in those times kept bells or gongs on the sterns of their boats to use on foggy days, to keep other boats at a distance so they could get home safe."

"How clever of you, Yonie. I'm afraid I didn't find out much more. All I got from it was a lonely feeling, as if it's brooding about something."

Yonie stared at the gong. She reached forward to touch it, and LaRue's paw lashed out, swatting her hand away.

"You used claws!" Yonie sucked on her scratches indignantly.

"I do apologize." LaRue sounded shaken. "But I can't help my reflexes. From what little I've learned, we would be wise not to strike this gong without knowing more about it. In fact, I'd like you to wrap it back up. That's right, get it good and muffled. Even a mosquito hitting it might be enough to stir it. I'll be glad to see it returned to M'sir Gerard. When did he say he'd be back?"

Yonie glanced at the window-cloth, which no longer glowed with even the embers of sunset light. "Hours ago." She felt a ripple of unease, like the trace a water moccasin might leave in a still pond.

CHAPTER TWO

THERE ISN'T much meat on a bat. Yonie's stomach gurgled and growled the next morning as she untied the *Dragonfly* and threaded her way through the water-alley out into the open canal.

The air was already steamy, and the water was dark jade under the shade of the gum trees that lined the sides of the Petty. Traffic slid past: rowboats frog-kicking along, slim canoes darting and weaving, low-riding water carriers and wood barges nudging in to the banks.

"I don't think well of this man for breaking his appointment," LaRue grumbled from her usual perch atop the bow seat. "I wish there were some easier way of getting this unsightly relic off our hands."

"You don't have to come along, LaRue."

The cat looked regretfully upward into the tree branches, the aerial roadways to her best hunting grounds. Then she glanced down at the ugly swaddled lump on the canoe bottom below her.

"I'd better come, child. I don't trust that gong."

Yonie sent the *Dragonfly* down the canal with an expert twist of her paddle. Splashes of sunlight fell onto her wiry shoulders as she pulled the canoe under tangles of branches and flowering vines. The *Dragonfly* had been a gift from her father when she was barely big enough to paddle it. It was quite old, and its inkwood sides had darkened over the years to a satiny black.

"LaRue," Yonie said softly, "we're coming up on the Ford."

"Oh, yes — thank you." LaRue stepped down to the bottom of the canoe, avoiding the trickle of bilge, and nosed her way behind Yonie's skirt until she was concealed from view. They would have to slow to cross the Ford, and plenty of people thought it was funny to throw water on a cat.

As the water got shallower, the boat traffic thinned. A sheet of sky-mirroring water spread out, stitched down the middle with a straggling line of wagons, horsemen, and travelers on foot. Harness jangled and drivers sang. Walkers, spattered by wheels or hooves, cursed and told passing carts to go to Under Town.

Barefoot peddlers of cool drinks, sugared pastries, and cheap handicrafts flocked around the richer carriages as they slowed to cross the water. The spicy smells of barbecue and skewered crawfish drifted from the roadside booths on the far shore.

The water in the Ford reached barely higher than a knee-boot or a horse's hock. Yet the slow, clumsy ferries did a brisk business. Many foreigners were too wary of swamp-guile to wet their feet in bayou water, or even to risk a splash from a carriage wheel.

Yonie sent the *Dragonfly* skimming neatly between a brewer's cart and a mail coach. She dug in her paddle and soon had left the gabble of the Ford behind.

The Damnables lay well within the Circle of Commerce, that area of the Delta in which a person could travel to the city and return home the same day. In less than an hour, with only two stops for directions, Yonie had reached Damnable Swamp.

The village was a scattering of stilt-houses, gathered under the shade of looming cypresses whose trunks flared in wooden folds. The houses were no more than huts with wraparound porches, much like the one where Yonie and LaRue had grown up. Children scooted around the knobs of cypress knees in coracles, and old folks mended nets under porch awnings.

"Andry Gerard? You're not the first one to wonder where 'e's got to," said one sun-weathered old woman.

Yonie's stomach felt hollow, and not just from the woman's ominous tone. She had been looking forward to the sand crabs Gerard had promised her.

"Don't know where 'e is exactly, but I'll tell you one thing," the woman said dourly. "'E's tracking 'is wife. She left yesterday, up and left 'im with a four-year-old to look after! I always told 'im, you never can trust a foreigner, but would 'e listen? 'E would not."

The old woman aimed her brown twig of a finger across the inlet. "I reckon you should speak with 'is sister. Michelle Fontaine. She's got charge of 'is boy, poor little lamb."

Gerard's sister was a tall, grave woman with a current of gray running through her dark hair. She gave Yonie tea on the shaded balcony of her house, and even set down fresh rainwater for LaRue.

From inside the house came the stubborn sobbing of a small child. "I'm 'oping 'e'll settle down and take a nap. I've told 'im 'is folks'll be back soon, but I don't know if 'e believed me. Don't know if I believe it myself."

Fontaine shook her head slowly. "I was the last one to see 'er, you know. She wasn't 'erself, anyone could tell. Katja's got a good 'ead on 'er shoulders, and she wouldn't just leave like that without a good reason. 'I must to go 'ome,' she kept saying in that sweet little voice of 'ers, like something terrible would 'appen if she didn't. She didn't 'ave supplies in the boat, no water, nothing. Barely took the time to drop 'er child off 'ere. I just can't understand it. She's told me time and again, there was nothing left for 'er in the North after the war."

Yonie lifted the gong out of the canoe onto the balcony and flipped back the cloth, holding the dished metal so it couldn't ring. "Did your brother ever show you this?"

"Nay. But I knew 'e must 'ave 'ad something like. Yesterday afternoon I 'eard a sound ringing out over the water, like what this ought to make." She started to flick it with her fingernail, but Yonie caught her hand.

"Sorry, ma'am, but I think you'd best not." Yonie could feel her voice slipping into the same groove as Fontaine's, the musical, softly slurred bayou speech she had always used with her father. "I don't know what might 'appen. Your brother brought it to me for a Seeing, and I found out it's a very cunning thing."

"Are you a pearly, then? And you so young?"

Yonie nodded uncomfortably. "Can you tell me what it sounded like? 'Ow did it make you feel?"

Gerard's sister twisted her hands in her lap. "It was nothing but lovely," she said. "Melancholy, though. Made me glad to be 'ere in my own good 'ome, where I was born and raised."

"But your sister-in-law, Katja—she grew up in the North?"

The other woman's hands grew still. "Up in Hark, in the Icejaws." She looked down at the gong as if it were a cottonmouth that had reared up in her path. "I tried to stop 'er," she said. "But it was like she didn't 'ear me at all. It was this gong, wasn't it? The sound of it's beguiled 'er, and it's making 'er go 'ome."

A few minutes later, Yonie and LaRue were alone again, drifting among reeds near the empty cottage Fontaine had pointed out as the Gerards'. The wrapped gong lay in the bottom of the canoe, surrounded by green bilge water. Unsurprisingly, Gerard's sister had not wanted it in her home.

"That poor family," Yonie burst out. "We can't just leave the gong on their doorstep. It's a public danger! I say we drop it in the Hellbog, and good riddance." She picked up the dipper and began absently to bail.

"Wait." LaRue stopped her. "The thing's been stewing in that water all day. Let's see what more I can see." The cat gazed down into the threads and specks of green that floated around the bundle.

"I think I understand now," she said at last. "This gong, as we know, was designed to get people safely home. It must consider that an obligation."

Yonie had never been able to find any useful books about guile. Apparently it was not considered a fit subject for respectable research. Even historical volumes on the ancient Northern nations of C'thova and Gry (now known as the Shunned Lands) did not discuss guile. Authors marveled at the wondrous "chiridou" artifacts those ancients had created, while they scrupulously ignored the trouble-some guile that seeped down from the headwaters of the River Skulk.

The writings about guile that did exist were usually designed to appeal to prurient interests, and were scooped up quickly by private collectors. Yonie had tried reading *The Wily Bedknob,* but after three pages had thrown it into the Petty Canal.

From sheer personal experience, though, most bayou residents knew the main characteristic of guile: it liked to work.

"But, LaRue, the North isn't that poor woman's home anymore. Why would the gong send her there?"

"I'm not saying it did right, but I think it's trying to help. Give a thing enough guile, and there's no telling what lengths it'll go to to do its job. That's why we get expert swimmers with gills or canoes that sometimes balk at cross-ing the Ford because they hate to scrape their bottom." She gave the *Dragonfly* a reproving glance.

Or pet cats, thought Yonie, *who learn to speak so they can be better companions for lonely little girls.*

"But of course you're right, dear, there's more to it than that." LaRue gave a pink-tongued yawn. "What else does guile do, besides try to work?"

"It lets wily things share their thoughts, a little bit. That's how you do Seeings."

"Yes. Well, sweet, I was not quite right before, when

I said the gong was lonely. It's homesick. It wants very badly to go home, and evidently its home is the first place it remembers. And it's sharing that thought rather strongly indeed."

"Then we'll take it home!" Yonie gestured with the dipper, accidentally flinging drops of water onto LaRue. "That might even break the beguilement on M'dam Gerard! We can figure out where the gong came from and put it back."

The cat flicked droplets off her ears. "That's one way to get rid of the wretched thing," she conceded. "We can inquire with M'dam Fontaine, I suppose. And I do believe, with all the trouble we've gone to already, she might consider paying us."

The sand crabs were still in their cage on the porch of the Gerards' deserted home. Yonie took them back over to Michelle Fontaine, who steamed them and served them with some leftover marsh-rice. Yonie remembered her own mother preparing the same dish, telling her that no grand High Town household served anything better.

"Your brother never told me where 'e found the gong. Well, actually, 'e said 'e found it in a fish." Yonie spread her hands.

Fontaine laughed sharply. "'E would. Andry's a good enough fisherman, but whenever the water gets low, 'e just can't keep away from the ruins. 'E's always 'oping to strike it rich."

The trade in ancient artifacts was widespread around Wicked Ford. Most visitors returned home with at least one dinner plate or necklace in the ancient style, some even bearing nicks or dents testifying to their antiquity. These had generally been crafted by artisans in the Cloudy Canal manufactories a few days earlier and purchased at the water market or the stands at Road-end.

Genuine relics fetched a higher price but came with risks, which was why professional relic hunters typically consulted a pearly about their finds. Amateurs like Andry Gerard, however, were often ill-prepared for the wiles an object might carry.

Yonie fingered the end of her braid, clicking her thumbnail against the wooden bobbles. "Do you 'ave any idea where 'e's been looking lately?"

"I'd say Vile Basin. I've seen 'im coming 'ome with 'is boat all streaked in white mud." Fontaine gave Yonie a sober look. "M'dam Watereye — if you can bring them 'ome safe, I'll never forget it."

Yonie pressed the other woman's hand in hers. "I'll do everything I can," she promised.

CHAPTER THREE

VILE BASIN was a fetid body of water blanketed in dense green slime. Its edges merged gradually into pale, gluey mud, and only the most sluggish of currents eddied through the reeds. Mosquitoes snarled and droned over the water.

Yonie guided the canoe around decomposing logs and through stands of swamp plants that lured their insect prey with the odor of rotting meat. She was glad to have LaRue along. In spots like these, you never could tell how wily the plants might be, and human skeletons had been found stuck to the sundews.

"Look, LaRue! I'm sure this mud's been churned up by someone's feet."

The *Dragonfly* slid into the shade of great, gnarled ink-trees shaggy with moss. Roots and damp earth rose up until Yonie was paddling through a narrow sunken channel.

In the gloom under the trees, LaRue's pupils were enormous. "Yonie, look! Up ahead."

The boulder jutting into the waterway was curiously angular. As Yonie drew level with it, she saw that it was ancient masonry, the top of an archway leading into wet darkness. A heavy stone door-slab, bearing the very fresh marks of a crowbar, leaned against hairy tree roots nearby.

"You found it, LaRue!"

"Not so loud, dear. Give respect. This may well be a tomb."

The entrance was mostly submerged, with barely a head's height of clearance above the water. Yonie ran her hand along the layers of blackened grime that striped the doorway's arch. Under the waterline, strings of soft algae trailed from the stone.

"This must be below water most of the time." Yonie laid down her paddle. "Are there alligators around, LaRue?"

The cat communed briefly with the channel. "None close enough to concern us."

Yonie slipped off her skirt and blouse, leaving on her undervest and drawers to protect her from leeches, and let herself down into the tepid, waist-high water. With slow-motion steps, she walked over squashy mud and ducked to pass under the stone arch.

Suddenly she was treading water, spitting swamp scum out of her mouth. "I'm fine," she called, splashing back to the canoe. "The bottom drops away under the arch."

"Then it was only recently opened. Otherwise the floor would be silted up to the level of the channel bottom." LaRue switched her tail. "It's highly likely this is the right place. M'dam Fontaine should be able to find it with no trouble."

"What do you mean? She won't need to come out here at all after I put the boat-gong back."

"Yonie, you're not thinking of going in there? You've done more than enough for these people already."

"But she can't do it. She's got that little boy to look after. And what about M'dam Gerard? She's beguiled, and she's all alone!"

LaRue sniffed. "Honestly, my dear, I never will understand humans. The lengths you'll go to for someone who's not even family! And from what I've seen, you're worse than most."

"It'll be easy for me. I'm a good swimmer — you saw to that." Yonie waved a wet hand at the stone doorway. "And don't you want to know what's inside?"

"Curiosity. Now that's something I do understand." LaRue began to wash, as she always did when she was pleased. "Huh! Most children your age wouldn't dare go into a place like that."

"I'm sixteen," Yonie said, somewhat irked. "Hardly a child."

"Of course, dear. All right, you may put the gong back yourself, if you're not afraid to go in alone."

Yonie eyed the opening. Now that she thought about it, it was obvious that LaRue couldn't go in with her. "It should be safe, shouldn't it?"

"I would think so. That stonework looks sturdy enough that nothing short of an earthquake could shake it loose. As for the snakes — don't bother them, and they won't bother you."

Yonie was silent a moment. "LaRue, can you light my way?"

"Let me see what I can do." The small cat raised her head alertly. In the shadow of the doorway, a bubble wavered upward, burped through the surface of the water, and blossomed into a blue glow that lasted several seconds. "Well, there's not much mud inside, but there should be enough swamp gas for light, if we're sparing."

Calling the bluefire was not common in the city, where pearlies had long since squeezed every sizable pocket of gas from the mud. Seeing LaRue summon light reminded Yonie of earlier days, sneaking out past her parents' room late at night, paddling with LaRue out behind Evil Island so the cat could practice her skills. Yonie had always wondered if, on that last night, her parents had had time to see that she was gone.

Yonie picked up the gong and tied the corners of its wrapping around her waist. More gingerly than before, she waded toward the archway and sank down inside until she was swimming in place.

The air was cooler under the stone ceiling, and though the water around her kicking legs was lukewarm, it was free of the streamers of pondweed that lined the channel. The dank scent of moss and dead leaves faded as she swam along the passage, leaving only the sterile smell of wet stone.

The gong was heavy, and the sweat on Yonie's face began to turn clammy.

"Light please, LaRue!" Yonie's voice bounced hollowly between the roof and the surface of the water. She could hear the sound spread out into a larger space ahead. A moment later, she felt a tickle as a bubble of swamp gas swept by her. It exploded into a soft blue flare.

The chamber ahead was not much larger than the garret she shared with LaRue. Nothing showed above the water except for a curious structure in the center of the space.

"I'm in a room," she called back down the passage in a low voice. "There's something in the middle — kind of like a gondola, but with a closed top." She swam forward until her hands rested on smooth stone.

"LaRue, I think I'm in a burial chamber, and this is a coffin boat. I've read about them — the ancients thought they could carry the soul to the next world."

Yonie backed away, treading water again. Every tiny

splash she made was magnified in the half-drowned room. "Now I just have to figure out where to put the gong."

Another swamp bubble flamed blue, and Yonie spotted a rectangular indentation on the coffin boat's stern, just where her history book had said these gongs belonged. She worked her way around the carved stone side until she reached the place.

Awkwardly, she felt for the knots that tied the gong around her waist. She couldn't manage them one-handed, and it would be extremely difficult to do while treading water. And what if she dropped the gong? At the thought of diving blind into the black water under her feet, Yonie found herself clambering up to crouch on the coffin lid.

"Sorry, I don't mean any disrespect," she whispered. Her wet braid lay like a dead eel against her neck. Under her bare feet, the stone boat was almost as warm as the swamp water.

Yonie worked the gong out of its wrapping and slid it along the stone deck of the burial ship. It fitted neatly into the hollow in the stonework.

Yonie took a deep breath. She could go back out in the daylight now, climb up into her canoe, and think about how brave she'd been. She didn't have to kneel here anymore, in a lightless room right above the dead body of an ancient whose coffin boat might or might not have helped him into the next life.

"Yonie! Are you all right?" Another swamplight burst

from the water behind her with a moist gurgle. Startled, Yonie swung her head around. Her braid whipped out, and the beads at the end clanged into the gong.

At first it was just an insignificant, tinny sound. But it deepened into a dolorous note that filled the chamber. It was pure and sad, like a distant steamboat whistle on a foggy night. Yonie fumbled for the gong and held the rim tight to damp the vibration, but even after the metal lay dead in her hands, the sound kept ringing in her head.

Yonie whimpered. Not since her parents' death had she felt so out of place and alone. She had failed. The gong was still yearning for its home.

CHAPTER FOUR

THEY HAD left Vile Basin behind them hours before, but Yonie was still digging in her paddle until her muscles burned. Her kerchief was matted with sweat, and her ankle was purpling where she had bashed it against the stone coffin in the dark. It hadn't been easy swimming out of there with a heavy weight in one hand, but she wasn't about to leave the gong. Not when she could still hear its somber cry.

"There could be dozens of those crypts back there," LaRue growled. She shook her head as if her ears were hurting. "Who knows how many your M'sir Gerard plundered? I say we leave the gong on his doorstep after all."

"We'll come back and do that, LaRue, right after we get home."

"Yes, of course, we must get home."

The canoe skimmed over the water, its bow pointed away from the city, headed toward the shifty, weed-choked maze of the Sloughs — the place where both Yonie and LaRue had been born.

The gong note sang in the dusty corners of Yonie's mind. It sang about a cottage on the water, with the warm sunset light draped over its log sides and thatched reed roof. Papa's fishing boat and Mama's green canoe rested at the dock, and the smell of bubbling chowder drifted out the open door. Mama was singing one of the fancy trilling songs that none of the other mothers knew, one that she had learned back in the Academy when she was studying to be a Proper Young Lady. Papa was sitting on the balcony watching Yonie paddle laboriously across the cove and back, with her kitten curled up like an extra-fuzzy apricot on the bow seat of the *Dragonfly*.

Yonie yanked the canoe through narrow shaded waterways and open pools where crowds of water lilies watched the sky. Her swamp-slimed clothing had dried now and was crunchy to the touch. The ringing of the gong felt so loud and real, Yonie was surprised it didn't set the moss swaying overhead.

But she was almost home. Off to the left was the marsh where she and LaRue had hunted yellow frogs and where the cat had put her life into Yonie's hands with her first guileful word. Down that way was the stand of cypress where she could almost always elude her taunting cousins.

The *Dragonfly* shot out of the Bitterway, a long tunnel columned with sweet gum trees. For the first time in two years, Yonie saw what was left of the cottage that had been home. Fire-blackened stumps of pilings protruded from the water, and the naked stone chimney pointed toward the sky. The water meadow behind showed only remnants of the old kitchen garden—a hint of raised beds and fallen fences.

They floated between the old dock posts, looking down through tea-colored water. The charred beams were furred with algae now, and minnows swam over and around them.

Yonie slammed the water with her paddle, frightening away the fish. "This gong still won't leave me alone! What does it want, LaRue? This is the closest to home I can get! I don't have any memories earlier than this!" She flung the paddle down into the canoe and hunched over, squeezing her eyes shut and covering her ears with her hands.

"I still hear it too." The canoe shifted as the cat got to her feet. "But that's only to be expected. I should have known, my dear, I should have known. This is not the earliest place that I recall."

Through the noise in her head, Yonie dimly wondered what she meant. LaRue had always been with her. Purring on her lap by the hearth on damp winter evenings, listening intently to every word her parents said. Stalking over her quilt-draped body in the middle of the night. Riding in her canoe as she went exploring, out to the hidden places where the cat could dare her words and wiles.

Yonie barely heard the splash over the sound of the gong. By the time she saw LaRue's wet head bobbing in the water, the cat was already a half dozen canoe lengths away.

"LaRue, what are you *doing?*" She had never seen LaRue swim except for the few times Yonie had overturned the *Dragonfly*. Although LaRue had forced Yonie to practice until she could swim better than any of her cousins, the cat herself had always refused to go in the water. She said that she had already come as close to drowning as she ever wanted to —

Yonie's eyes widened. "No, LaRue!" she screamed. "Come back!"

The canoe's side crashed against a dock post as Yonie slewed it around. She knew where the cat was headed.

The gong had forced Yonie back to the earliest place she remembered. But LaRue's first memory was not of their cottage. It was of the bottom of the Bitterway, and the inside of a sack.

Yonie's mother had never failed to get teary when she told the story. "Simply barbaric, my dear, to dispose of a whole litter that way! Our neighbor might not have wanted those kittens, but I did. I only wish I'd gotten there in time to save them all." Yonie had always felt sure that it was this near drowning that had concentrated so much guile in LaRue's tiny kitten body.

LaRue's head was no longer showing above the water. Yonie stabbed with her paddle, urging the canoe forward. She cast about wildly, scraping lily pads off the surface.

The gong still wailed in her head, driving her back toward the ruins of the cottage. Clearly it was not satisfied with returning her to her home — it wanted to keep her there.

And LaRue? Would the gong keep the cat below the water, even if she found the rotted scraps of that long-ago sack?

A cry of anguish tore out of Yonie's throat. She glared at the gong where it lay gleaming in the bilge, still droning its forlorn song. "Sink you! *Drown* you! I'll send you to Under Town, you flooding thing!"

LaRue would never have permitted her to use such language. But that didn't matter now.

The canoe wobbled precariously as Yonie dragged the gong toward her. She heaved it up onto the stern of the canoe and grasped the horns to tip it over the side.

Then she halted.

The gong was radiating contentment.

It was back on the stern of a boat, Yonie realized, right where it belonged. And the homesickness that had maddened it was completely gone.

The ringing in Yonie's head had stopped. All she heard was the buzz and clack of insects, the plop of diving frogs, and the soft breathing of wind through cypress branches.

That, and the sudden sputter and mewling of an enraged, swimming cat.

Yonie had dried LaRue off as best she could with her blouse and skirt, but the cat's tail still looked skeletal with the fur plastered down.

"That's quite enough, Yonie! Now for goodness' sake, cover yourself. This is a public waterway."

Yonie rebuttoned her blouse obediently, still grinning with relief.

The cat hopped onto Yonie's lap and examined the boat-gong. "Hmm. Well, now we know — this gong's first home was on a real, working boat. Sitting idle in a tomb must have been agony for it. Perhaps it belonged to whatever poor soul was buried there."

"That makes sense," Yonie said. "It's too ugly to have been designed as a funeral ornament."

"You'd be surprised what some people like. I'm sure M'sir Gerard will have no trouble selling it when he and his wife get back."

Warily, Yonie touched the gong with one hand, the other holding the tail of her braid in a tight grip. "Can he sell it, though? Isn't it still dangerous?"

The cat stared into the rapidly drying pool of water

around the gong's base. "I'll need more water to be sure, but I'm hoping that my experience made an impression on it through the guile-link. It should understand now that not everyone's first place-memory is of their home." The cat shuddered. "Certainly not mine."

"I'm just glad the gong feels at home on the *Dragonfly*. Its original boat is probably mud by now."

Yonie glanced back at the ruins of the cottage. The sun was low enough to send rosy bars of light across the scorched pilings. "Come on, LaRue. Let's go home."

Now home meant the city: that glorious tangle of boardwalks and bridges and stinking canals and flowery avenues. Thousands of faces, thousands of voices calling out in a dozen accents or in foreign tongues, to the tune of the riverboats' whistles day and night. Wicked Ford, where her snug garret and her soft mattress were waiting for her . . .

"We'll never make it back before dark," LaRue said. "And you're exhausted. The last thing you need is to spend the night bumping around lost."

Yonie flexed her shoulders and winced. LaRue was right —trying to find her way back through miles of dark, mazy swamp would not be wise. However, it sounded less night-marish than imposing on her nearby relatives.

"Nobody wants me here, LaRue. They all told me to stay in the city and not come back."

"My poor little kitten, they're your family. They have to at least let you spend the night."

Yonie gazed at LaRue a moment. The cat was licking the water out of her tail with a weary motion quite unlike her usual brisk comb strokes.

"All right. I'll try Aunt Elisa."

Yonie's family, like many in the Delta, had been pared down by an influenza epidemic that had ripped through the area when Yonie was too young to remember. But the family had started out large enough that there were still quite a few members around, and some even lived close by. Aunt Elisa, the widow of Papa's brother Stephan, had been fond of Yonie at one time, she was sure. The same could not be said for her sons, who were a few years older than their cousin Yonie. With a little luck, they would have moved out of the house by now.

The water lanes had changed in the last two years, and by the time Yonie had backed out of several scum-clogged dead ends, it was full night with only moonlight and LaRue's occasional dollop of bluefire to steer by.

Yonie liked to think she had grown up with less fear of the dark than most bayou children. Due to her mother's influence, Papa had restricted his storytelling to the more humorous and cheerful of the traditional tales, and though her cousins had tried hard to make up the difference, only a few of their scare stories had made a big impression.

However, with LaRue huddled small and silent, and her clothing clammy against her skin, Yonie couldn't help recalling some eerie characters. There were the come-kiss-mes who would lead you astray with sweet voices. There was M'sir Teeth. There was Jenny Dangle, a little girl who liked to swing from a tree branch by her knees, with her long green hair hanging down—and woe betide the traveler who felt her hair brush against his face. (This tale was especially effective in areas with lots of trailing moss.)

Most of Yonie's nightmares, though, had involved the Apple Sharer, which could look like anyone—*anyone at all*. It would show you an apple and offer you half, if only you would lend it your knife. What happened then was almost too gruesome to describe, though the cousins had done their best.

When Yonie finally spotted the outline of Aunt Elisa's cottage with lamplight warming the windows, she actually felt relieved.

The house looked like any other Slough dwelling, but the carvings Cousin Gilbert had chiseled into the dock pilings were unmistakable. Yonie could see the remains of a skunk with her own face on it (so recognizable that Yonie had tried to whittle it off one night when the family was asleep). And there was the bee tree her cousins Gage and Gustave had dared her to climb, with disastrous consequences, and the rock like a giant fist in the water where Gregory had once stranded Yonie, terrorizing her with false alligator sightings.

The *Dragonfly* bumped against the dock.

"Aunt Elisa?" Yonie's voice echoed over the water.

The lantern bobbed in the window, and the door of the cottage banged open. Bare feet padded across the balcony and down to the dock.

"'Oo's there?"

Yonie squinted against the lantern light. Peering down at her was the astonished face of her cousin and childhood persecutor, Gilbert DuRoy.

CHAPTER FIVE

"SINK IT, is that Yonie?" Gilbert frowned. "You're s'posed to be living in the city."

"I do live in Wicked Ford, yes," Yonie said in her haughtiest accent. "But I occasionally come this way on business, and today I, er, lost track of time. Would it be too much of an imposition if I stayed the night?"

Gilbert's eyes widened. "Family's always welcome," he said at last. He held out a hand, and reluctantly Yonie took it. The calluses on their respective palms scraped together as he helped her onto the dock. Yonie was gratified to find that she was now tall enough to look Gilbert straight in the eye.

Inside, the cottage was more orderly than she remembered. But the same tired rag rug still lay on the floor, refusing to die, and a piece of embroidery Yonie had executed herself was still tacked in an undeserved place of honor on the log wall.

The Elders' alcove near the door held the familiar age-darkened likenesses of the family's dead. There were also two newer figurines. Yonie looked quickly away as she recognized her parents.

Aunt Elisa was nowhere to be seen. Yonie's other three boy cousins were missing as well, as was their old hunting dog, Smoky. Yonie wondered uncomfortably when they might appear.

"'Ave you eaten?" Gilbert demanded.

"Not recently."

"I'll get you something, then. You look 'alf starved."

"I've been doing just fine for myself," Yonie snapped.

Gilbert held up his hands. "'Ey, now. You look right good, Yonie, truly. I 'ardly recognized you."

Seething slightly, Yonie settled onto a chair and watched Gilbert slice up a lumpy sausage. His black beard had thickened since she'd last seen him, creeping up his cheeks to create a mask-like effect. He reminded her of a lanky, bright-eyed raccoon.

Gilbert looked up, and Yonie quickly shifted her eyes to the wooden salt-and-syrup set in the center of the table. The containers were shaped like two characters from folklore — Jack-of-the-Mire and Curly Dog — and were rather charming.

When Gilbert reached around Yonie to set the food on the table, she flipped her braid over her shoulder protectively.

"Aw, Yonie, it's been years since I yanked your 'air."

"It's been years since I saw you," Yonie retorted. She picked up a round of sausage (Gilbert hadn't provided a fork) and bit down.

Feeling her cousin's eyes on her, Yonie touched the syrup pot, where Curly Dog's tail coiled like the tip of a fern. "Nice work," she said stiffly. "You could sell these."

"I 'ave been. There's a fellow up by Fever Creek gives me a good price. Takes 'em up to the city to sell."

"Do you ever take them up yourself?"

Gilbert shrugged. "Been to the city. Didn't like it. Lot of stuck-up people there."

Yonie chewed. The sausage tasted wonderful. LaRue purred in her lap, far more comfortable than the situation seemed to warrant.

"I guess your brothers took Smoky out hunting?"

"Nay." Gilbert looked down at the table. "You remember 'ow 'e was getting, even before you left. 'E was already on Granny Pitchers's 'ook, and it wasn't long before she 'auled 'im in."

"Oh — I'm sorry," said Yonie insincerely. She hadn't been fond of Smoky, who had treated LaRue much the same way his masters treated Yonie. "It won't be the same without him," she offered.

"That it won't. 'Ey, LaRue's looking good, though."

While Yonie was profoundly grateful for the prolonged vigor the cat's guile seemed to be granting her, she did worry that as time went on, those who knew LaRue's true age might suspect the truth. She quickly changed the subject.

"So, er — when are your brothers getting back?"

"What, didn't you 'ear? They're gone. They're all married."

Yonie gaped.

"Aye! Gregory went first — Cecile Roach, no surprise there. Then Gage — girl called Yuhanna from Moily Neck. Then Gustave married Lydie Rowbear, and they moved down near Charwater."

"I had no idea." Yonie felt hurt that no one had told her, though to be fair, she had never provided her relatives with an address. "How about you? Any plans in that regard?"

"Nay," said Gilbert tersely.

"Maybe if you shaved," Yonie suggested helpfully, but broke off when she saw that Gilbert's face had darkened. He rose, sawed off more sausage with greater force than necessary, and returned to the table.

"There's more news," he said after a moment. "Lydie's in the family way. Mama's down there with 'er now."

The thought of Gustave even holding a baby, let alone caring for one, alarmed Yonie so much that she was slow to absorb the other awful implications. "Your mother's gone for the night, then?"

"She's gone for good. Lydie said she could use some 'elp once the baby came, and that's all Mama needed. Not much to keep 'er round 'ere anymore, after . . ." His voice trailed off. "So I've got my own place now."

Yonie's face flushed, and she pushed back from the table so quickly that as she stood, LaRue was left swinging by her claws from Yonie's skirt. "Well, in that case, I can't possibly stay the night. Thank you for your hospitality, but I should be getting back while there's still some moon to steer by."

"Sunken wrecks," Gilbert said in disbelief. "Don't tell me you're worried about your *reputation?* I'm your cousin, for fortune's sake! Do you always 'ave to be such a proper little society girl?"

"In case you hadn't noticed, I'm not a little girl anymore."

Gilbert averted his eyes in a guilty way that suggested he had indeed noticed. "You won't get more than a mile before you're lost," he objected. "Do you really want to spend the night sleeping in your canoe?"

"I've done it before."

"What if you brush up against some scourge oak?" A

childhood mishap with the shrubby vine had given Gilbert a fiendishly itchy rash all over his body. ("*All* over," he said darkly whenever he spoke of it.) The rash had faded after three weeks, but the memory had not.

"I'll chance it."

"Aaagh! You'd rather do that than stay with me?" He grabbed his shaggy hair and pulled at it. "Well, go ahead, then! I guess you really are better off back in the city, Yonetta DuRoy."

"I go by Yonie Watereye now."

"Oh, aye? That's prob'ly a good idea."

Yonie stalked out without another word and unmoored the *Dragonfly* with a vicious yank at her slipknotted bow-line. If it hadn't been for LaRue, she would have been well away before Gilbert even got out the door.

As it was, the cat was still adjusting herself on the seat when Gilbert came stomping out of the darkness, carrying what looked like a bunched-up blanket.

"This here's so the skeeters don't suck you dry," he said brusquely, throwing it down into the canoe. "And 'ere." He tossed in the rest of the sausage.

Yonie almost refused, but the background whine in the damp darkness, and the hopeful rumble from her stomach, were loud enough to change her mind. She gave a curt nod and pushed off into the nighttime swamp.

By the time Yonie had found a place to tie up, the mosquitoes were in full swarm and she was feeling reluctantly grateful for Gilbert's loan, an old quilt which she hastily draped over the top of the *Dragonfly* to create a canoe-shaped cave. That feeling lasted all the way until morning.

Yonie felt as if she'd spent six hours sleeping in a damp trench, as she in some sense had. Bird calls ratcheted from the trees above. Inches from her face, sunlight was glowing through lozenges of blue, orange, and green.

"Oh, *no*." Yonie sat up and uncovered herself, violently rocking the canoe. A patch of coziness around her ankles abruptly disappeared, and moments later LaRue emerged, fur bristling.

"What on earth is the matter, Yonie? I was sleeping!"

"This is one of Aunt Elisa's quilts!" Yonie brandished a fold of fabric.

"Her sun and stars pattern, I believe — though why you should find that so vexing, I certainly don't know." LaRue paw-patted the quilt where it lay across her seat, then stepped onto it and began to wash.

"Because now I have to return it! If it was some raggedy old thing, maybe it wouldn't matter, but this is beautiful."

"Then I suppose you'll get to say good morning to your dear cousin. Maybe he'll ask us to breakfast."

"It's not *funny*, LaRue! I can't go back there. I should think that would be obvious."

LaRue looked up from her washing. "There's no need to hold your braid that way, love. It's not going to escape. In any case, shouldn't you launder that quilt before you bring it back?" The quilt was stained green along one edge where it had brushed the water.

"Yes — that would only be polite, wouldn't it! I'll return it next time I'm in the neighborhood."

Though when that would be, Yonie thought as she paddled sore-muscled toward home, she did not know. In the past two years, she'd almost managed to forget how she'd parted from her relatives, but now those memories were all pouring back.

She'd always felt like a bit of an outsider among the Slough folk: that odd book-reading DuRoy girl with the city mama. But she had thought her aunts and uncles cared for her, at least. That was why it had been so painful when they fervently embraced her idea of moving to the city and brushed off her promises to visit with a notable lack of enthusiasm.

Gilbert was right — she was better off in Wicked Ford. There was nothing left for her here. Nothing but blackened timbers covered in snails and slime.

The *Dragonfly* rounded a bend and glided into a stretch of open water so still that it exactly mirrored the sky and leaves above. Yonie's breath caught. The canoe seemed to be sailing through the air, suspended magically in the center of a sunlit clearing.

She lifted up her paddle and let the *Dragonfly* coast. The illusion was perfect, the reflection of the scene above completely hiding everything below the water's surface. But Yonie knew she was seeing only half the picture. Below her was a whole underwater landscape full of activity and life.

Yonie's thoughts twirled like flecks of algae in an eddy of current.

She had been brooding over how much it hurt to be rejected by the only relatives she had left. But they *weren't* the only ones.

Yonie's mother had never talked about her side of the family, who had disowned her for marrying Papa. Even so, an entire half of Yonie's ancestry lay somewhere in Wicked Ford.

She didn't even know her mother's maiden name. But she could find out. She could find those shadowy high-society connections Gilbert had mocked her about.

Yonie hauled on her paddle, piercing the mirror surface as she swept the water of the Sloughs behind her. So what if her father's family all thought she belonged in the city? Maybe she did.

Maybe her mother's family would think so too.

CHAPTER SIX

THE NEXT morning found Yonie striding through the aisles of the Grand Market with LaRue on one shoulder and her knapsack on the other. The air was already sultry with summer heat.

The Grand Market was an expanse of paving stones possible only here in the high part of town, and Yonie, more accustomed to the clop of boardwalks and the creak of rope bridges, marveled as always at the silence beneath her feet. She never shopped here — the Grand Market was for luxuries, not groceries — and she had never attempted to do business here as a pearly. But her financial situation was growing desperate, and setting up here might help. Perhaps she would even get a chance to ask after her mother's people.

Yonie strolled past the scents of marsh-mint and Northern sword pepper. She paused to admire a raccoon carved from a swamp root and whistled at the asking price. Gilbert's carvings were as good or better. His reseller was likely making a fat profit.

Yonie passed a craggy graybeard in a fisherman's smock, shaking a pair of turtle-shell rattles and crooning in an unintelligible backwater patois. As a young man, Yonie's own father had sometimes brought his fiddle to the Grand Market. Papa had loved to tell about the day Mama stepped up beside him and began to sing along.

There were other performers as well, jugglers and tumblers and versifiers. And of course there were the pearlies.

"That one's a charlatan," Yonie muttered under her breath, and got a confirming squeeze on the shoulder from LaRue's claws. The scales on the woman's forehead were painted on, and she was telling fortunes to tourists.

Yonie, like most locals, knew that guile could go to great lengths in carrying out what it considered its work. It could even alter the shape and behavior of things that it imbued. Guile sometimes shared its thoughts with the folk around it, and had an affinity for other guile, which was how Seeings were done. But it couldn't tell the future.

When Yonie reached the antique sellers' area, she saw several pearlies whose bodies marked them as genuine.

Here was an old man, canal-dredger's muscles turned to fat, beard carefully shaved to display the ring of gills around his neck. Over there was a leathery, shrewd-faced woman whose thumb showed a fishhook scar alongside her fingers' tracery of web.

Yonie unshouldered her knapsack and took out a platter and a jar of scum-filled Petty Canal water. Immediately she was bombarded with glares from the nearest pearly, a woman with bulging fishy eyes. Yonie decided to move on.

After some wandering, she established herself near the antique stand of a sharp-eyed husband and wife team.

"Glad to have you, sugar," said the woman, who introduced herself as M'dam Finchum. "It's good business, having a pearly nearby." She helped Yonie arrange her square of folded blanket as Yonie filled the platter she had brought. The green of the canal water showed up well against the white glaze, which seemed to gratify the Finchums. They were even more pleased when they noticed that Yonie's blouse was missing one sleeve.

This had been LaRue's idea. "You need some touch of the unusual about you," she had opined the previous evening. "You don't look like a typical pearly, and in the daylight it'll be even harder to create that air of mystery."

"How about a tail?" Yonie suggested. "Just a hint of one? I could sew something underneath my skirt —"

"Absolutely not!" The cat had swept her own majestic plume about her. "You're far too young to have strangers staring at that part of your body. Tail, indeed."

The blouse had solved the problem that morning when the seam gave way. Yonie wasn't sure what people imagined her covered arm to be like, but if anyone asked, she planned to slowly shake her head.

Yonie sat cross-legged on her blanket, watching the occasional customer browse through the Finchums' jumbled wares. Someday, Yonie vowed, she would have her own antique stand, much better than this one. The charade of being a pearly could end, and LaRue would no longer have to work to support her.

She stared down at the empty tip bowl on her blanket. She was sweltering from the direct sun and the warmth of LaRue hammocked on her skirt. If she didn't get a customer soon, she was thinking of defecting to another stand.

But a young couple was approaching her. They were from the Coast, judging by their sober yet expensive garb, and though they were comically mismatched in height, they had the same glowing expression on their faces. A tarnished pewter vessel dangled heavily at the end of the man's arm. It was rather large to be carrying one-handed, but his other hand was clasped fondly with the woman's, and obviously he would need a very pressing reason to let go.

The man cleared his throat. "Good day, ma'am. The

fellow over there tells me that you are, er, that you can perform a, a Seeing, he called it? We have this fruit bowl, here, that we're thinking of buying."

"For our new house," the woman put in shyly. "We have some lovely things already — everyone was so kind — but this is the first time we've been west, and we want something to remember our trip by. The gentleman said this piece is oh so historic, from the time of the ancients he thinks, and probably full of, you know." She lowered her voice. "Guile."

"Of course I will 'elp you," Yonie told them, in her father's bayou accent. (*Your mother's way of speaking is all very well for impressing our usual customers,* LaRue had advised her, *but when it comes to educated folk, you'll do better to put it away. Be the mystic seer-woman from the bayou, with fish blood on your hands and swampweed in your hair.*)

Yonie settled the couple's potential purchase onto the platter. "You must 'ave patience; it can take time to see if a thing is wily" — LaRue dug her claws into Yonie's leg — "though in this case, the answer is clearly yes."

"And what sort of, er, wiles does it have?" the man asked diffidently.

How on earth she could find that out without talking to LaRue, Yonie did not know. She snuck a glance at the cat, who was gazing down into the swamp water with sleepy eyes. They had agreed on a system — claws for yes, none for no — but now that Yonie was actually faced with it, the idea of playing score-o'-questions in front of customers seemed ludicrous.

Any more visible communication would be deadly dangerous. In Wicked Ford, and indeed throughout the Devil's Foot, slyfolk might be suspect, but slybeasts were slaughtered.

Yonie had once seen a dog hanged by a mob down at the docks. A man with his nose streaming blood had been weeping and screaming in a foreign accent that his dog was a Harkene water spaniel, and it was normal for that breed to have webbed toes. There had been absolutely nothing Yonie could do.

Luckily cats, because of their aversion to swimming, were the least likely animals to be suspected of harboring guile. So long as LaRue limited herself to kneading Yonie's leg, the worst that would happen today would be failure and embarrassment for Yonie.

That, and possibly being turned out of their garret by M'dam Teabow if she couldn't pay the rent.

Yonie studied the pewter bowl. It had a wide, flat rim like an overturned hat, and a rounded base supported on five beautifully molded little duck feet. Yonie was certain she had seen something like it in one of her books. Was it in *Ancient Households, Ancient Ways?*

Aha.

"What you 'ave 'ere is indeed from the time of the ancients," she told the couple. "It's in the Stillwater style, and it's very well-preserved."

"Oh, that's marvelous! Darling, imagine having some-thing that old sitting on our dining table."

Yonie's mouth twitched. "Ma'am, I 'ave to tell you — the ancients would've been more likely to keep this under their bed."

The lanky young man wrinkled his brow. "Look here — do you mean to say it's a, a *chamber pot?*"

"I 'ope you're not disappointed." Yonie detailed the advantages to be gained from a wily chamber pot: how it might resist tipping, maintain a pleasantly neutral scent, and remain unobtrusive wherever it was placed. After mak-ing each point, she felt the reassuring needle-pricks of LaRue's kneading paws.

"And 'ow much are the sellers asking for it?" Yonie gave a low whistle. "You could 'and this over to a collector for ten times that price. My advice is, go buy it quick before they change their minds. And, ma'am, sir, my best wishes to you for a marriage full of 'appiness."

The couple conferred briefly, then deposited a generous tip in Yonie's bowl. "We never even told her we were newlyweds," Yonie heard the woman whisper in an awed voice as they hur-ried back to the Finchums' stand to make their purchase.

A few minutes later, Yonie and LaRue were sharing an overpriced but delicious grilled eel purchased from a pass-ing vendor. LaRue was purring in Yonie's lap, and M'dam Finchum had come over and brought her a cup of tea.

Yonie's next customer was a careworn lady with the

pale complexion of a Northerner, who plunked a grubby brooch down into the platter hard enough that droplets of water went spraying over the side. "M'dam, I must to know, what are the wiles of this brooch? Those merchants, they say it will make me look younger. Absurd, would you not say?" Her eyes wanted it to be true.

"I've 'eard of jewelry like that," Yonie told her cautiously. But the claw-stabs never came. She wondered if LaRue was still awake.

"A beautiful cat," the woman remarked, and Yonie nearly yelped as LaRue's claws spiked into her thigh. "But does it not distract you from your work?"

"Nay," Yonie replied through gritted teeth. "She 'elps me to *relax*."

Yonie handed back the brooch. "I'm sorry, ma'am, but as far as I can tell this 'as no wiles at all." She winced as LaRue confirmed the verdict, and hoped the cat had not drawn enough blood to dot through her skirt.

"It is what I thought." The woman nodded morosely and dropped a modest coin in Yonie's bowl.

The next thing Yonie knew, M'dam Finchum was storming up to her and snatching back her empty teacup. "What d'you think you're doing?" she barked. "She would've paid silver for that piece!"

"It wasn't wily," Yonie explained, rising to her feet as LaRue clambered onto her shoulder. "She didn't want it once she found that out."

"It was wily as anything, you little liar!" M'dam Finchum shrilled, stepping back to look up at Yonie's face. Passersby were pausing to watch the confrontation.

"You must 'ave been misinformed," Yonie said doggedly. "It 'ad no trace of guile."

"And what do you know? You're no real pearly, not at your age. What's the matter with you? That first sale went so well —"

"I know what it is," M'sir Finchum said darkly, coming up beside his wife. "Miss Greedy here couldn't wait till the end of the day for her taste — thought she'd teach us a lesson."

Yonie's face flushed. "I work for my customers, not for you!" she said hotly. "You ought to be ashamed o' yourselves, trying to pass junk off onto people by telling 'em it's wily —"

"That's enough!" M'sir Finchum roared. "I want you out of here now!"

"Gladly," Yonie spat, scooping up her possessions and stalking away. She took some small satisfaction in hearing an argument between the Finchums erupt behind her over the "fruit bowl" and how much they should have charged for it.

Obviously, she had misunderstood the relationship between Grand Market merchants and their pearlies. Now that she thought about it, there was no reason to assume that even the genuine pearlies were giving real Seeings. LaRue must think her hopelessly naïve.

This would be her last time working at the Grand Market, Yonie promised herself.

"Excuse me! M'dam Pearly?"

The girl was near Yonie's age, smiling anxiously up at her from under a floppy beret. The beret was an unfortunate shade of yellow-green, as were her skirt and the ribbon bows at the throat of her white blouse and on the ends of her two black braids.

No one would choose such clothing. Yonie realized that it had to be a school uniform, like the ones in stories from her mother's childhood. This was not just a girl, but a Young Lady.

"Ma'am, I thought it was wonderful the way you told off those people back there," the girl confided. "I don't think there's another pearly in the whole market who would've done that."

"I reckon not," said Yonie, stomach rumbling. The eel-on-a-stick already seemed like a long time ago. "Mind you, they might be smarter than me."

"Oh, don't say that! You're honest; that's the difference. That's why I want to hire *you*."

CHAPTER SEVEN

Y ONIE'S PROSPECTIVE customer was named Justine
Cordell. She was fifteen years old and in her third year
at the Bellflower Academy for Young Ladies, where she
had to watch her behavior to an unfair extent due to her
father's position there as headmaster. She had an older sister,
Nadine, who lived in the upriver town of Sinister Bend with
her husband and, as of a week ago, a new baby boy.

Yonie learned all this while sitting on a cold wrought-
iron bench under the Grand Junction Bridge. When paddling by this spot on previous occasions, Yonie had seen a
quiet, relatively trash-free area with a few beds of flowers

struggling in the shade. If Justine had not informed her, she might never have recognized it as a nexus of illicit activity, where the more daring pupils from the Academy met with boys from the DesMaray School or even, sometimes, *Low Town men.*

Why this made it an inconspicuous place for the two of them to talk, Yonie was not sure.

"So," Yonie said, cutting off Justine's nervous chatter. "What is this wily thing we're dealing with? 'Ave you got it on you?"

Justine squirmed. "Actually, I don't know what it is. I just know it exists."

Yonie raised her eyebrows.

"It all started when Mother went up to Nadine's to help with the baby. Father started acting — odd. It's so unlike him, there has to be something, you know, something *sly* going on. But no one will believe me."

In Yonie's experience, people could act out of character for a wide range of reasons, even without the interference of guile. "What is 'e doing, exactly?"

"Well, at first he was just very vague and daydreamy. Sometimes he'd call me by my mother's name — that sort of thing. I thought maybe he was just missing her. But now —" Justine pulled off her beret and kneaded it in her fingers. "He's — making improper advances to women. Even some of the older girls at school! It's just awful. If he keeps on this way, he's going to lose his job, and what other school would hire him after that? It would just destroy him!"

It could destroy Justine's prospects as well, Yonie assumed. She wondered if the girl had thought of that. "It's possible some wily thing's to blame," she allowed. "'As anything new come into 'is possession? It's usually boat stuff or antiques — furnishings, tools, coins, jewelry . . ."

"Not that I know of. He doesn't care for jewelry at all, I've never seen him wear it, and he hates shopping. But there's got to be something!"

"I'm sorry, but I don't know what more advice I can give you. I can't do a Seeing without the thing itself."

"Maybe you could come to our house and, er, look around? That is — can you see guile like that? Would you need to dunk everything in swamp water?"

"Nay — for deep Seeings, it's 'elpful to surround the object with loose guile, but I don't need that just to sense if a thing's wily or not." Yonie paused. The whole venture sounded like a chase after a marsh-candle. But it was a job. A High Town job.

"I would expect pay even if there's nothing cunning in the 'ouse," she warned. "You're sure your papa won't mind me poking around 'is things?"

"He doesn't need to know. He'll be at school the rest of the day, and our housekeeper quit yesterday." Justine's mouth turned down. "You can imagine why."

* * *

"I'm really more used to water taxis," Justine confided as she settled onto the bow seat of the *Dragonfly*. "There's a nice boy who often takes me down to the market on half days — he was surprised to see me this morning!" Justine had told Yonie she was missing class at the moment, something she never would have contemplated "in a million years" if it weren't such a desperate situation.

The Grand Canal slid between steep flowered banks, where ladies clustered like petals around the dainty tables of waterfront cafés. Justine's pointing arm turned the canoe down progressively narrower canals whose names grew progressively longer. By the time they reached the Canal DeVillaincourt, the high banks were blocking the mid-morning sun, and the band of sky overhead was frequently interrupted by bridges that smelled of wet brick. Yonie was glad to leave the claustrophobic tunnel of canal and climb up the stone steps to the bright street above.

The Cordell house was a white and pink concoction that sat right down on its foundation like a cake on a plate. Yonie watched with interest as Justine took out a key. Her garret's only security arrangements were the decrepitude of the steps leading up to it and M'sir "Two-Hats" Shambly on the first floor, who was slightly unbalanced on the subject of thieves.

As Yonie toured the Cordell house with LaRue balanced watchfully on her shoulder, she could not help comparing it to the cottage where she had spent her childhood. Instead of the grassy smell of reed thatching and the ever-present whiff of fish, there were the smells of furniture wax and wool rugs. Instead of the crooked stripes of chinked log walls, there was painted plaster. And there was room after room after room.

Yonie had grown up thinking that her own house was unusually large. Mama, with her city sensibilities, had insisted that Papa add on a separate bedroom for the two of them (unwittingly enabling Yonie's nighttime forays). Now Yonie could not help wondering if her mother had been raised in a house like Justine's. If so, how had their snug little two-room cabin looked to her?

After a surreptitious conference with LaRue in the garderobe, Yonie sat down with Justine in the parlor to give her the news.

"Justine, I'm sorry, but I've been over the 'ouse from top to bottom, and there's nothing wily anywhere. Except for that one copper goblet in the back o' the dish cupboard — the one with all the dents. I can tell it spent most of its life as a bailing scoop."

"So that's why it spills all the time! But we've had that old thing for ages. It couldn't be causing the, the problem with Father." Justine blinked rapidly, and looked away through a glass-paned window.

Seeing the back of Justine's bowed head, with the

clumsy part running crookedly down between her braids, Yonie could vividly imagine the girl that morning, braiding her own hair without her mother or sister's help, frightened by her father's behavior, feeling very alone. Yonie couldn't bring herself to take her pay and go.

"I can think of one other place to look," she said. "Does your father 'ave a private office at the Academy?"

"Of course!" Justine brightened, then frowned. "But he'd never let you in. It would be quite a trick even getting you onto the school grounds — it's staff and students only, and you're too young to be staff—"

Justine gave Yonie a speculative look.

So it was that Yonie found herself up in Justine's bedroom, trying on the uniform of a Bellflower schoolgirl.

"It's lucky for us that Nadine's pretty tall," Justine said as she surveyed the effect. "We'll still need to take down the hem of the skirt, though. I don't think we can do much about the blouse." The blouse was loose in the bosom, short in the cuffs, and tight as a sausage skin around Yonie's biceps — evidently Academy students did not spend much time paddling canoes.

Less than an hour later, Justine had altered the skirt with a speed that astonished Yonie, whose own sewing was of the accurate but painstaking variety. Yonie's shoes were polished as black as two watermelon seeds, and her hair was freshly washed and trimmed.

"There, that's nice and even." Justine set down the scissors, took up a brush, and started smoothing Yonie's hair with long, gentle strokes.

The last person to have brushed Yonie's hair for her was her mother, who had constructed braids so tightly engineered that the skin of Yonie's face always felt stretched back until well into midmorning. Justine's hair brushing was a more physically pleasant experience, but still Yonie felt her eyes tearing up. To distract herself, she looked down at the rawhide hair tie she was holding in her lap, but that was just as bad. The luck-beads on it had been a gift from Papa, carved for her one rainy evening.

"I'll fasten it back with a clip," Justine was saying. "That's what most of the older girls do." She held out a tin hair clip for Yonie's inspection. It was in the shape of a jolly duck, with a smile that was physically impossible for a beaked creature. "M'dam Watereye? Is that all right?"

"Aye, that'll do fine." Resolutely, Yonie draped Nadine's beret over the top of her head.

CHAPTER EIGHT

As the two girls walked down LeFever Street, Yonie adjusted the borrowed school satchel, making sure it was cinched only partway shut. She still felt guilty about confining LaRue, but she was already conspicuous enough without a cat on her shoulder. Justine, luckily, had accepted LaRue's presence as simply adding to the drama of their endeavor.

The Academy was just down the hill, Justine had told her, in the Grove. Yonie had often seen the silvery treetops of the Grove peeking over the grand houses and storefronts of the central district, but she had always regarded them as a landmark rather than a destination. In this she was no doubt influenced by the words of the guidebook she had purchased soon after her arrival in Wicked Ford:

The exotic Blue Gum Trees of Fabian's Folly, or The Grove as they are coming to be known, stand in a Soup of Muck and Fallen Bark that will quickly deter Merrymakers seeking a Shady Stroll. The imported Saplings, planted in this low-lying Acre of the otherwise pleasant High Town, have proved to be every bit as useless at draining Swamp-land as they are commercially as Timber, scuttling M. Fabian's Dreams of founding a Fine Furniture Empire.

Yonie had bought this guidebook used with its covers and outer pages missing, so she had never known its publication date. She suspected it was not exactly current, as it referred to Wicked Ford as "Wycke's Ford," a name that the peculiar humor of the inhabitants had by now all but erased from memory.

Upon seeing the Grove up close, Yonie reclassified her guidebook from reference work to collector's item. The "Saplings" were of impressive girth, and their height had been masked by the depression in which they grew. The blue gums were like no other trees she had ever seen, with silvery, scythe-shaped leaves and ribbons of bark curling down from the trunks.

"The real entrance is over on Morechain Street," Justine said as she led Yonie into the dappled light under the trees.

"It's got a boardwalk. Try not to get your shoes too muddy, or everyone will know we sneaked in the back way."

The blue gums had been planted in a grid, and now that they were forest height, they formed unnaturally straight aisles of sunlight and shadow. The branches began high up, giving the smooth trunks the look of pillars. The stately effect was somewhat lessened by the squelch of the ground underfoot.

"Here we are!" Justine patted the blue gum trunk before her, which had sections of branch nailed across it like ladder rungs on a dock post. About ten feet up, mostly concealed by foliage, was a platform with four trees supporting the corners.

"The school supplies usually come in the front gate," Justine explained as they climbed, "but when the water's up, they float them in from the back."

From the end of the dock, a walkway slanted upward into the gray-green leaves. Yonie trailed a cautious hand along the rope guardrail as they ascended about twenty feet. "Now, if your papa's in 'is office when we get there, 'ow do we get 'im out?"

"Well, I stayed home sick this morning, supposedly," Justine said. "So it'll seem natural for me to fall ill again after I get to school. I'll just go out where a teacher can see me, and collapse or something, and beg for Father. Then they'll send for him, and while he's gone, you can get into his office. Do you need the directions again?"

Yonie fingered the spare key Justine had filched from her father's desk. "Nay, I remember. And anyway, I reckon 'is name is on the door?"

"Er, yes." Justine was obviously startled to learn that Yonie could read.

The sound of muffled laughter drifted down, and glimpses of yellow-green uniform appeared among the silvery leaves and gray-brown branches.

"Don't worry. I'll handle this," Justine hissed as two schoolgirls came into view.

The first was around Yonie's age, with her hair artificially reddened and her beret jammed carelessly into a skirt pocket. Trailing her was a chubby, cheerful-looking younger girl.

"Justine?" exclaimed the younger girl. "What are you up to *now?*" She giggled. "Did you go meet that taxi boy, the one who's madly in love with you?"

Justine smiled glassily. "Hello, Pia. No, I —"

"Who's this?" asked the older girl. She cocked her head at Yonie. "And what's with the uniform? You're not from Bellflower."

"She is now," Justine put in smoothly. "Her family just moved here from Sinister Bend, and she's going to be joining the fourth class. Father asked me to show her around."

"Quite the scenic tour," the redhead drawled. She glanced coolly at Yonie's handed-down outfit and worn

shoes. "Well, welcome to prison, I'm sure. I'm Lacey Wynne
— you'll hear about *me*. What's your name?"

"Her name's Yvette Morrow," Justine said swiftly.

"Let her speak for herself, why don't you?"

Justine sent a desperate glance at Yonie and opened her
mouth, clearly about to explain why Yvette sounded like a
swamp fisherman's daughter.

But Yonie was quicker.

"How do you do, Lacey, and was it Pia? Justine's been
giving me a simply fascinating tour, and I'm sure I'm going
to enjoy it here immensely . . ."

Justine forgot to close her mouth as Yonie rolled out
pleasantries in a crisp accent identical to her own.

Lacey took out a comb and sent it snicking through her
hair as if she were sharpening a knife. "Huh! I hope Justine's
telling you the whole story. Like watch out for Hautain —
she teaches etiquette, and she can practically breathe fire.
And then there's Turcoat, the music master — look out or
he'll want to give you private lessons, if you know what I
mean. Those little practice rooms are so cozy, and sound-
proof too —"

Pia gasped out a laugh. "Lacey, you're awful! He's completely harmless!"

"Oh, I *suppose*. Nowadays it's the headmaster we have to
watch out for. Isn't that right, Justine?"

Justine's face reddened.

"And then there's Sauvage, for dance," Pia put in loudly, glaring at Lacey. "I hear he used to train dogs."

"All right, all right." Lacey put up her hands. "See you around, Yvette. It's not such a bad place, if you don't mind wearing a lily pad on top of your head." The two girls edged past Yonie and Justine and hurried away down the ramp.

"That Lacey is a Bad Example," Justine said, in what sounded like a verbatim quote. She gave Yonie a sidewise glance. "How did you learn to talk like that?"

Yonie smiled mysteriously.

Then she stopped, suddenly tired of the pretense.

"My mother went to a school like this one. Maybe it *was* this one, for all I know. When I want to sound High Town, I speak like her." Yonie shifted her tone. "But my papa, 'e grew up in the bayou, and when I 'ave a 'ankering to sound that way, I talk like 'im."

Justine's eyes sparkled as if she'd just seen a carnival trick. "M'dam Watereye, that was marvelous!"

"You might as well call me Yonie," Yonie told her recklessly. "I'm only a year older than you."

The Bellflower campus was a mix of standalone classrooms supported by a tree at each corner and newer amalgamations where several buildings had been joined together. As Yonie followed Justine along the necklace of walkways and suspended bridges, the ground was a shadowy presence far below.

"Here's the back door to the administration building," Justine announced. "Wait here a few minutes while I go raise a fuss. I'll keep Father away as long as I can."

At almost the moment Justine entered the building, Yonie felt the vibration of footsteps on the walkway, though the blue gum foliage still screened her from view. What would happen to a stranger in a school uniform who was found trespassing? Yonie's cousin-avoiding reflexes took over, and she swarmed up the trunk of the nearest tree.

". . . how we're going to pull it off without the Barzilay girl," came a smooth male voice. "She's our strongest soprano."

Yonie froze. If they looked up they would see her. But the branch she was crouching on had several waxed-paper toffee wrappers wedged under a strip of bark, so perhaps the teachers here were not so observant in the upward direction.

"How long is she suspended for this time?" a woman asked.

"Indefinitely! And then the rain leaked in and ruined a third of the sheet music."

"You poor thing. If there's anything I can do—"

"Ah, M'dam LaRue, you are the soul of kindness," the man's voice said suavely.

Startled by the name, Yonie just managed to glimpse the two figures before they passed out of sight. There was a pale, lanky middle-aged man with a blond-and-gray goatee, and a rotund woman whose coloring was even more exotic, with freckles and a head of apricot-colored curls.

Yonie gazed thoughtfully after them until she heard the headmaster's name being shouted in the building below.

One whole wall of the headmaster's office was golden-brown with the wood of filing cabinets and the spines of leather-bound ledgers. Across from the door was a broad desk on which papers were neatly stacked.

"Did you hear?" she asked the cat excitedly. "That teacher's name was LaRue! I think Mama must have named you after her." Yonie lowered the satchel to the floor and loosened the drawstring.

"Ginger-haired, was she?" LaRue vaulted onto the desk and inspected a letter opener, a bottle of ink, a teacup, and a saucer, which Yonie hastily filled with water she'd scooped from the DeVillaincourt Canal.

"Very! So this really must've been Mama's school."

As LaRue nosed about the room, Yonie turned away from the desk and came up facing the filing cabinets. She reached reflexively for her luck-beads, but found her hair hanging loose down her back.

Student records were confidential. Yonie certainly would not want some interloper poking around in her private documents. But the question was, would *Yonie's mother* want to share this small part of her history with her own daughter?

Mama had always avoided talking about her life before meeting Papa. But she'd promised that when Yonie was older, she would tell her more.

Yonie was older now.

The file wasn't hard to find. There was only one Valery Estee within the possible timespan. The surname was Bruneau.

Yonie settled into Headmaster Cordell's chair, a wheeled swiveling affair that under other circumstances could have amused her for some time. Before her lay five years of her mother's life. Here were the classes she had taken, ranging from the prosaic (Household Accounting) to the obscure (Crewelwork and Tatting) to the tantalizing (Advanced Etiquette: Dealing Gracefully with Faux Pas, Rudeness, and Social Disasters).

Valery had gotten her best marks in Literature and Voice. The occasional Disciplinary Report recorded only minor infractions, but described with frustration how the young Valery refused to testify against her classmates, even when they had been the cause of her troubles. The year-end evaluations from her teachers drew a picture of a studious, stubborn, fiercely private person.

Yonie reached the final year, and her fingers tightened on the page.

Instead of a packet of evaluations, there was a Notice of Withdrawal stating that Valery Estee Bruneau had left the Bellflower Academy four months short of graduation. The last line said only *Reason: Marriage.*

Mama hadn't completed her schooling? That seemed very unlike the determined woman who had kept Yonie at her lessons while her cousins fished and roamed.

Yonie reread the notice, searching for any additional clue — and found it in the date at the top of the page. Valery Bruneau had quit school only five months before Yonie was born.

"Well, I've found nothing," said LaRue, jumping onto Yonie's lap. "How about you?"

At that moment, a key clanked in the lock.

CHAPTER NINE

A TIRED-LOOKING MAN with the same fine features as Justine hurried into the room, but stopped short when he saw the intruder. His eyes narrowed.

"I thought I knew all my students — I *do* know all my students — and I don't know you."

Cordell came around the desk and spun the chair sideways to face him, causing LaRue to reflexively clamp onto Yonie's skirt. "Who are you, and how did you get in here?"

"Justine let me in," Yonie stammered out. "We only wanted to, to —"

Cordell's expression suddenly softened like a candle in

the sun. "Of course," he said. "She wanted to surprise me. And she certainly did." He reached out and tucked a strand of Yonie's hair back behind her ear. "I'm thrilled to see you, cherie."

Cordell's hands were on the armrests of the chair, trapping Yonie inside. His vague, tender expression held her paralyzed. Wasn't he even curious about the cat in Yonie's lap?

Justine was correct. Something was very wrong with this man.

He leaned down, lips parting slightly. His chin was carefully shaved. His collar gapped open at his throat to emit a waft of soap scent and an unsettlingly intimate glimpse of a fine chain lying against his skin. "It seems like I've been waiting for you forever," he murmured. He leaned closer, and though Yonie twisted her head and uttered a strangled noise, he managed to place a warm kiss along her jaw.

LaRue's paw lashed up and incised three red lines across Cordell's collarbone, right next to the golden line of necklace. "Meeeerow!" she said emphatically.

Suddenly, Yonie recalled Justine's voice from earlier that day: *He doesn't care for jewelry at all. I've never seen him wear it.*

She reached up, hooked her hand under the necklace, and yanked.

Yonie had expected the chain to break. Instead she

jerked Cordell's head sharply toward her, so that his fore-head clonked into hers. It was almost as painful as colliding with an attic rafter. The chain cut into her hand, and if her skin had not been callused from the canoe paddle, it might have drawn blood.

"Aagh!" the headmaster burst out (with a lack of pro-fanity that set an impressive Good Example). "Cherie, what are you doing?"

"I have to look at this," Yonie told him apologetically, forcing the chain up over his head. His ears presented an obstacle, but the besotted expression never left his face as she dragged awkwardly at the necklace and finally got it free.

The chain was unremarkable, but from it dangled a golden locket the size of a small mussel shell, its cover pocked and scarred.

Yonie popped the locket open with her thumbnail. Inside was a miniature portrait of a gracious-looking woman with hair as black as the night sky.

"It's a wonderful likeness — almost as beautiful as the real thing," Cordell said fondly. "Such a thoughtful gift, my darling!"

Removing the locket from M'sir Cordell had not removed his odd behavior. He was still looming over her, and the misplaced warmth still shone in his eyes. Yonie put her heels to the floor and rolled the desk chair back so she was momentarily out of his reach. She ripped Justine's clip from her hair and pried at the portrait with the bill of the duck.

The oval of heavy card sprang loose and fell to the floor with a barely audible *plip,* and the happiness drained out of Cordell's face. He gawked at the sight before him: a lean, overtall sixteen-year-old in an ill-fitting uniform, and a slit-eyed mass of bristling orange fur.

"Great waters below," he said hollowly. "*What* has been going on?"

Yonie tossed the empty locket and chain onto the desk and stood up, arms cradling LaRue. "Sir, you should really hear the story from Justine."

"Justine? What does she have to do with this? She's not well — just threw up all over M'sir Sauvage in the hall. I had Matron take her to lie down."

"Send for her, M'sir Cordell. She'll come."

Bemused, he looked at Yonie's face, then at the duck clip lying on the desk, before he nodded and left the room.

By the time Cordell returned with his daughter, the Valery Bruneau file was back in its drawer. The empty locket was in the saucer, staring up through a layer of green canal water, and LaRue sat nearby smugly washing her ears.

"M'dam Watereye, I understand I owe you my thanks," said Justine's father, offering his hand. "Do I owe you an apology as well? Justine tells me I've been behaving rather badly. All I really remember is how much I was missing my wife, Cherie. I suppose the locket was — amplifying that, somehow?"

"That was certainly part of it," said Yonie. "Guile wants to work, and what is the job of this sort of locket? To remind the owner of someone who's far away."

"But *that* much would have been fine!" Justine burst out. "Why was it making Father act that way?"

Yonie picked up the wet locket and held it in her hand. "This is one of a pair," she told them. "It belonged to a soldier, who gave the other to his sweetheart before he left on a campaign. But he never returned."

Yonie rubbed her thumb over the cover of the locket, which featured an engraving of two muskrats with tails entwined. "This locket spent countless years soaking in guile-water, pining for its mate. Guile wants to work, but it also shares its thoughts. You know how, when you miss someone badly, you keep thinking you see them everywhere? In a crowd, or a stranger's face? That's what was happening to you, sir — to an extraordinary degree."

There was a moment of silence.

"It's a good theory," Cordell said, "but I'm afraid you're mistaken. When Cherie sent me this, her note said that she had the matching locket. She got the set of them at a riverboat stop just north of the city — bought them from a portrait artist who did her miniature."

"It must not have been a matching set," said Yonie, with the absolute confidence of one who had grown up with LaRue.

"Well, never mind about that. I'm very grateful to you, M'dam Watereye, and I'd like to reward you for your help."

Yonie put the pickerel she had just finished cooking into a dish and set it down by LaRue, who was sprawled on the sun and stars quilt.

Then she straightened up. "Oww! Sink it!"

"Yonie!" the cat said in scandalized tones. "Language!"

"Sorry," she muttered, rubbing her head. "Stupid roof beam."

"My dear, you can hardly complain. If you'd accepted the first reward M'sir Cordell offered you, we could have spent the morning looking for new lodgings." LaRue rolled to her feet and took a shred of fish delicately between her teeth.

"I know. But there must be thousands of books in the Bellflower library! That's worth a few head bumps."

"I'm surprised he agreed. I'm sure he doesn't grant library visiting privileges to just anyone." LaRue licked another morsel from her dish. "I still don't approve of the risks you took in this whole business, but I must admit you handled things rather well. With the exception of M'sir Cordell's romantic advances, which seemed to leave you completely at a loss—"

"Oh, LaRue, haven't we been over that enough?"

"You are of an age, Yonetta, when you will encounter men who try to take liberties—"

"I've encountered men like that already."

"I'm not speaking of ruffians lurking under a dock. You've always handled that type of situation entirely to my satisfaction. But you may someday meet men whom you wish to discourage by more subtle means than a canoe paddle to the head."

"Yes, LaRue."

"Don't roll your eyes, please. We shall return to that topic another day. But all in all, that last job did turn out well. Our rent's paid for another month, there's food on the shelf, and I wouldn't be surprised if we got more work from that Academy crowd." LaRue settled down again. "So what's wrong, dear? I don't think you slept a wink last night, and today you've been jittering like a pot lid over boiling water."

Yonie sank down cross-legged onto the rug near LaRue. "I keep thinking about Mama," she admitted. "What she must've gone through."

"Well, that's what you get for snooping in her records. I do think you have at least a cat's worth of curiosity in you."

"She never would talk about her parents. I'd always thought they disowned her — that's what everyone said — but I never knew why. Now I know. It was because she had a biscuit in the oven before she got married."

"You should be aware that that expression is not used among refined folk," said LaRue neutrally. "And I'd assume it was your mother's choice of husband that her family objected to, more than the actual pregnancy. Even among the High Town families, you'd be surprised how many first babies are born 'early,' and how remarkably large they are despite that disadvantage."

"You remember the story," Yonie said. "How Mama and Papa used to meet in the Grand Market, and he would play his fiddle while she sang, and that's how they fell in love. It's just so hard to imagine them sneaking off to some hotel before they were even married, to—er—"

"For an intimate liaison," LaRue put in smoothly.

"Yes! It seems so unlike them."

"A lady does not speculate on such things—at least, not aloud. I agree that it does seem out of character for such a proper young woman, and such a gallant and romantic young man. But you'll find as you get older, Yonie, that this area of human behavior is full of surprises."

Yonie wound the end of her braid tight around one finger, until the wooden beads dug into her skin. "So her family disowned her. But Mama must have disowned them as well," she said. "Otherwise, wouldn't they have wanted to at least meet their granddaughter? Look how far Justine's mother traveled to see her grandson—all the way to Sinister Bend. And Aunt Elisa—she moved in with Cousin Gustave and his wife, and the baby's not even here yet! My grandparents might be happy to meet me. I just don't know."

LaRue gave a cat sigh. "I have a feeling," she said, "that you won't rest until you find out."

CHAPTER TEN

Yonie had never seen so many books. The shelves of the Bellflower library marched in ranks and lined the walls and were equipped with attached rolling ladders that bore stern signs indicating their correct use. In the center of the room a tree-pillar rose upward, encircled by a spiral staircase which was, disappointingly, closed off at the bottom with a brown velvet rope.

Barring Yonie's way to the books was a wide desk with a large, busy-looking woman stationed behind it. The librarian's expanse of ruffled white blouse was immaculate, and her gray-and-black hair was worked into a frighteningly complex series of looped braids. If this woman had done her own hair, keeping the library holdings in good order would be well within her capabilities. Yonie felt very conscious of her own clothing, which was well-worn and bore signs (both visual and olfactory) of having been laundered in canal water.

The librarian examined Yonie's letter from the headmaster (and, Yonie suspected, the cleanliness of her hands).

"How interesting. I'm pleased to make your acquaintance, M'dam Watereye. I'm Adele Pierpond, the head librarian here, and I'm happy to make you welcome, as M'sir Cordell says, as long as you behave yourself." She gave Yonie a level look. "Just to be clear — you haven't been granted checkout privileges. You'll do all your reading here, and I'll inspect your bag on the way out."

Yonie's face flushed. "I understand," she said curtly.

"Now, do you have any particular research interest today?"

"I'd like to learn about the leading families of Wicked Ford, past and current. Especially those connected with this school," she added offhandedly.

"I'm afraid our Bellflower collection is off limits, except to senior students. But you might try the genealogical works over in history. And of course there's always *Bellamy's* in reference. *Bellamy's Social Roster?* It lists the members of the most prominent local families. It's got some background on each one, plus births, deaths, and marriages. There's a new edition every year."

The blue spines of the social roster covered a tall shelf in the reference section. Yonie extracted the most recent volume and flipped to the B's.

Yes — there was an entry for Bruneau!

The Bruneaus, she learned, had made their fortune in real estate during the early days of settlement, and were noted for their accomplishment in the arts. Family members currently numbered five, with no one in Yonie's generation.

Their given names seemed strangely familiar, and after a moment, Yonie realized that they were also the names of Low Town canals. She wondered if the ancestral Bruneaus had established those neighborhoods. It was entirely possible, Yonie thought dizzily, that the venerable piers her own lodgings stood upon had been put in place by one of her ancestors.

Yonie approached one of the ladders and rolled it stealthily into position, refraining from, as the warning sign said, ANY TYPE OF HORSEPLAY. She returned to the ground with several dusty volumes of the social roster.

Yonie's own birth was not recorded, and her mother's name did not appear in that year's edition either. Going farther back, though, she found entries that included her mother, and eventually determined that the surviving Bruneaus included an aunt, a couple of aged cousins, and both of Mama's parents.

While paging through the volumes, Yonie had noticed names like Oldroyd, Yves, Colegrove, and DesMaray, names already familiar from storefronts, delivery vans, banknotes, and so on. These families got upward of a dozen pages apiece. The Bruneau entry was less than one page, suggesting that they were no longer prominent. Had that real estate fortune been poorly invested?

Yonie sat back, constructing visions of a modest but cozy home into which her lonely grandparents, Madeleine and Jacques Bruneau, would welcome her as their only grandchild.

The next morning, Yonie crunched down a gravel walkway and stood looking up at a dove-gray house that wore on its eaves the fancy cutout designs of a bygone era. A surprisingly unassuming front door presided over a flight of white-painted steps half a story high. A tall hedge bristled around the house like a respectable collar.

Yonie's blouse was still clammy from last evening's laundering. She missed the weight of LaRue on her shoulder, but the cat had not consented to come. "I don't want any part of this," she'd said primly, "but I'll be home by sunset in case you need a shoulder to cry on."

Yonie's shoes clopped hollowly as she climbed the steps. The door featured a small gauzily curtained window, behind which a shadow appeared soon after the jangle of the bell had died away. A long moment later, the door opened.

"Good morning," said Yonie, standing up as straight as she could. "Is M'dam Madeleine Bruneau at home?"

"I am she. Are you the Eggleston girl?"

Yonie's image of her smiling, snowy-haired grand-mother (based on memories of her late Granny Charlotta DuRoy) tattered and whipped away. She suddenly remembered just how young a mother Mama had been. The slim, smartly dressed woman before her could not have been much over fifty. She was brown-haired, with a speckling of silver roots barely visible at her hairline. She was not smiling, either.

"You've probably heard that I do not tolerate tardiness, but undue earliness is very nearly as bad. Next time try to be merely prompt. You may come in and sit in the music room until it is time for your lesson." Madeleine Bruneau made an imperious follow-me gesture and swept away.

"I'm not the Eggleston girl," Yonie called, hurrying after her.

The hallway was papered with a design of lilies and saturated with floral perfume. Glass-fronted cases held platoons of ivory statuettes and rows of painted plates like staring faces. Yonie passed room after dark room overflowing with opulent furniture.

Only a few days ago, she had admired Justine's spacious, sunny house and wondered if her mother had grown up in similar surroundings. She knew now that the answer was no.

Madeleine Bruneau sailed ahead of Yonie into a room containing four divans and a spinet, inlaid above the keyboard with inkwood designs. The mantel over the fireplace supported an ornate gilt clock, which M'dam Bruneau indicated with a meaningful wave of her hand. Another clock hung nearby on the wall, as if to back up the message.

"I'm afraid you've mistaken me for someone else," Yonie said breathlessly, managing to block the doorway before the older woman could leave the room. "My name isn't Eggleston. It's Yonetta DuRoy —"

"DuRoy? Should I know you?" M'dam Bruneau's forehead wrinkled beneath her subtly applied cosmetics.

"No — I mean, I'm hoping you'll want to know me." Yonie inhaled, feeling the cloying perfume coating her throat. "You see, I'm the daughter of Valery Bruneau —"

The woman's face iced over. "Valery is dead."

Yonie nodded heavily. "So you heard about the fire. I didn't know if you would have —"

"She died sixteen years ago," Bruneau said harshly. "We never speak of it — and certainly not to strangers."

For a moment, there was only the tick of the mantel clock and the softer tick of the clock on the wall.

"I'm not a stranger," Yonie said hotly. "I'm your granddaughter —"

"As far as I'm concerned, you're a very rude person who has barged in where she's not welcome, and it's high time you took your leave."

A door across the hall banged open behind Yonie, revealing a heavyset gentleman gripping a newspaper in one fist. "Shame on you!" he roared. "Look how you're upsetting my wife. You can just go on back to whatever muckfoot shack you came from. You're not getting anything from us, and if you have any brothers or sisters, you can tell them the same!"

"It's just me," said Yonie in a small voice. "And I can't go back —"

M'dam Bruneau stepped closer. Her eyes were as hard as two copper gill coins. "You heard my husband. There's nothing here for you. Go to your father for money, if you dare."

"He died in the fire, too —" Yonie choked out.

"Gracious, girl, I don't mean that lump of swamp mud your mother conned into marriage!" The woman let out a razor laugh. "She never told you? Then that's one thing she did right. Now get out of this house, and don't you go harassing the rest of the family, either, or we'll have the law on you, *Yonetta DuRoy.*" Her voice put a vicious twist on Yonie's name.

Yonie retreated down the hallway, gagging on the floral scent and also the under-smell it was probably meant to cover, the moist odor of rot. Behind her she heard M'sir Bruneau say in disbelief, "She named her *Yonetta?*"

Yonie hauled open the front door and threw herself into the fresh air.

One step from the bottom of the stairs, she caught her toe and went flying. Her arms came up too late to do more than smash her elbows into the gravel walk, and her face slapped the ground to the side of it. She tasted blood.

The door slammed above her, but when she turned her head, all she could see was the wooden step a few feet from her face.

She had been prepared to have the Bruneaus doubt her identity. She hadn't expected — *that.*

Yonie got to her knees, which were burning from gravel scrapes. She wiped her eyes on her sleeve, blinked to clear them — and found herself still staring curiously at the steps.

They looked relatively new, but the paint had been slapped on, and the planks were splintery and uneven. No wonder she had tripped.

Why had this recent addition been so poorly made? Yonie didn't know carpentry, but she knew something about antiques, and even if the Bruneaus had no other funds, any of the collector's items she'd glimpsed in the hall could have more than paid for a quality stairway.

Yonie went up to the hedge that screened the bottom of the house and parted the prickly foliage. It was gloomy under the leaves, and for a moment she couldn't understand what she was seeing. Two jaggedly fanged mouths gaped at the base of the wall, drooling mud onto the roots of the hedge.

They were windows — rotted windows with daggers of broken glass around the edges. Only the upper halves still showed above the ground.

The Bruneau house was sinking and was already up to its waist in mud.

The rooms Yonie had just been in must have originally been the upper floor, but were now the only part of the house still habitable. If one could call it that. No amount of perfume could mask the smell wafting up from a downstairs filled with sinkhole sludge.

Yonie's hands curled as she thought of her grandparents living in that damp, doomed house. Why did they endure it? They had that trove of antiques. Madeleine Bruneau had music students — enough, evidently, that she could afford to be rude to them. Surely they could be living in a perfectly decent apartment in some less fashionable part of the city.

But of course that would mean giving up most of their belongings — all those clocks and divans and statuettes, the furnishings of a large house now crammed into half the space. It would mean giving up their High Town address.

And it would mean giving up their home — a house that, according to *Bellamy's Social Roster*, had been in the family for generations.

Yonie stomped back down the eerily silent street, noticing now the crazy tilt to so many roofs and walls. How many neighbors still remained?

Madeleine and Jacques Bruneau, clearly, were people who held tightly to what they had. Had they tried to hold their daughter that tightly too? Mentally Yonie applauded Mama for her extraordinary escape.

The Bruneaus had been right about one thing, she decided: they certainly had nothing to offer Yonie. Nothing except nasty insinuations about Yonie's paternity — and she would not let those words bother her.

She would not.

When LaRue dropped down through the roof-door that evening, she found Yonie scrubbing the garret's floor with a soapy rag, something she had felt compelled to do upon moving in but not since.

"Oh dear, did it go as badly as that?"

"Worse." By the time Yonie finished recounting her visit to the Bruneaus, she was weeping, though not actually on LaRue's shoulder.

"So I spent the rest of the afternoon just paddling around, thinking," she concluded.

"About what, my sweet?"

"Mostly about Papa. How he used to hug me, and the buttons on his coat would dig in — it was really uncomfortable, but I didn't care. How he taught me to dance the maroky, and I didn't find out till the DeGaults' wedding party that he didn't really know the steps; he was just making it all up. How he looked when he was playing the fiddle in the evening, with his eyes all crinkled up and happy, and then after I was in bed, he would tell me those stories — 'The Frog Sisters' and 'The Boat of Stars' and all the ones about Jack-of-the-Mire and Curly Dog. I thought about all that.

"And — I didn't want to, LaRue — but I thought about what M'dam Bruneau said. I just couldn't help it."

Yonie looked down into the cat's golden-green eyes. "I remembered some things Mama and Papa said that just seemed a little strange at the time. Like once when Mama was brushing my hair, she kind of muttered, 'You certainly got my hair, thank goodness.' I never understood why she would say that, because I would have been just as happy with curly black hair like Papa's.

"And then there's my middle name. Sebastienne. It's not common to name a *girl* after her father, is it? But Papa insisted. As if he was working extra hard to say *this is my daughter.*

"But mainly, I was remembering something Papa used to say." Yonie lowered her voice and let it take on a bayou burr. "'After I met 'er that first time and 'eard that angel voice, I knew she was the only one for me. It was only two months before I made 'er my wife, but they were the longest two months I can recall.'

"But now I know she was four months pregnant when she left school, and she wasn't married until then, so how could she have met Papa just two months before?"

LaRue regarded Yonie with an unblinking green gaze. "Ah, you've been doing arithmetic. I must tell you that where matters of procreation are concerned, genteel people are expected to entirely forget that ability."

"LaRue." Yonie's voice dropped to a painful whisper. "Was Papa really my papa?"

"Listen to you! Is your canoe your canoe? Yonie, dearest, do you think I care what tom sired *me?* I care about the folks who loved me and raised me. That's all I need to know, and the same goes for you." LaRue rubbed her cheek against Yonie's tear-streaked one, leaving behind several threads of orange fuzz.

But it was different, Yonie thought that night as she lay awake on her pallet. She might not care for her own sake if Papa had sired her, as LaRue put it. Plenty of Delta children were adopted — during the flu epidemic, as the saying went, Granny Pitchers had been fishing with a net.

But Yonie cared that her parents hadn't told her, and she cared a great deal about what they might have suffered. Forgetting what Madeleine Bruneau had said would not be so easy.

CHAPTER ELEVEN

YONIE VISITED the Bellflower library frequently over the next few weeks, following her own curiosity. The authors' names embossed on the spines of the history and archaeology books became friends: T. E. Verville (leading authority on ancient industry), Robert Jacks Jr. (eminent art historian), and the archaeologists D. & J. McKnee, who had handwritten a dedication to the Bellflower library in each volume of their work.

The librarian's stern attitude gradually melted into fondness. "Yonie, honey, I think there's still time for a cup of tea outside before it starts pouring," M'dam Pierpond told her one humid morning. "Would you like to keep me company?"

After they stopped by the school kitchens, Pierpond led Yonie down a rope-suspended walkway. Yonie was surprised when the librarian halted in a spot that was scenic but had no benches. Then she saw that several nearby blue gum trunks bulged out into burls that could be used as seats.

"Make yourself comfortable, honey," said Pierpond, majestically lowering herself down with a motion that set her braid-loops swinging. "Now, tell me, what have you been reading about lately?"

"The Sky Tower of Rheniol."

The librarian raised her eyebrows. "I knew you had an interest in antiquities, but C'thovan relics? That's about as old as it gets."

"It's just so mysterious," Yonie said. "The way the wood and the steel are preserved, and how they blend into each other without a seam. And those relics from Gry, too, like the Glowing Jars of Sarun! How on earth did the ancients get those effects? None of the scholars even want to speculate. They label everything mysterious as 'chiridou,' which is just another word for magic."

"Not exactly," Pierpond said dryly. "Magic doesn't exist. Those relics do." She sighed. "Honey, you can't expect people to enjoy dwelling on powers that we don't have, from places that are still tainting our river." She took a sip of tea.

"You must have learned in your trade that the, ah, unique qualities of our local water are even more of a taboo subject among the educated class than they are among the general populace."

"Not so much in my, er, trade," Yonie hedged, not wanting to admit that so far her High Town clients had numbered one. "But I've certainly noticed it among the students here at Bellflower."

"Oh, yes, you've been eating your lunch with Justine Cordell, haven't you?"

It had been gratifying when Justine sought out Yonie's company — and soon her classmates had followed. As it turned out, Yonie could make an entire circle of girls erupt in hushed giggles by recounting a few professional anecdotes, which they all seemed to consider deliciously naughty.

Having a group of friends her own age was a new and precious thing for Yonie, and was a direct result of her library privileges. Yonie hoped that Headmaster Cordell, if he heard of these gatherings, would not regard her as a Bad Influence. She shifted guiltily on the blue gum burl.

"I'm sorry, honey. Should we find ourselves a bench?"

"Oh, this is perfectly comfortable," Yonie said, absently patting the whorled wood of her seat. "It's as if the tree remembers that M'sir Fabian intended it for furniture."

The librarian's eyes widened, and Yonie realized too late that referring to guile could be considered risqué.

Then Pierpond gave an earthy chuckle. "It's a rare

student here who knows how the Grove came to be planted. Fabian's Folly, eh?" She dumped the remains of her tea over the side of the walkway. "Let's get back to the library. There's something you deserve to see."

"I'm allowed to use my own judgment about who gets access to the Bellflower Collection," Pierpond said as she unhooked the brown velvet rope from across the bottom of the central staircase. "And frankly, I think you're more responsible than a lot of the senior pupils I let up here for special projects."

At the top of the stairs, Pierpond unlocked a door and gestured Yonie inside. "We have to lock it — that rope down there might as well be cobwebs, for all the good it does. Be sure to let me know when you leave," she warned. "And, honey, if you should feel like organizing anything — please be my guest."

Yonie managed a thank-you as the librarian retreated down the stairs. The square room was as large as the entire downstairs of the library, but its walkable space was much less, due to a hodgepodge of tables that formed a maze.

The windows were as plentiful as the ones downstairs, but the panes were covered by curtains of vines that gave the room a green-lit, underwater feel — an Under Town for old, forgotten things.

A few tables near the entryway held neat stacks of books and book-repair materials, but as for the rest of the room, Pierpond had evidently adopted the same attitude as the gardener had about the vines.

There were crates of papers stacked up to five high. There were trophies with figurines that danced, wielded paintbrushes, or presented perfect loaves of bread. There were helmets from some antiquated sport. There were three dressmaking dummies and a ceramic head with insets of real hair that had suffered a cruel shearing. There were bins of fabric remnants in eye-twisting patterns that had probably only benefited from their years of fading.

Any hopes Yonie harbored of finding traces of her mother had fizzled the instant she set foot upstairs. The heat alone was oppressive enough to put a time limit on her stay. Swinging open a window was out of the question — some of the vines were as thick as her wrist.

But to humor M'dam Pierpond, Yonie felt she should linger at least a little while. And as she edged her way along the makeshift aisles, she realized that to locate anything in the Bellflower Collection, one had to adopt the outlook of a geologist rather than a librarian. If she could identify the stratum of her mother's era, she might actually find something.

Some time later, face coated with sweat and dust, she did.

The charcoal sketches from some long-ago art class were of varying quality, but the one of Yonie's mother would have been unmistakable even without *V. Bruneau* neatly lettered at the bottom. The quirky smile, the slight lift of one eyebrow, the hand pressed to her cheek — Yonie had seen that expression a thousand times in the course of her childhood. The schoolgirl who had captured that likeness was a gifted artist, and Yonie hoped her talent had not been suffocated in her adult life.

Yonie knuckled her eyes, snuffed deeply, and wiped her sweaty hands on her skirt. It would not do to smudge this picture. Trying not to think too hard about what she was doing, she carefully transported it over to her knapsack and closed it between the pages of her notebook.

Adele Pierpond's glance into Yonie's knapsack as she exited the library was perfunctory, far different from the inspections of a few weeks ago. The librarian might have been just as glad to see Yonie taking her dust-smirched clothing and cobwebby hair safely away from the orderly lower floor.

The clouds were deepening to purple as Yonie hurried toward the main gate. There was no time for lunch, she decided. Her knapsack would protect the sketch from a light rain, but not a downpour.

The sweat from Yonie's hour in the attic was barely cooled on her face when she encountered Headmaster Cordell, stumping along with his fists pushing out the pockets of his coat.

"M'dam Watereye! Would you have a moment to talk with me in my office?"

* * *

The headmaster opened his desk drawer and pulled out the muskrat locket. "I want to apologize for doubting your skills," he said. "After you removed this from me, I wrote to my wife the same day. If she was going to hear stories about my behavior, I wanted her to hear from me first. I also told her not to blame herself for the trouble her gift had caused."

He let the locket clunk onto his desk, the chain slithering down around it.

"Today I got her reply, and it was very troubling. You see, she had never heard of any locket."

"What? But wasn't there a note with it?"

"There was — but I can see now that it's not her handwriting." He set a sheet of paper on the desk. "See how it's almost illegible? And then farther down, the writer apologizes, saying the river was choppy that evening."

The headmaster of a school, Yonie was sure, would have to be a man of even temper. But she could tell that inside, Cordell was raging.

"M'dam Watereye, would you be willing to help me again? For additional pay, of course."

"Do you mean another Seeing?"

"Not necessarily. Mainly I just need someone who can do a little poking around. A person who's discreet, and who is not, er, constrained by the demands of a rigid schedule. You see, I know now that someone is trying to get me dismissed from my position, and I would very much like to know who.

"What do you think, M'dam Watereye? I know it's not much to go on, but you can take the note and the locket. And here's the portrait that was inside." He showed her the small oval of card, then swept all three items into an envelope. "I'll pay you three gallons a day."

Yonie's eyebrows rose. The most expert fish cleaners at the cannery made two.

Then she shook her head. "I'm sorry, sir, but I couldn't take your money. I'm just a pearly. I'm not the person you need." A few streaks of rain were beginning to dot the windowpane behind him.

"Well. That's a disappointment." Cordell looked down at the envelope, then slid it toward Yonie. "Take these things, anyway, in case you change your mind. Or even if you don't. I can't stand them near me anymore."

Yonie fitted another stick of firewood into her tiny box of a stove. Her wet clothes hung from hooks on the rafters nearest to the fire, spread out like enormous bat wings.

The entire way home, she was expecting to find her notebook and the sketch one sodden mass. But her oilcloth raincoat wrapped around the knapsack had kept the contents dry. She had reverently removed the stolen charcoal drawing and secreted it under the large front cover of *The Unlucky Prince* on her shelf.

When LaRue came in not long after, somehow the

sketch got omitted from Yonie's story of her day, which was already eventful enough.

"You turned down a job offer?" LaRue licked the last tuft of fur dry. "This may be a first."

"I turn down 'jobs' every time I walk down Marsh-stair Street after dark."

"Very funny. But still, I'm surprised."

"I wish I could help him. But I wouldn't be any use, and to tell the truth, LaRue, the whole thing scares me."

"Of course it does," said the cat. "It was unsettling enough, seeing a wily thing twist up that poor man the way it did. But knowing it was done deliberately! I only hope there are no consequences to you."

"What do you mean?"

LaRue's tail swished against the floor. "Well. Today you learned that in helping M'sir Cordell, you did not just avert an accident. You deflected a precisely aimed weapon. Whoever planned that attack will not be pleased with you. Not at all."

CHAPTER TWELVE

ON THE next Saturn-day morning, the rising sun stabbed Yonie's eyes as she tied up her canoe outside her neighborhood pub.

The Mole-in-'Ole wasn't seedy enough to entice slumming travelers, but was sufficiently dubious to make newcomers examine the mugs for cleanliness. It did, however, attract a faithful group of frugal dockworkers and fishermen, and thus was open most hours.

The placard outside its door featured a jolly squint-eyed mole peering from its burrow, one long-clawed paw clutching a pint glass. The fumes of fermenting merryberries wafting from the DesMaray Brewery across the way added to the ambiance.

There was probably no ideal time for a sixteen-year-old girl to visit an alehouse, but early morning was better than most. There were a dozen or so customers inside, evenly divided between what Yonie thought of as Day People and Night People. The Day People were mostly fishy-smelling folk from nearby villages who'd been up since before dawn transporting yesterday's catch to market. They were gulping tea and scraping fried eggs off tin plates.

The Night People were sweaty cargo men just come from unloading barges and shady characters whose smell was sweeter but whose professions were less savory. They were drinking Wicked Ford's signature ruby ale or more exotic liquors imported from up the Skulk.

"Hey, Yonie! Are y'here to have a drink with me, at long last?" called out one of the younger Night People, flashing her a grin. It was Luc "Lucky" Lazard, an agreeable enough fellow who, as Yonie understood it, made his living by providing entertainment to tourists — entertainment that usually resulted in his winning money at cards.

"Give it up, Lucky. She'd drink you onto the floor and out the door," bawled a heavyset fisherman who went by Cattail Jack.

Two years earlier, as a skinny fourteen-year-old, Yonie had entered the pub and politely asked for a bottle of their strongest brandy. The story had not been forgotten, and had in fact taken on a life of its own. Yonie was sure that by now, even the men who had been in the pub at the time recalled her draining the entire bottle in one draft. Her later protestations that she hadn't bought the brandy for drinking had been met with winks and laughter — even by the pub's owner, Serge Molyneaux, who had helped her use it to disinfect the knife slice on her hand.

(That had been the end of her employment gutting fish down at the water market, and a good thing too. She could never match the speed of the professionals, and as LaRue said, it was hazardous to put herself where her pride made her try.)

"M'sir Molyneaux, good morning!" Yonie greeted the squat, muscular man behind the bar. "I don't suppose you've got any letters for me?"

"Woo, la-di-da — she's got customers who read, now?" called Johnny Fought-Askew from his usual corner, blinking at her over his loaf of a nose.

"I can hope, can't I?" Yonie shot back. Most of her customers were illiterate, but Molyneaux was kind enough to take messages. This was also the address she had given to Headmaster Cordell, since her garret — and her entire building — were, as far as she knew, unnamed.

"That fellow Gerard came in," Molyneaux rumbled. He passed over a scrap of brown paper on which he had recorded the fisherman's note: *My Wife is home safe. Thank you Mam thank you. You kepe that gong I dont want it back.*

Yonie sighed and felt one burden lighter.

"There's more." Casually, the proprietor passed his hands under the counter and then attempted to make an envelope appear out of Yonie's ear. The trick was clumsily done, as always, but Yonie was careful to act surprised and delighted.

In fact, she *was.* The envelope was petite and creamy and stamped with the green hoofmark insignia of the Leaping Deer Delivery Service, one of the city's most reliable (and most expensive).

Yonie whipped her belt knife from its sheath and sliced the envelope open. She heard murmurs behind her as she put away the knife and could almost feel the blade growing six inches and acquiring a cougar-bone handle stained with blood.

Dear Mme. Watereye,
My husband's colleague Roger Cordell has recommended your services for a special inspection I need done in my place of business. If you are interested, you can find me during daytime hours in my shop, Therese's Treasures, at the junction of the Grand Canal and Shoveler Row.
Yours sincerely,
Therese Turcoat

A smile dawned on Yonie's face.

"Look, it's from one of her admirers," shouted One-Eye Belowdeck.

"It's about a job," Yonie told Molyneaux, turning her back to the others. "Thank you, sir, for holding the letter."

Luc Lazard sighed theatrically. "Should've known she wouldn't smile that way for a love letter."

"Yeah, she gets so many, see, they don't make an impression anymore," agreed Big Remy, his neighbor at the bar.

Yonie's cheeks were flushed as she strode out the door.

Therese's Treasures had a narrow storefront in what looked to be a very desirable location, just up the Grand Canal from where the black iron statue of a horseman stood overlooking Shoveler Bridge.

Therese Turcoat had gone to some trouble to make her shop inviting. Broad panes of high-quality glass showed passersby a constellation of brooches, rings, and earrings on midnight velvet, clouds of fine scarves, and brush-and-comb sets inlaid with pink shell. There were inkwood carvings and fabric patterned in merryberry dye, as well as a number of mysterious gadgets of just the sort to pique Yonie's interest.

Above the door hung a freshly painted sign lettered in green and gold, its edges carved in ornate curlicues. "Therese's Treasures — something for everyone," Yonie read aloud for the benefit of LaRue on her shoulder. "Huh. Something for every wealthy female, more like."

The slim woman with a glossy coil of dark hair atop her head had to be the owner, Yonie guessed, from the way she raised her head with deer-like alertness when Yonie entered the shop. Yonie was gratified by the warm welcome she received, even after she explained that she was not a customer.

"M'dam Watereye, I'm so glad you got my letter. Please, come in back and I'll explain." M'dam Turcoat swept Yonie into a room full of boxes and a wide worktable. "Here, now we can speak in private. Not that it's terribly unprivate out there. That's the whole problem, really—it hasn't been busy, not for months. People come in, wander around one or two minutes, and then leave. I've never seen anything like it. Even in the slow season, people usually browse."

Turcoat gave Yonie a haunted look. "I lost my assistant. She just didn't feel comfortable here anymore, she said. After three years with me! I would have had to let her go anyway—I'll be lucky if I can pay next month's rent—but I started to wonder. I do get a number of antiques through here, and things from the backcountry too."

The shop owner's face betrayed a slight flush. "I've never employed a—a person of your talents before, but I don't know what else to do. It took me years to open this shop. If I lose it now, it'll just break my heart."

"I understand completely, M'dam Turcoat," Yonie said. "I'll be as thorough as I can."

"M'sir Cordell said you were very, er, perceptive. I wasn't sure what you'd need in the way of equipment — will this do?" She gestured toward the table, one end of which was covered with a pale green linen cloth. A gleaming silver basin rested next to a carafe of murky green canal water, which had a matching green satin bow tied around its glass neck. A basket of folded white hand towels was set out nearby.

"Er — that should do nicely, ma'am," Yonie said.

Turcoat agreed to a fixed fee, with Yonie's assurance that she would be able to finish the inspection by the end of the day. Yonie was delighted that they had not settled on an hourly rate, since her scruples would then have compelled her to work efficiently. As it was, she anticipated a leisurely day of looking at beautiful and fascinating things.

So why, Yonie wondered as she worked her way methodically through the shop full of Treasures, cat on shoulder, was she not having a good time?

She knew she was welcome here. The shop itself was open and well lit. Why did it seem so oppressive? Why did she feel as if coming here had been a terrible mistake?

Yonie felt a furry cheek rubbing insistently under her ear, and blew out her breath. LaRue had found the problem, and soon they could get paid and go home.

"Ma'am?"

The shop owner looked up eagerly from her paperwork. "Yes, M'dam Watereye? Have you found anything you need to inspect — er — more closely?"

"Not yet, ma'am. I thought I'd step out for lunch before I start on the back room."

"Oh, of course. I can't join you, I'm afraid — I need to pick up my new gown — but I highly recommend Truffaut's, on the corner of Shoveler and Jollifee. Their quiche is just divine."

"Thank you, ma'am," said Yonie politely.

Five minutes later, she was squatting in the shadows under a nameless bridge where Shoveler crossed the Pig Alley Canal, eating lukewarm beans and rice out of a jar. Next to her on the damp ground, LaRue licked at the jar lid that held her portion. The chattering of the pedestrians above, Yonie hoped, would be enough to mask the sound of their conversation, and the heap of sour-smelling refuse nearby should discourage visitors.

Upon exiting the shop, LaRue had streaked away, and it had become clear that she had signaled Yonie not because she had discovered anything, but because she needed to, as she put it, "answer Nature's call." Yonie had always been a little curious about where LaRue went to accomplish this, but knew that the cat would consider it very indelicate of her to ask. (Yonie was also slightly jealous, having paid two gills to use the public "convenience" at the end of the block.)

"So there is a problem in the shop, then?" she asked the cat.

"Definitely. I'm used to feeling unappreciated in certain establishments — the fishmonger's, for instance — but I felt quite remarkably unwelcome in that place. Didn't you? I only hope I can locate the wily thing by the end of the day."

The windows of the shop's back room were beginning to darken. Yonie rolled her shoulders, which were cramped from unpacking and repacking endless crates and sacks. LaRue paced wearily along the tabletop, studying the last batch of items Yonie had set out.

They had looked at bells and inkwells, egg scales and thimbles, fish servers and asparagus tongs, perfume bottles and feathered fans, metronomes and tuning forks, egg slicers and apple peelers, as well as a bucketful of jewelry. Of them all, only four had carried more than a trace of guile.

There were two hand mirrors, one that gave an overly flattering reflection, and one that pointed out the minutest facial flaws. There was a porcelain doll's head, whose painted eyes seemed to gaze lovingly back at the onlooker. And there was a bronze paperweight in the shape of a malproportioned swan, which was much heavier than expected.

Turcoat had been flustered but fascinated to have the wily features pointed out. But they were still no closer to finding the source of the uneasiness that pervaded the shop.

The doll's head, to tell the truth, was slightly creepy, but LaRue had ruled it out.

Yonie rested her forehead in her hands. That morning, she had been sure dozens of High Town customers lay in her future. But how could she ever build a reputation when she started with this sort of failure? And poor M'dam Turcoat — it hurt to disappoint her so badly.

The door swung open.

"M'dam Watereye, it's unfortunate, but I really can't stay any longer. I've already missed dinner, and I'm attending a concert tonight, my husband's advanced vocal ensemble. As it is, I'll have to change here." Turcoat crossed the room and took down the long dress box she had returned with that afternoon.

"Pretty, isn't it?" she said, unlidding the box and lifting the gown up toward the fading light. "I ordered it back before this trouble started. Don't know how I'll pay for it now," she added, half to herself.

Yonie, though no expert on clothing, had to admire the deep brown velvet, and the spiraled gold cord that decorated the collar like coils of miniature rope.

Brown velvet. Rope . . .

Yonie fumbled for the end of her braid and squeezed the luck-beads tight as she tried to hold on to the connection that had just formed in her brain.

"I was so hoping you'd able to help me," Turcoat said. "But I suppose you might as well go."

"M'dam Turcoat, wait just one minute!" Yonie dashed out the storeroom door, through the shop displays, and out the front door into the street, with LaRue at her heels.

Outside, the oppressive weight of you-don't-belong-here lifted, and the memory came clear as rainwater. In the Bellflower library, M'dam Pierpond was unhooking a brown velvet rope from the bottom of the spiral stair, leading Yonie up toward the Special Collection and saying, *That rope down there might as well be cobwebs, for all the good it does.*

A velvet rope. Easy to step over — a psychological barrier only, and ineffectual at that.

But what if such a barrier was thick with guile? Even if it had no physical power to bar the way, its effect on the mind might be very strong indeed.

Yonie scooped up LaRue and raised the cat above her head. The cat's whiskers came forward, and she slitted her eyes at the signboard above the shop door.

"Yessss," LaRue said, in what might, in an ordinary cat, have been taken for a hiss.

CHAPTER THIRTEEN

ARE YOU quite sure?" asked Turcoat. "It's such an attractive sign, and brand-new. I just got it —" She paused and gave a short puff of a laugh. "A few months ago. Right before business started going down."

Yonie nodded. "It's freshly painted, but anything with that much guile is not new. I expect it used to say *no trespassing* or something like that. I can't give you the details without getting it into some guile-water, though, and it's so big that'll mean dipping it in a canal. Of course, you could just remove it and see if business improves."

"No," said Turcoat tightly. "I need to be sure." She

fetched a screwdriver and a stepladder, and they were soon lowering the signboard to the brick sidewalk.

"I should be back in about ten minutes," Yonie said. "There's a small canal nearby that should do."

"Should I — accompany you?"

Yonie hoisted the sign onto her shoulder. It was heavy, but not as heavy as a canoe. "I'll be all right, ma'am. Besides, don't you need to change?"

"Oh!" Looking horrified, Turcoat dashed back into the shop.

The sides of the Pig Alley Canal, Yonie had noted earlier in the day, were a gruel of mud and algae, a likely lurking place for guile. She let the sign down with a splash.

LaRue stared intently at the signboard, pupils stretched so wide that they looked round as a human's. Yonie was not sure if LaRue's Seeings involved actual seeing, in addition to intense concentration, but if so, it was fortunate that she had the night vision of a cat. It had been shady under the bridge at midday, and now it was gloomy indeed. The only light came from a lantern outside a restaurant on Shoveler Row, half a block away, and the bridge cut a dark swath through that lantern-shine.

Yonie wished she had not chosen to go under the bridge, even though there were stone steps leading down to the water. The signboard standing upright in the mud looked like a door leading down to Under Town itself.

"It's old," LaRue said in a low voice. "Terribly old. If

it weren't so wily, it would've fallen to pieces ages ago. The original paint is long gone. But it still remembers — oh, yes, it remembers what it used to say. It was not in our language, but I think I can understand . . ."

Yonie's eyes had adjusted well enough for her to see the fur along LaRue's back and sides standing out like flames. When LaRue finally spoke, her voice rang out like a bronze bell.

"Let not the unworthy pass this way, lest their skin be peeled from off their flesh and cured into armor for the sons of Lanakilimn, and their bones be carven with flowers and pierced for necklaces to delight the daughters of Oukharath, and their cartilage —"

A scream gashed the air, and a chunk of darkness rose up under the bridge only a few feet away. A moment later, Yonie found herself on top of the bridge, her hands scraped from the stone steps and her throat raw from the shrieks clawing their way out.

From the other side of the bridge, a ragged figure shot out and ran pell-mell down the street. In the light of the lantern he looked like an ordinary, if terror-stricken man, and suddenly Yonie felt rather foolish.

"Poor man," said LaRue, sauntering up to join Yonie. "He won't sleep again tonight, I'm sure. I didn't even see him behind that rubbish heap. I suppose I could have translated just the words, and not the tone — though it was compelling, don't you think?"

* * *

The pile of banknotes was deliciously thick in Yonie's hand, and the shop now felt friendly and welcoming, with a lamp lit in the front room and a curtain pulled cozily across the display window.

"I've added a little extra for your trouble," Turcoat told her, eyeing the canal-slime that coated Yonie's shoes, hands, and sleeves. "It's well worth it, to have a full report. Now I won't need to hold back tomorrow when I talk to the man who sold me that sign."

"Oh, I'm sure he had no idea—"

"M'sir Weatherley owns that big antique store on the corner. He's been trying to put me out of business for years." The shop owner wrapped a lacy shawl over her shoulders and secured it with a sharp jab of the pin. "He can't seem to understand that having me nearby actually brings in more customers. Myself, I'd love it if this whole block became known as Antique Row—" Turcoat stopped herself on the brink of what was obviously a favorite spiel. "Anyway, when he offered me that sign at a discount, I was fool enough to think it was a peace offering. He said he'd bought it for himself, and it turned out to be too small for his storefront. Hah! Not that I can do much, since no judge would admit testimony from a pearly. No offense, M'dam Watereye."

Yonie looked down. She thought it very unlikely the sign was part of a sinister plot. In her career as a pearly, she had encountered only a handful of wily things that were truly harmful, and she had never seen one used in malice.

Except for M'sir Cordell's locket, of course.

Turcoat had regained her composure. "Do you know, I can feel the difference in the shop already? Well, now I must run, truly run, if I want to get to Bowdown Hall in time for the concert. I do hope I'm not late, or it will be the first time in nearly twenty years. And the advanced vocal ensemble is so special. Emile takes such time with the girls, especially the lead soprano, and the results are just spellbinding."

Turcoat put out the lamp and ushered Yonie out the door. As she turned to lock it, Yonie found her voice.

"Twenty years? If—" She cleared her throat.

"Gracious, what's the matter, M'dam Watereye?"

"It's just—if your husband's been teaching voice at Bellflower for twenty years, then he must have taught my mother. Valery Bruneau."

Turcoat's eyebrows lifted like a blue heron's wings. "Valery Bruneau . . . I *do* remember a Valery! Lovely girl— we had her to tea many times. Emile was extremely fond of her. He would go on and on about her exquisite voice. But she moved away, didn't she? Very suddenly? He was quite bereft. I suppose that's why I remember so well." She smiled at Yonie. "Perhaps we should have you to tea one day. But for now, good evening, M'dam Watereye, and a safe trip home."

Yonie watched M'dam Turcoat hurry away up Shoveler Row at a near run that still somehow managed to be graceful. Then she began to plod in the other direction, back toward her canoe.

Enticing smells drifted down from the restaurants farther up the street, making Yonie's stomach grind. She wished she could afford to go there. She wished she had someone to go there with.

It would be so pleasant to be like M'dam Turcoat: finely dressed, on her way to an entertainment, and going back afterward with her husband to a comfortable home. Far better than wearing threadbare clothes smeared with mud and facing a long paddle home in the dark to a cramped garret where she would have to eat cold beans.

At least Yonie wasn't sleeping under a bridge like the man LaRue had frightened away. But thinking of that poor man just made her feel worse. There were so many people who needed help, and she could barely take care of herself.

Could she even do that? Where would she be without LaRue? Papa had always said that so long as she was honest and did her best, she could feel proud of herself. What would he say about the life she was leading now, when her livelihood was based on deception and putting her best friend at risk?

It would not be for much longer, Yonie promised herself. She would get more High Town jobs, and someday, she had decided in the course of the afternoon, she would open her own antique shop.

M'dam Turcoat might even help her. She had already

invited Yonie to tea. Well, not exactly, but she might. After all, hadn't Yonie's mother been almost a family friend? One of her husband's star pupils, one of those lead sopranos with whom he spent so much time?

A memory surfaced in Yonie's mind. She was standing on an aerial walkway surrounded by blue gum leaves, hearing that rusty-haired Bellflower girl — Lacey Wynne, that was her name — gossip about the teachers. *And then there's Turcoat, the music master — look out or he'll want to give you private lessons, if you know what I mean . . .*

Yonie's mother would have had many private lessons with Emile Turcoat. Yonie's mother, of whom M'sir Turcoat had been "extremely fond."

Yonie walked faster, threading her way through crowds of cheery restaurant-goers as LaRue scurried to keep up. Instead of the brick sidewalk under her feet, she could almost feel the peeling bark of the blue gum branch she had perched on that day at Bellflower, while two teachers passed by chatting below.

She had heard M'sir Turcoat's voice, smooth and suave. Hadn't he been charming M'dam LaRue into doing something for him? A persuasive man. And Yonie had glimpsed him as well, his silvered blond hair (*You certainly got my hair, thank goodness,* Mama had said) and his height (unusually tall, just like Yonie). He would not have been so very much older than Valery then, even if he had already been a married man . . .

Yonie stopped so suddenly that LaRue trotted right into her ankles. "Was it him?" she said aloud in an anguished voice, causing several passersby to cut her a wider margin.

A horribly plausible story spun itself out in Yonie's mind. Her mother had trusted and admired the dashing young music master, and he had seduced her. She had not dared to tell anyone — or possibly she had told her parents, and they had blamed her. Maybe she even blamed herself.

Then she had discovered she was pregnant. Yonie could not even imagine how terrifying that would be for a young woman in that stratum of society, and in that particular family.

When young Valery had met Sebastien DuRoy, it must have been like the sun coming out after a storm. He had rescued her from the whole mess and turned out to be as good a husband and father as she could ever have hoped for.

It all fit, sickeningly well.

Again the memory came to her: the tall figure of Emile Turcoat, striding down the walkway beneath her tree-branch perch. She had never seen his face clearly. How she regretted that now! If they shared some prominent feature (unconsciously, Yonie fingered her nose), it might put her doubts to rest.

She could seek him out at the Academy. The prospect of meeting with him filled her with dread, but she knew she would not sleep until she had seen his face.

But wait — why search for him at Bellflower? Tonight,

at least, she knew exactly where he was. A well-lit public place, where she could stare at his features as long as she wished, and no one would think anything of it.

Yonie turned and started back up Shoveler Row, fists at her sides, shoe soles hitting the sidewalk like hammers.

CHAPTER FOURTEEN

BOWDOWN HALL had been constructed to mimic the Iblonian style, which favored white marble, fluted columns, and roof domes. This had been a tall order to carry out in wood, and even in the twilight, Yonie could tell that the whitewash on the exterior was in need of refreshing. Indeed, the only part of the building that was truly a dazzling white was the top of the dome, where a large flock of doves was currently (and, Yonie assumed, frequently) at rest.

Yonie's experience of musical performances had been limited to backcountry weddings and fish fries, and to the buskers of varying skill who played at the markets around

Wicked Ford. So it was a shame, she thought as she paid the surprisingly high admission fee, that on her first visit to a real concert hall she should be entering late, too distracted to listen to the music.

The hall was stuffy, smelled of cologne, and at the moment was filled with the rushing-water sound of applause. Up on the stage the advanced vocal ensemble, wearing fluffy white dresses piped with Bellflower green, stood arrayed on risers. The shorter students had been placed in the front row, and Yonie recognized her friend Justine beaming self-consciously at the audience.

M'sir Turcoat stood to one side, looking dapper in a butter-colored vest and gray cravat. There was the tall physique and graying blond hair Yonie remembered seeing from above, and the stylishly trimmed goatee.

Yonie walked down the aisle toward the stage, eyes fixed on Turcoat's face. Yes—a distinct falcon's beak of a nose, much like the one Yonie had seen as a child whenever she picked up Mama's tortoiseshell hand mirror.

Here was the man who had overturned her mother's life.

Yonie's fingernails dug into her palms. Up onstage, Turcoat had paused by Justine. Casually, he placed a hand on the schoolgirl's puffed sleeve, bent, and spoke into her ear before walking smoothly to the center of the stage.

Yonie's blood hammered in her head. That possessive touch on Justine's shoulder—if Turcoat would do that in public, how might he treat her if they were alone?

She could not allow this to continue. Turcoat had gone for sixteen years without any consequences for his actions. He would not go longer.

"Thank you so much," Turcoat told the audience in a voice as sleek as a newly shined shoe. "Our next piece will be 'Over the Mountain, Under the Stars.' This is a traditional ballad about love and honor, from the shepherds of the Kashtan hill country —"

"'Ow *dare* you!" Yonie found herself at the foot of the stage, chin raised to glare up at the music master. "You ought to be ashamed to even 'ave the words *love* and *honor* in your mouth!"

M'sir Turcoat gaped. "Young lady, I don't know who you are, but —"

Yonie vaulted onto the stage, the loose sleeves of her blouse flaring out like the wings of a raptor stooping upon its prey. "Aye, you don't even know 'oo I am — and me your own daughter!" she snarled. The excellent acoustics carried her voice to all corners of the hall.

The vocal ensemble gasped and craned their necks. One girl on the back riser teetered too far forward and had to be caught by her neighbors.

Yonie stalked closer to the music master, who was looking desperately in all directions. "You don't know me," she spat, "but you knew my mother way too well, you piece of slime. 'Er name" — she stabbed a finger toward Turcoat's chest —"was Valery Bruneau!"

Emile Turcoat's eyes found her face, just as hands came from behind Yonie and seized her by the upper arms.

As the ushers hustled Yonie out of the hall, she could hear "Over the Mountain, Under the Stars" getting off to a shaky, but under the circumstances quite creditable start. She did not resist as the ushers shoved her out into the dark street and was only vaguely aware of their threats to toss her in the canal if she returned.

All Yonie could think about was the expression she'd seen on Turcoat's face in those last moments. It hadn't been rage, or shame, or fear. It had been pure bewilderment.

M'sir Turcoat, quite clearly, had had no idea what she was talking about.

Yonie stumbled down the sidewalk, feeling as if she had indeed been thrown into cold canal water. What had she been thinking? There had never been any real evidence against M'sir Turcoat.

She had wrecked the concert, which the students must have been rehearsing for months. She had probably wrecked her own chances of ever getting another High Town job. And she might have wrecked M'sir Turcoat's reputation, maybe even his teaching career.

Numbly, Yonie let her feet carry her back down Travers Street, past the golden-lit windows of a café whose occupants looked happy and carefree. Two of the customers, she couldn't help but notice, had noses like Emile Turcoat's.

A wet fog was rolling in off the marshes, and the boats along the Canal Angelique had lit their bow lanterns. Yonie's clothes were clammy with sweat from her run. The caked mud on her sleeves, on the other hand, was dry enough now to flake off. A fine apparition she must have made, raving in front of all those people. LaRue had always said that Yonie's quick temper would get her in trouble someday, but she never could have imagined this.

The fog touching Yonie's face suddenly chilled right through to her skull. *Where was LaRue?*

Yonie whirled around, already knowing the cat had not been at her heels for a long time.

When had she last seen her?

LaRue had bumped into her ankles down on Shoveler Row when Yonie had suddenly changed direction. And then Yonie had dashed off up the street, dodging along a crowded sidewalk.

She'll be peeved with me, but she'll be all right, Yonie told herself. Surely the cat would go wait in the *Dragonfly,* instead of striking off through an unfamiliar area to try to find her way home through the dark.

And the fog.

And the feral dogs that ranged along the overgrown canal banks, and the drunken bargemen who liked to kick cats with their steel-toed boots.

* * *

Yonie forced her weary body up the stairs to her garret. LaRue had not been waiting in the *Dragonfly*. None of the diners or strollers along Shoveler Row had noticed her, nor the taxi men waiting at the bridge.

"LaRue?" Yonie called hoarsely.

The slant-ceilinged room was dark and empty.

Yonie shuffled over to her pallet, let her knapsack slide off her shoulders, and crawled under Aunt Elisa's quilt without bothering to remove her clothes.

She lay there listening to the night noises: the creak of oars from the Petty Canal below, the rise and fall of voices from nearby windows. The pitter of mosquitoes butting against her window-cloth and the rustle of the dried reeds in her mattress every time she turned.

One sound that she did not hear, no matter how hard she tried, was the smooth scrape of a cat squeezing under the loose shingle on the roof, and the springy *thunk* of paws hitting the shelf below.

Less than an hour after lying down, Yonie rose and descended the stairs to the boardwalk that led along the Petty Canal.

She was not often out and about at this hour, but she was not surprised to find things quiet. Her neighborhood's chief reputation was as a cheap place to sleep, and most of the residents seemed to be availing themselves of this attraction.

The Kimball sisters' bakery was shuttered, and the

air outside its door smelled only of damp wood. Queen Obergine's Hairdressing Palace was dark. As Yonie made her way along the tangle of piers and catwalks and makeshift bridges that passed for streets in the Low Town of Wicked Ford, the neighborhood felt quite unlike itself, and by the time Yonie finally climbed the steps up to the lamplit murmur of the Mole-in-'Ole, she felt unlike herself as well.

The pub was full of voices and clinking glasses and the smell of ale. Molyneaux was not in evidence, and a man she didn't know was busily filling glasses behind the bar.

"Hey, it's our Yonie!" cried Luc Lazard from his usual seat. "Have you come for a drink with me, sunshine?"

Yonie walked over to the bar. "Do you know," she said, "I suppose I have."

CHAPTER FIFTEEN

I T FELT strange to be sitting on one of the tall stools, resting her elbows on the sticky wood of the bar. Yonie took a swallow of the ruby ale Luc Lazard had ordered for her.

Most drinking establishments in Wicked Ford were willing to serve anyone old enough to reach the top of the bar. The backwaters of the Bad Bayous had no shortage of alcohol, though much of it was homemade. The fact that Yonie had never before tried ale was therefore something of an anomaly and was due chiefly to the influence of her mother and LaRue, both total abstainers.

"I'm surprised to see you here, M'sir Lazard," Yonie said. "I thought this was your work time."

Lazard smiled lazily. "Yeah, most nights I'd be down at Road-end, showing the latest netful of tourists how to play cards."

Many travelers regarded Wicked Ford as the last outpost of civilization before a tedious journey, and the business owners of Road-end did all they could to encourage this impression. To northbound travelers they described the interminable looping ride up the River Skulk, broken only by fueling stops at tiny one-dock towns whose inhabitants would scrabble to sell them homemade trinkets. To the southbound travelers, they detailed the arduous trek by horse-drawn wagon or mule train over the mountain wall and down to the cities of the coast, through sleepy farmland where the only hope of entertainment would be a ball game on a village green or perhaps a country dance where all the girls had large, well-muscled brothers standing by.

The Road-end district catered to this feeling of desperation with its hard-drinking taverns, its gambling hells, and, according to LaRue, plenty of That Sort of Place where unfortunate women provided That Sort of Thing.

Yonie rested her eyes on Lazard as he spun her a story of a tableful of cheating Coastmen and a game gone horribly wrong. Frankly, it was hard to see Lazard as a slick Road-end denizen. He would probably have looked much younger without his stylish little mustache.

". . . So now I can't go back to the Last Chance till the next steamboat and the next caravan leave town," he finished. "I really made a wreck of it. Then again, if I hadn't, I wouldn't be sitting here next to you."

He raised his glass to Yonie and drained his remaining inch of ale. "M'sir! Another two rubies, if you please."

The new glass felt cool against Yonie's fingers. "You think you made mistakes tonight, M'sir Lazard? I bet I've got you beat."

Luc raised one eyebrow. "Never bet with me, sunshine — but now you've got me curious. What does it take to get the cool, calm Yonie Watereye so bothered?"

Yonie began with the antique shop job, editing automatically to remove any mention of LaRue. Then she needed to explain her suspicions about M'sir Turcoat, which would probably have been more painful if it weren't for the distancing effect of the ruby ale.

Luc was a good audience, probably professionally so, and Yonie's day looked very different through his eyes. By the time she got to the confrontation at Bowdown Hall, they were both laughing so hard that Yonie spilled her third ale all over her skirt.

"And you said all this — onstage?" Luc gasped.

"Aye, really belted it out!"

"How many people were there, again?"

"I reckon maybe two 'un — two hundred. I don't know what got into me. I lost my temper *and* my common sense."

Lost . . . Yonie's helpless laughter suddenly turned into tears. "Oh, Luc, that's the worst part of tonight — I lost my cat. I left 'er near that shop, and now I can't find 'er any-where—" She put her arms down on the bar and let her hot face rest on them as she gave out great snuffling sobs.

Then she threw up.

"Aw," said Lazard. Then he was gone, and she could hardly blame him.

But then he was back, with a damp cloth, which was what she wanted most in the world right then. He was talk-ing to the barkeeper, handling everything, and soon she was seated in a real chair at a clean table, and across from her was Luc, asking her when she had last eaten.

"He was so sweet," Yonie told LaRue, sitting forward on the reed mattress with the quilt rumpled around her. "He got them to fix me an omelette, and I felt a lot better after that. And he told me you'd probably be back by morning, and he was right! I thought for sure you'd gotten lost."

The cat flourished her tail. "No fear of that — I used the boat-gong! Do you know, once I rang it, I could actually feel the garret pulling me like a fish on the line? It was as good as a compass for keeping my bearings. Not that my paws aren't sore, mind you. And do you have any idea how tricky it is to get a decent sound out of a gong using only one's claws?"

"I suppose I don't. LaRue, I can't even tell you how sorry I am for running off that way —"

"Please, my dear — we've had enough tears for one morning, and I have no desire to be crushed a second time. Just let this be a lesson about what can happen to your judgment when you skip dinner." The cat cocked her head. "To be fair, you had been marinating in the atmosphere of that sign all day. I'm sure it affected your behavior."

"Even if it did, I can hardly use that as an excuse. Mentioning guile would only make me seem more crude."

"Well, I'm just glad you didn't get into worse trouble, out drinking ale on an empty stomach with that Lazard character." LaRue's whiskers twitched.

"He was very kind. He even walked me home — he said the streets weren't safe at that hour for such a pretty girl."

"Oh, merciful waters. I hope he didn't take any liberties with your person?"

Yonie's thoughts went back, as they had several times already this morning, to that moment at the foot of the steps. "So when will I see you again, Yonie?" Luc had asked. "I hope it won't take another disaster." His teeth had looked very white in the darkness.

She had mumbled something about coming back to check her mail, and he had said, "I hope you check it soon, sunshine." Then he had leaned over and kissed her on the cheek, in such a casual, friendly way that she had not had the heart to object. His face had been warm and very smooth, as one would expect from a man who had probably shaved only hours ago. Except for the mustache, which had been a little tickly.

"He was a perfect gentleman," Yonie maintained.

"Hmf. In the future, when a young 'gentleman' compliments your looks, you would do well to take his comments with a dollop of mustard."

Yonie was silent a moment. "Do *you* think I'm pretty, LaRue?"

The cat narrowed her eyes until they almost disappeared in peach-colored fur. "I hope you realize," she said, "that that is not a question a lady should ever ask. It puts the interviewee in a very awkward position. But as you don't possess a mirror, I shall regard it purely as a request for information. So: no, you are not pretty. 'Striking,' I might say. In a few years, you may graduate to 'handsome.'"

"Er — thank you," said Yonie, who had been expecting something more along the lines of *you'll always be beautiful to me.*

"But regardless of your looks, I don't like the idea of your being alone with this Lazard fellow. Remember, I spend most of my waking hours observing Human Nature, and believe me, there are things in this city I wish I'd never seen. Even back in the Sloughs, I overheard plenty of stories that the adults didn't share with you."

The cat's voice softened. "I suppose there is one rose among the thorns here. Without this little infatuation to occupy you, you'd be moping about for days, thinking about that concert —"

"I'm hardly *infatuated,* LaRue. I just enjoyed his company, that's all —"

"But as it is," LaRue went on loudly, "you probably won't even remember to write that poor teacher an apology unless I remind you."

"I'll write it now!" Yonie declared. "And post it before breakfast."

"Eager to return to the pub, are we?" LaRue yawned. "Even though it's Sun-day, and there's no mail? I can tell you now, Lazard won't be there. He'll be sleeping. And you should do the same, my dear. Then you'll be all rested tomorrow, and you can go up to Bellflower and deliver your letter in person. You know it's the right thing to do."

LaRue curled up next to Yonie and began to produce a steady, almost inaudible purr.

Emile Turcoat's classroom was easy to find, which was fortunate, because Yonie was not feeling up to asking directions. Her face already felt even hotter than the day would warrant, and the letter of apology in her hand had acquired some sweat marks in just the few minutes she had been hesitating outside the door.

The muffled fluting music seeping from the classroom squeaked and suddenly stopped. Yonie opened the heavy door a crack. Four sleepy-looking older students sat in a half circle, holding instruments Yonie had never seen before — black tubes in various lengths, twined with silver fittings. The music master's back was to Yonie as he bent and spoke to a red-faced girl, putting a sympathetic hand on her shoulder. It was the exact gesture that had so inflamed Yonie on the evening of the concert, but today it looked gentle and teacherly.

The students had already spotted Yonie, so she hastily entered the music room, stubbing her toe agonizingly against the doorjamb as she went by.

Turcoat turned. His neat goatee began to quiver.

"M'sir Turcoat, I came 'ere to apologize for what I said at the concert — none o' that was true —" Sink it, her swamp accent was coming to the front. "It was inexcusable, and I don't expect you to forgive me," Yonie said, enunciating with extreme care.

Her face was roasting in this stuffy room. What else had she intended to say? Yonie looked around at the students, who now showed no sign of drowsiness. "I'm sorry I was so 'orrible," she blurted, then thrust her letter at Turcoat.

As she hobbled to the door, she heard the whispers rising behind her:

"— drunk, do you think?"

"— was that the same —"

"— get through the gate, anyway?"

"— practically falling down —"

Yonie stumbled down the hanging pathway. Only when she was entirely alone did she slow and gasp for breath and rub her stubbed toe.

Well, that was a fine idea, LaRue, she thought. *Now I'm a crazy woman and a drunkard, too.*

The library was a refuge of peace and shade. Yonie took a moment to breathe in the smell of paper and leather before heading back to the chair she now considered her own. She spotted the sky-blue form of M'dam Pierpond in the fine arts area and gave her a friendly wave as she went by.

It was quite a while before Yonie realized that Pierpond had not waved back.

Yonie's next greeting was met with a cool look.

Finally, Yonie cornered the librarian at her desk. "M'dam Pierpond? Is something wrong?" she asked, feeling her stomach crumpling up inside her.

"Not at all, M'dam Watereye. You have every right to use the library. You and M'sir Cordell made an agreement, and until I hear otherwise, that still stands."

"Oh," said Yonie. She cleared her throat. "Are you in the mood for tea? Maybe —"

"It's late, and I have a lot of work to finish up." Pierpond meticulously squared the corners of a stack of papers on her desk. "Besides," she said quietly, at last raising her eyes to Yonie, "today I don't seem to have much of an appetite."

Outside the library, blue gum leaves hung motionless

in the heat, and flowers dangled languidly from their vines. A distant bell sounded, and students filtered out onto the boardwalks and hanging bridges.

The lunch deck was a maelstrom of schoolgirls. Yonie skirted the crowd, trying to be as inconspicuous as a very tall non-uniformed person could be in a sea of chartreuse. Finally she caught a glimpse of black hair and pointed chin. Justine was embroiled in an argument with a girl Yonie didn't recognize. As Yonie approached, it erupted into a clawing tussle over what looked like a small newspaper.

The other girl had been getting the better of the petite Justine, but when Yonie appeared, she scuttled away, letting the paper drop where it was immediately trampled by dozens of feet.

"Yonie! I'm sorry, I can't talk to you." Justine gave her a pleading look. "I'm dying to hear the whole story — I saw how upset you were. I know there must have been some reason — but Father says I have to stay away from you, you're not a Good Influence, and if you bother me, then he might not even let you use the library anymore, even though he's a man of his word, because some things come first —" She ran out of breath, and gave Yonie a wretched look before she hurried off.

Miserable as Yonie felt, curiosity compelled her to pick up the battered newspaper, which was easily done due to the space that had opened up around her. It was the *Society Bugle*, a publication of which she had previously been unaware, and it sported stories such as "Heiress's Debut Marred by Grease on Floor!" and "Risqué Cake Stuns Wedding Guests — Bride in Tears!"

Yonie didn't realize its true significance until she came to the third headline on the front page: "Swamp Gal Storms Concert, Tells Conductor 'You Sired Me!'"

Appalled, Yonie saw that the reporter had questioned many of the students who had attended the event, learning that "although she gave her mother's name as Valery Bruneau, the lean, hawk-faced young woman calls herself Yonie Watereye, an alias that some say alludes to a most unsavory profession."

The reporter had fortunately not discovered the actual historical link between Yonie's mother and Emile Turcoat, and refused (several times, at length) to speculate on the truth of the accusation.

Yonie took some small comfort from the fact that she had evidently not ruined the performance after all, since "many students in the audience declared it 'the best concert ever.'"

It was not until Yonie's shaky hands were loosing the *Dragonfly*'s bowline that the knot in her chest started to unfold into anger.

The anger was mostly against herself. She couldn't fault Cordell for wanting to protect his daughter, especially when he already felt under attack by an unknown enemy. But it hurt to think that now the headmaster no longer considered Yonie an ally.

Yonie pulled grimly at her paddle. That, at least, was something she could change. She still wouldn't take Cordell's money to investigate the locket — but that didn't mean she couldn't do it for free.

CHAPTER SIXTEEN

THE LOFT over the tailor's shop was half full of art supplies: pieces of lumber, heaps of paint-spattered sheets and rolls of canvas, bottles of yellowish oil and sharp-smelling solvents.

The other half of the loft was full of light, from wide windows obviously transplanted from a grander building. A draped table held a bowlful of pears, which, judging from the partial painting on the easel nearby, must have looked delicious about a week before.

"Other projects, don't you know," said August Bassompierre, apologetically waving away a fruit fly. The old man shrugged. "Most of my customers choose to have their portraits done in their own homes. Can't fathom why — the light's never as good. Now, how can I help you, ma'am? Would you like to sit down?"

Yonie's feet were aching, but she declined the chair; its seat was flaky with dried gray paint. "Sir, I'm told that you're an accomplished painter of miniatures, among other things. I was wondering if I could see a sample of your work."

"Of course, of course." Bassompierre turned to rummage in a drawer, displaying paint-stained trousers that might have been a victim of the same accident as the chair. "Here are a few. Now, you understand, these are the ones that didn't turn out well. Or I wouldn't still have them, eh?"

Bassompierre was a refreshing change from the other portrait painters Yonie had spoken to today, with their tidy little shops and their carefully framed sample paintings on the wall and their reluctance to waste their time on a Low Town girl with patches on her skirt.

He was also, judging by the work he had just shown her, a brilliant artist, and she could see why the other painters had all mentioned his name. Yonie looked at a tiny oil painting of a boy, eyes alive with mischief, and two jewel-like pictures of women, both with the same coloring but utterly different in their faces and expressions. If he was dissatisfied with these portraits, she would have liked to see the ones he was pleased with.

None of them, however, had the tightly controlled, intricately twisting strokes Yonie was looking for.

She drew out the envelope that she had retrieved from her garret earlier that day. "Would you be able to produce something in this style?" Yonie watched Bassompierre's face as she displayed the oval of painted card that had come from M'sir Cordell's locket.

There was not the faintest flicker of recognition.

The old man took the portrait onto his creased palm and examined it. "Very nice work! Cressy? No, not with that brushwork. Who was it, then?"

"I was hoping you could tell me."

Bassompierre shook his head. "No one I recognize. Certainly no one local. Any fellow this good, even an amateur — I would know him."

Yonie sighed and flopped down onto the crinkly seat of the chair. "I was afraid you'd say that. I've been tromping around all day, and nobody will admit to painting this. And I didn't see this style anywhere, either."

Bassompierre raised his curly gray eyebrows. "You have a fine eye for detail, if you could tell that. Are you studying art?"

"Oh, no, I've never been to school at all. I grew up in the Sloughs."

"That makes it all the more remarkable!" The old man looked at her as if he'd found a silver piece in the bottom of his teacup. "The bayou folk have a rich tradition, but it tends heavily toward the three-dimensional. . . ."

Yonie ended up talking with Bassompierre for almost an hour. When she emerged from his studio, her notebook held a list of museums and galleries that she "simply could not neglect," as well as the name of a dealer who might be interested in Gilbert's carvings.

But she hadn't learned enough to get back in Cordell's good graces. It didn't help to know that the portrait painter wasn't local — it just made things more scary. M'dam Cordell had said she'd never sat for that portrait. Either she was lying, which would be awful, or someone must have been spying on her, which would be awful too. Had some foreigner been making furtive sketches of the woman in a park or café?

Yonie spent the next two days talking to all the antique dealers she could find (except for Therese Turcoat, whom she could not bring herself to face). None of them seemed to recognize the locket, though several offered to buy it. None of them admitted to knowing any other dealers who could read guile, and one man nearly slapped Yonie for asking if he himself had that talent.

The most interesting conversation was with M'sir Weatherley, the man who had sold M'dam Turcoat her forbidding, guile-laden sign. Yonie had entered his ornate showroom and inquired discreetly about "special" items. When that brought no results, she began ladling on the hints until Weatherley's cheeks nearly matched his maroon waistcoat. "I run a d-decent shop here," he sputtered. "If you want that kind of thing, g-go look somewhere else." He flapped his hand toward the door as if Yonie were some noxious flying insect.

"Perhaps you might direct me to someone who could help?" Yonie tried.

"Absolutely not!" His hostile stare propelled her through the doorway.

Many folks got flustered at the thought of guile, Yonie mused as she walked back down Shoveler Row, but Weatherley's reaction had been extreme. His embarrassment would make sense, though, if he had in fact deliberately made use of a wily item against his competitor.

There were also the words he had muttered to himself as Yonie went out the door. She had caught only the last two, which had sounded a lot like "afford it."

Yonie had until now steered clear of the other pearlies of Wicked Ford. She had no wish to exchange shoptalk with a mountebank, or worse, with a genuine seer who might recognize Yonie as a sham. And naturally she had no need of their services.

But now she had questions that LaRue could not answer.

"'Ave you ever 'eard the like?" Yonie asked Simon Bojoe (known as Slyman Bojoe throughout the water market, though not to his face). "A thing so cunning, and aimed like a weapon right where it'd 'urt a man the most?"

Along the flank of the pier, flatboats bobbed, and fish-mongers shouldered past with sacks of writhing eels and kicking crabs. Two women ladled scoops of shrimp from a tub, their bare arms sheened with sweat. The air was like a warm wet cloth on the skin.

Bojoe squatted frog-like atop a wide dock post, his folded legs casting long angular shadows in the low morning sun. He turned his head to gaze out over the water, and Yonie saw a transparent film flicker across the curve of his eye.

"I been diving since I was a lad, and I've seen my share of slygoods over the years, so I can tell you, daughter, you've no need to fear. I don't know where you 'eard that story, but that sort of power would take 'undreds of years to grow. Someone goes looking for that sort of thing a-purpose, they're not going to find it."

In the next hours, Yonie spoke with Granny See-Green, a tiny wizened person whose green bandanna was tied suggestively high around her presumably gilled throat; a stout laundress named Clarice, who lectured her about washing in rainwater only; and "Webs" Gustovy, an elderly potter with red clay under the nails of his umbrella-like hands.

Like Simon Bojoe, they had never heard of anyone selling wily things as weapons, and opined that things that guileful and dangerous would be extremely rare. As for targeting the item directly to the victim—well, it made a good story, but in reality, the lack of inventory would make it impossible. Granny See-Green in particular said this with a mildly wistful air.

Yonie's notion of some criminal mastermind supplying both the locket and the shop sign was looking more and more unlikely. And yet she couldn't forget what she had seen.

It was time to talk to a different set of pearlies.

Once she reached the Grand Market, the answers changed dramatically.

"Reminds me of that poor woman last spring." Auntie Malvo adjusted her shawl to further shadow her dappled face. "Combed 'er 'air for three days straight before me and 'er sister forced the wicked thing out of 'er 'ands, and 'er all screaming to get it back, though by rights what she should've wanted back was 'er 'air, which was mighty thin on 'er 'ead by that time. Never did find out 'oo left it on 'er dresser."

M'sir Riverlover peered at Yonie out of ice-colored eyes completely devoid of lashes or brows. "What no one can figure is where the drowned things — sorry, ma'am — where the things could be coming from. Family I know stopped leaving the 'ouse of an evening — scared to be out of the light of their new lantern. Course it wasn't new. It was a sly old thing, but by the time they came to me, the gentleman 'ad already lost 'is seat on the Council. Missed too many meetings, you see."

And there were even darker tales, like the one of the

bracelet, anonymously given, that had pinched off a bride's hand.

Perhaps the caliber of storytelling was simply higher among Grand Market pearlies. But if Yonie did not dismiss all their accounts, she could see a pattern.

All the cases involved a High Town victim. That would make sense if the wily weapons were being secretly sold to a select clientele, as Weatherley's parting mutter had hinted. The incidents had all taken place within the last two years, starting not long after Yonie's arrival in the city. She hadn't heard of them before now because she had only recently begun to move in the High Town world.

Maybe the police could track down this . . . this *guile-monger* if someone could just convince them of the threat. But, sadly, those pearlies who had spoken with the authorities had not been believed. Yonie, with her High Town accent and the new clothes she'd purchased after the Turcoat job, might have had more luck, but the *Bugle* article had probably destroyed her credibility.

Yonie stared out over the Grand Market, that miniature delta flowing with heads and sun hats and bright kerchiefs, and wondered who among the cheerful shoppers might next encounter a cunning trap set by a secret enemy.

CHAPTER SEVENTEEN

"GOLDEN SNAIL, please," Yonie told Molyneaux the next morning. She passed him the letter she had written to Headmaster Cordell, which described Yonie's locket inquiries and guilemonger suspicions.

"Not Leaping Deer?" The barkeeper raised one heavy eyebrow. Golden Snail, the cheapest message service, drew its name from the fable of the snail and the greyhound. Sadly, it adhered more closely to the first part of its "slow and steady" motto.

Yonie shrugged and looked away. "I don't know when I'll get that kind of money again."

"Hey, sunshine, what's the matter?" Luc sang out as he emerged from the crowd.

"She's worried about her business prospects," said Molyneaux. "But maybe she shouldn't be." He pulled out an envelope and attempted to spin it on the end of his finger.

Yonie scooped the letter up from the floor. There was no sender's address on the envelope. The single sheet inside was written in a clear, self-assured hand:

Dear Mme. Watereye,
I am in need of your services. Kindly present yourself at 1 Amelie Terrace, The Heights, at your earliest convenience.
Regards,
Felix DesMaray

Yonie was at first irked by the imperious tone of the letter, but once she reached the signature, it made more sense. The DesMarays were not only the wealthiest family in Wicked Ford, they were also one of the oldest and most prominent.

Their biggest enterprise lay outside Wicked Ford: the vast bogs of "baie du marais," commonly known as merryberry, which employed hundreds even in the off season. But within the city, their influence was also broad. A man might work all day at the DesMaray cannery, walk home past schools and parks endowed by the DesMaray family, and then spend his evening drinking ruby ale from the DesMaray Brewery. The very coins and banknotes used in Wicked Ford were issued by the DesMaray Merchant Bank and backed by the family's most popular product.

Yonie kept staring at the letter. Should she whoop or scream?

It occurred to her that the pub owner would be a DesMaray business associate. "M'sir Molyneaux? What can you tell me about Felix DesMaray?"

Luc whistled upon hearing the name. Since he'd already been peering over Yonie's shoulder, she assumed that his reading abilities didn't extend beyond the numbers on playing cards.

"Mmm," said Molyneaux. "I mainly deal with his brewery man, but I know Felix runs just about everything, now that his father's passed. Very shrewd man, a little slippery, some say, though I've never had a problem. They say he's a bad enemy to have, but if you deal straight with him, he'll treat you right."

"Hey, Yonie, we ought to celebrate!" said Luc. "Tell you what, they're having a Swamp Night at the Starry Plough next Saturn-day. I'll take the night off, and we can go dancing. What d'you say?"

"I'm not much of a dancer —"

"Come on, you grew up in the bayous, you've got to

at least know the maroky. I bet you know steps I've never heard of."

"Yes," Yonie conceded, "that's probably true."

She was not quite sure how she had agreed to it, but by the time they parted on the steps outside the Mole-in-'Ole, the plan was set.

It took Yonie only a few minutes to paddle home, change into her newer blouse, and tie a fresh kerchief over her hair. It took her two hours to find LaRue, who'd been hunting mice in the cheesemongers' shops along Frommidge Street.

LaRue and Yonie had scouted out discreet talking places in most nearby areas of the city, and shortly Yonie was sitting cross-legged in the Chapel of Holy Eglantine on Gleese Avenue, LaRue curled on her lap.

Yonie gazed up at the fresco on the wall above her, which depicted Lady Eglantine with arms outstretched, supporting half a dozen wild birds that would never consort with one another in nature.

Although Yonie's mother had taught her only a dutiful outline of the faith she was brought up in, Yonie did know that Lady Eglantine was associated with healing, as well as a love of animals. The people on the more crowded side of the chapel wouldn't look twice at the girl bent over her pet, so long as Yonie spoke in the soft cadence of prayer and LaRue kept her voice down and didn't look too lively.

Quickly Yonie filled LaRue in on the contents of the

DesMaray letter. "I hope we can get some time alone there to talk. The Grand Market signals will never do for something this important. Oh, LaRue, what if they don't allow animals in the house?"

"Yonie, darling, try to calm down." LaRue stopped to breathe raspily as an elderly lady shuffled by.

Yonie stared up at the fresco. The artist had had a very generous opinion of Lady Eglantine's arm strength. Even the arm with the duck and great heron showed no signs of strain. Come to think of it, the perching abilities of certain species might have been overestimated as well.

"I'm all right now."

"Then let's not waste any more time." The cat sprang up from Yonie's lap and bounded for the door.

As they passed into the sunlight, Yonie heard several voices from inside exclaiming "Glory be!" and "Praise the Lady!"

The DesMarays' city residence, 1 Amelie Terrace, proved to be three pale pink stories with a roof of imported blue slate, set in a broad lake of lawn. The house was shaded by venerable gum trees that probably predated most of the city, and its elevation was such that a breeze off Lake Leery flipped the triangular tail of Yonie's kerchief up and down and dried the sweat on her neck as she walked up the drive.

A servant took Yonie's name and ushered her into a side room that contained four padded chairs and a low table with a dish of peanuts and dried merryberries. A narrow window admitted a drift of rose scent from the gardens outside.

Yonie was relieved to see no newspapers in evidence.

She balanced herself on the edge of a chair and let LaRue slide down from her shoulder. "Do you think I should get some cards made, LaRue? That butler or whoever he was seemed to expect one. I hope they don't keep us waiting long."

"You're chattering, Yonie." LaRue bumped Yonie with a furry shoulder. "Try to relax."

Yonie twiddled her hair-beads. "But we need this job! We're running out of money again, and I have to buy some fabric for a dress."

"My dear, what's wrong with the skirt and blouse you're wearing? I've been so careful with my claws —"

"They're fine, for everyday. But I want something nicer for special occasions."

"Special occasions."

"Yes." Yonie did not elaborate. There was no reason LaRue had to know every detail of her life.

"Oh, Yonie. It's that Lazard fellow, isn't it? What has he talked you into?"

"Why do you assume he talked me into anything? Maybe I actually *want* to go out dancing and have a little fun."

"Merciful waters! I can imagine what that man's idea of

fun might be. Next thing you know, he'll be trying to give you jewelry." LaRue's tail swished fastidiously. "He is *not* a wholesome companion, and I don't approve of your spending more time in his company."

"Then it's a good thing I don't need your permission," Yonie retorted. "I'm going. And don't you dare follow me."

The cat studied Yonie. "You might not need my permission, dear, but plainly you need my advice. Where relations between the sexes are concerned, I'm clearly far better informed than you."

"You mean you're more cynical."

"That does follow as a result, yes. Yonie, don't you understand I'm just looking out for you? I'll say it again: you should not be seeing that man."

"You can't tell me what to do!" Yonie burst out. "I'm six years older than you!"

"Wisdom is not always measured in years," the cat said austerely.

"You are *insufferable!*" Yonie jumped to her feet. "You used to be my friend. But now you're acting like my mother, and you're not! You're just a cat!"

For a frozen moment, Yonie's last sentence hung in the air. She met LaRue's wide eyes.

Then the cat flowed down off the chair, slunk over to the window, and squeezed out through the opening to vanish under the rosebushes outside.

CHAPTER EIGHTEEN

Y ONIE STARED out the window into the garden, not seeing the green of the lawn or the pink of the blooming roses. Never before had LaRue simply left an argument without having the last word.

When the door opened a few minutes later, Yonie was sitting motionless with unfocused eyes, clutching her knapsack.

"M'dam Watereye? I'm Felix DesMaray."

Yonie blinked. DesMaray was a towering, broad-shouldered man with startling coppery hair, which he wore in a fashionable tail down his back. His face was weathered brown up to mid-forehead, where an unusually fair complexion revealed itself. Yonie guessed that he must spend many hours outdoors on his acreage, with only a hat to shade him. He was currently clad in well-tailored business attire, and his handshake was perfectly measured.

DesMaray took a seat across from Yonie. "I must say, you're the youngest pearly I've met. How old are you, if you don't mind my asking?"

Normally Yonie answered this question with an enigmatic smile, but she remembered Molyneaux's advice. "Sixteen," she admitted. DesMaray himself looked to be in his early forties.

"I'm delighted to meet you, M'dam Watereye. You do prefer that name? I understand it's something of a working alias."

"It's not the name my parents gave me, sir, but it's what I've been using since I came to the city." Yonie had expected DesMaray to be imposing, but he was rather easy to talk to.

"So you're not a native of Wicked Ford, then? Where did you grow up?"

"The Sloughs. It's out beyond the Foulwater."

This was the point in conversation where most people remarked on how glad or clever or fortunate Yonie must be to have escaped that place.

"Ah, yes, let me see — jackfish, croaker. Catfish, of course. And mullet. Am I right? I've had some of my best fishing out that way. A very rich area."

DesMaray's intense blue eyes made him seem extremely interested in everything Yonie had to say, and she found herself actually exchanging fishing anecdotes with him.

"It sounds like your father is a fisherman by trade."

"Yes, sir, he was. He passed away."

"I'm sorry to hear it. And your mother?"

"I'm afraid I lost my mother as well."

A shadow passed over DesMaray's face. "So did I, a long time ago." For a moment he looked far away, and Yonie wondered how old he had been when his mother died.

Then he stood up. "Well, M'dam Watereye, I've heard a lot about you and your talents, and I'm eager to put them to the test. Come with me."

Until now, Yonie hadn't considered the immediate consequences of LaRue's desertion. "Sir," she said miserably, "I don't think I can help you."

DesMaray's red-blond eyebrows lowered a fraction. "You've come this far, madam. At least do me the courtesy of trying. I would hate to think you've been wasting my time."

A bad enemy, Yonie thought. She followed him on shaky legs as he led her deeper into the house.

They stopped in a spacious office with glass-paneled outer doors framing a view of city roofs and green branches. DesMaray led her to his desk, where an enameled vase filled with canal water sat on a lace doily. The vase also held several cheery sunflowers, which DesMaray extracted with a grimace and threw into a wastebasket. "Maids! Can't follow the simplest directions."

DesMaray closed the heavy office door, and the distant sounds of voices and footsteps vanished. Yonie swallowed as he turned the key in the lock.

"Right, let's get down to business." He gestured at the vase. "It's old, and it's been behaving very strangely. I'd like to know why."

Yonie's throat felt dusty. "What does it do?"

"It wilts any flowers put into it, within the hour."

Even under these conditions, Yonie couldn't help admiring the enamelwork, with its fanciful design of curious fish at the bottom looking up.

"It's a lovely piece, sir," she told DesMaray after a minute. "But I can't get anything out of it."

"Try again," he said curtly. "I reward hard workers."

Yonie could feel her face getting hot. "I'm sorry to disappoint you, sir, but I can't tell you anything about this vase that you don't already know."

"M'dam Watereye. You call yourself a pearly — is this how you usually treat your customers? I do not appreciate people who waste my time, madam, and I cannot abide quitters. We will stay here until you give me a Seeing."

Yonie could hardly recognize the genial DesMaray of the waiting room in this man who was now looming behind her with crossed arms.

LaRue had once told her that everyone in the Delta

had a little bit of slyness in them, and that being a pearly was only a matter of degree. After that, Yonie had tried for weeks to do a Seeing herself, without success.

But she was older now, with more swamp-stuff in her veins. Yonie squeezed her eyes almost all the way shut and glared at the vase as if she could intimidate it into talking.

Nothing.

She tried gazing dreamily, as if the vase might let some hint slip. She pictured guile leaching from ruined cities in faraway lands, washing down the Skulk, and finally coming to rest in the Bad Bayous. There was guile in that vase. There was guile in her too.

Ten minutes later, she had given up hope.

Should she make something up? With her experience of wily things, it would be easy enough. If she could only hold on to DesMaray's business, the next time she would surely have LaRue's help. Wouldn't she?

But even as the thought crossed her mind, Yonie knew she couldn't do it. She and LaRue had always done their honest best for their customers.

Yonie lifted her chin and faced DesMaray.

"Sir, I can tell you several things about this vase. From the shape, colors, and subject matter, I would say that it dates from the Bear period of the Iblonian Empire. And judging by the geometric touches on the fish, it's probably from a part of Iblonia near the border with Gry.

"What I cannot tell you, sir — no matter how much

you browbeat me — is anything about the wiles of this item. For that I apologize. There will naturally be no charge for this consultation."

DesMaray exhaled loudly, and the creases left his brow.

"Please pardon my temper. That was well spoken. In fact, I can't help wondering: how did a girl from the Sloughs ever learn that sort of diction?"

"My mother came from Wicked Ford. She was quite strict with me."

"I can imagine." DesMaray tilted his head. "Madam, I've been asking you a lot of questions — would you mind satisfying my curiosity about one more thing? I was wondering what provoked that peculiar outburst of yours at Bowdown Hall."

Yonie's face felt as if she were peering into a hot oven. "Does everybody in the world know about that?"

"Only everyone in Society, and though some people may consider that the world, I do not. But I would genuinely like to know. Having met you, I feel there must have been a reason."

"It was a stupid mistake, that's all." Yonie looked down at the floor. "It's a personal matter — but I'll tell you, if only to clear M'sir Turcoat's name. I recently got some information that caused me to, er, question my paternity. Then I learned that M'sir Turcoat had been close to my mother, and I jumped to conclusions. But I no longer believe he was anything to her but a teacher and a friend."

"I see. And are you still looking for your father?"

"My father was Sebastien DuRoy. But yes, of course I still want to know — who it was. How could I not? But going around making a fool of myself and making trouble for good people is not the way to do it. Sir."

She shouldered her knapsack and held out her hand. "I'm sorry I couldn't help you today."

Instead of shaking her hand, DesMaray gestured toward a pair of armchairs by the windows. "Please don't leave quite yet, madam. I have a proposition for you."

It was both disconcerting and flattering how DesMaray's entire concentration seemed to be focused directly on her. Yonie settled uneasily onto the cool leather seat.

"First, I must admit something." He leaned forward with his elbows on his knees. "I haven't been altogether truthful with you. I didn't actually invite you here for your professional skills, but rather to get some idea of your character." He grinned. "You get high marks in both, by the way — that's a perfectly ordinary vase, so far as I know."

Yonie's brows came down and she opened her mouth, but DesMaray was continuing.

"I also wanted to get a look at you and learn a little more about your background — more than I could get from newspaper articles. And now that I have, I'm completely satisfied. You're definitely mine, and I'd like to provide for you, if you'll let me."

Yonie could only stare dumbfounded at the man in

front of her — the long legs, the aquiline nose. The red hair that he had not passed on to Yonie, much to Mama's relief.

What had DesMaray said earlier, when she told him she'd lost her mother? *So did I, a long time ago.* He had been speaking of Valery Bruneau.

DesMaray chuckled. "I wish my Vivian could see your face. She was convinced you were some sort of schemer."

"All I want," said Yonie through gritted teeth, "is the truth."

"You deserve it," said DesMaray, more soberly. "So. Valery and I knew each other as children, in the vague sort of way that all the Society families do. I was older — eleven years older — and before she even had her debut, I was already quite the rake. I was far too charming for my own good in those days, and the wealth didn't help. Most of the ladies were after me for their daughters, and the rest were after me for themselves. As for the girls, they agreed with everything I said — or else they disagreed and pouted their lips."

DesMaray shook his head with a faint smile. Yonie felt that he was enjoying this part of the story a bit too much.

"Valery wasn't like that. She was quiet, but she spoke her mind. She had those huge deep eyes, and that scrumptious voice, and she seemed to see something worthwhile inside of me.

"Unfortunately, she was wrong. One evening I got her alone and gave her the best brandy from our cellars, and then, well, I was *awfully* persuasive. I don't think she remembered all of that night afterward, but she remembered enough to hate me." DesMaray ran a hand over his hair. "I offered to marry her once I found out she was expecting, but she wouldn't hear of it, even with her parents pushing as hard as they could.

"Then she ran away with a fisherman, and I never saw that beautiful face again. Although I must say, you look very like her. At least, from certain angles."

"Er — thank you," said Yonie.

"It's an ugly story, I know." DesMaray sighed. "I wasn't proud of myself, even at the time, and believe me, over the years I've only gotten more ashamed."

Yonie studied the man in front of her. He was still extremely handsome in a craggy sort of way, and she could see how her mother might have been overwhelmed. In fact, it was hard for Yonie to be as angry with him as she ought to be, with those candid blue eyes fixed on her.

"It was good of you to tell me," she said at last.

"I like to think I've improved at least a little." He smiled sunnily. "Now, I'm prepared to set you up with a monthly allowance. We can leave the details for a later date, but I was thinking maybe thirty gallons or so. Nothing extravagant, but it should help put some meat on your bones."

Yonie's current rent was eight gallons a month.

"I'll also arrange for your admission to Bellflower,

and for your tuition payments. I'm sure Valery taught you the best she could, and my people tell me you're quite the reader, but it would be a shame if your studies stopped there. Education for girls has progressed quite a bit since your mother was in school."

Yonie's hands were gripping each other tight. All those shelves of books in the Bellflower library — hers to check out and take home with her whenever she liked. Teachers to teach her history, and geography, and mysterious subjects like algebra that she had only recently heard of from Justine. Lunches with friends amid the blue gum leaves. And time to savor it all, without worrying about the next meal or the next month's rent or how much longer her shoes would last.

"That's a very generous offer, sir. I — I don't know what to say."

DesMaray cleared his throat. When he next spoke, his normally smooth voice was ragged. "The way I see it, it's the least I can do for Valery's daughter. For *my* daughter."

Before Yonie knew it, she was up out of her chair, hugging Felix DesMaray, one of the most powerful men in the Bad Bayous.

CHAPTER NINETEEN

ONE LAST thing," DesMaray had said as he walked her to the door. "I'd appreciate it if you didn't reveal our relationship to anyone for a few weeks. You see, I'm getting married at the end of the month. Vivian — my fiancée — knows about you, of course, but I don't want any ugly talk at the wedding. Vivian deserves better than that. Heaven knows, she puts up with enough from me as it is."

Yonie had agreed, but now, sitting across from Luc at an intimate table in the Starry Plough Open-Air Ballroom, she was finding it hard to keep that promise.

Above them, the knobby boughs of an enormous

magnolia tree were draped with lanterns, and here and there among the leathery leaves a few huge-petaled white blossoms still spread their fragrance. In the evening sky stars showed, as advertised, between the branches, and would doubtless be even more noticeable from the dimly lit dance floor in the center of the courtyard.

The dancers wore a jumble of strange outfits, which had puzzled Yonie before she learned that "Swamp Night" was meant to be a costume affair. The clothing varied from bizarre (bare feet and mismatched business attire with the cuffs shredded away) to well-meaning (patchwork frocks that showed the skills of a professional dressmaker) to insulting (flour-sack tunics of the sort worn by tiny children at home, cut so that the flour label was prominently displayed). How was it possible for city dwellers to be so ignorant about a group of people who lived only hours away by boat?

Yonie's own dress, which she had painstakingly stitched out of pink-flowered calico, had qualified for the costume discount at the door. She was still not sure how she felt about that.

But the music was highly energetic, and for the first time since Papa had died, Yonie found herself able to listen to the fiddle without being overcome by tears. In fact, she was looking forward to dancing. Luc, who fortunately had not known about the costume aspect of the evening, was looking handsome (if a bit sweaty) in a jacket with shell buttons. He also proudly sported brand-new alligator-skin boots.

Luc had even rented a pretty little white and blue canal skiff to get them to the ballroom, and though his rowing was not nearly as impressive as he seemed to believe, Yonie had appreciated the thought.

She had also admired his foresight after he nudged the skiff in to a willowy bank and joined her on the stern seat to enjoy a scenic view — and, as it turned out, another kiss. Such a maneuver might well have been hazardous in a canoe.

Brief as the kiss had been, Yonie could still feel its ghost on her lips, and every few minutes her mind whirled ahead to what might happen on the way home, when it was dark and the public gardens along the Rose Canal would be less populated. The thought was both worrisome and alluring.

"Now will you tell me about that DesMaray job?" Luc asked.

Their tiny table was covered with plates that held only fruit peels, mussel shells, and shrimp tails. Yonie could no longer plead hunger as a reason to delay her answers.

"I told you it went well."

"Yeah, obviously, or you wouldn't have insisted on paying for everything tonight. But I'm dying of curiosity. What did he want you to do?"

"I can't talk about it."

Luc sighed dramatically. His face was golden from the low table candle in its orange glass chimney. "Think he'll hire you again?"

Yonie hesitated. "Let's just say, we have an ongoing arrangement."

Luc reached out to take her hand, pausing first to stack the small plates (with surprising adroitness) where they would not be in the way. His palm was soft and smooth.

"That's great, Yonie. It seems like things are finally going right for you."

"Not everything." Yonie closed her eyes for a moment.

"Oh, yeah, your cat. Don't worry, she'll come back like she did before."

Yonie had not seen LaRue since the cat left her on Mercury-day, four days before. Yesterday Yonie had pursued a glimpse of ginger fur down an alley, only to corner an enormous spitting tom with torn ears. She had had to linger several minutes blotting her eyes on her sleeve before she reemerged onto the main street.

LaRue was fine, Yonie told herself constantly. She would be back when she felt like it.

Unless, of course, what Yonie had said was truly unforgivable.

"Hey, sunshine, I've got something that might cheer you up." Luc reached into his coat pocket and took out a small oblong package, wrapped in shiny pink paper and tied with a red ribbon. It was the size of many of the boxes she'd examined in Therese's Treasures, the ones that held necklaces and bracelets.

Immediately all traces of relaxation left Yonie's body.

This could only result in terrible awkwardness. LaRue's warnings aside, the last thing she needed was jewelry, and she hoped Luc hadn't spent much.

"Go ahead, open it," Luc urged.

It was bound to be inappropriate. But how could she refuse it without knowing what it was?

Yonie's knife slid through the paper and ribbon to reveal a plain cardboard box. Luc watched her hands intently as she lifted off the lid.

It was not jewelry. It wasn't immediately clear just what it was. Lying in a nest of tissue paper was a copper cylinder incised with patterns of shells, starfish, seahorses, and other oceanic motifs. A sea captain's spyglass? No, much too small.

Yonie lifted it out and turned it to the light. The copper was newly polished, but showed enough nicks and scuffs to reveal its age. One end had a small peephole; the other end was a rotating cuff capped with glass, but flat — not a lens. Tiny faceted beads and rods of colored glass and minute translucent shells shifted under the surface.

It reminded her of something she had seen for sale a few months before in a Road-end shop — a cheap tin toy she had played with until the shop owner made her leave.

"Do you know what it is?" Luc asked.

"It's an antique kaleidoscope!" said Yonie. "How marvelous!" She beamed at him. It was a toy, something the rules of propriety allowed her to accept from a man, and more than that, it was something she truly liked. How had Luc known?

Yonie turned the kaleidoscope in her hands, admiring the decorations, then aimed it toward the candle flame in front of her and set her eye to the peephole.

The end cap of the kaleidoscope was evidently filled with water, giving the jewel-like floaters a gentle drifting motion as they changed. Round pale beads bobbed like two cork floats, Yonie's and Papa's together in their favorite fishing hole at Burnt Rock. Chips of green and orange glass glowed in the candlelight like the setting sun through sweetgum leaves.

"Hey, sunshine, can I have a look?"

Luc's voice was like a mosquito droning in her ear, and she could hardly hear what Papa was saying.

"What a beauty! Careful now, 'e's a slippery one." Papa's white grin parted his beard as the catfish dropped into the creel with the others.

The catfish and snapper twitched against the wicker sides. Yonie stared as the fish thinned until they were like slips of paper, banknotes lying sodden at the bottom of the creel. She looked up at Papa and gasped. The slanting sunset light had turned his black hair to the color of copper, making him a stranger. She had a sudden urge to throw herself over the scarred side of the old fishing boat into the simple colorless dark beneath the water.

Yonie twisted her hand, and the pattern twirled and

changed. Cloudy green beads floated alongside tiny lozenges of light brown shell, like algae-covered water sluicing over Yonie's bare arms as she desperately swam.

"Hey, you going to look at that thing all night? C'mon, put it down and come dance." The kaleidoscope joggled under Luc's hand, but Yonie held it tight, hissing through her teeth. How could she ever catch up to the *Dragonfly* with this kind of interference?

The canoe was already far ahead of her, Cousin Gage paddling gleefully down the channel while Gilbert craned his neck to look back. Over the splashing of the water and the evil sniggers of the cousins, Yonie could barely hear the mewling of the orange kitten cowering under the stern seat.

"LaRooo! LaRooooo!" Gilbert howled, in exuberant imitation of Yonie's cries. "Faster, Yonie, or you won't see where we leave 'er!"

"Sure 'ope an alligator doesn't get 'er," Gage hollered, bouncing on the seat. "'Ope one doesn't get *you!*"

Yonie's muscles burned as she kicked her way through the water. Her mouth tasted like scum and mud. She didn't have any more breath to shout, but if she could have spoken to her cousins, she would have cried, "Can't you just leave me *alone?*"

"Well, excuse me, *M'dam Watereye!* I thought you were enjoying my company, but I guess I can find someone else to dance with."

The *Dragonfly* was out of sight, lost in the bends of the channel. She would never find LaRue now.

Yonie's face was hot with crying and exertion, but the water was cool. All she really wanted was to slip down into that coolness and escape from the noise and the glare.

"Oi, watch where you're going, lady!"

"Oww, my foot!"

"What's she doing? Is she blind?"

"Ma'am, if you won't let go of that thing, we'll have to help you to the door."

Yonie wandered, heels clopping on wooden sidewalks, polished leather toes crashing against storefronts and lampposts. She kept the kaleidoscope pressed tight to her eye, aiming it toward a streetlight here, a bright window there, as the shapes and colors shifted.

Flecks of blue appeared, surrounded by shiny black beads like the night sky reflected in still water. As Yonie coasted the canoe in closer to the bank of the island, the curve of moon overhead floated into a net of black branches.

"Yonie, this spot looks quite promising." LaRue was a dark shape at the bow of the *Dragonfly*. "Are you ready for our little experiment?"

Yonie put down the paddle and picked up a well-worn book. "Go ahead!"

Blobs of blue flame gushed up from the shallows around them, two and three and four at a time. LaRue's wide-pupiled eyes flared as they reflected the leaping light.

"*Aha, young prince,*" Yonie read out loud, "*you must be unaware of the curse attached to that very pair of boots. Unless, by chance, you chose to lace them with leather from the wing of a Bristletoed Bat?* It's working! LaRue, I can actually read by your bluefire!"

LaRue smugly began to wash. "I thought it was possible, but it's good to be sure. You never know when that might come in handy." A last few bubbles popped their flame into the night, and then the darkness folded them back in.

Over the black crowns of the devil oaks, back the way they had come, the sky was surprisingly pale.

"Huh. Looks like someone's lit a bonfire over by Sulky Spit," Yonie remarked.

"An awfully big one." LaRue switched her tail uneasily. "I don't know —"

"It's a signal fire!" Yonie cried. "Someone's in trouble!"

The *Dragonfly* lived up to its name as Yonie sent it darting down narrow channels and skipping its way over patches of mud. She set a reckless pace, picking out landmarks by the bursts of bluefire LaRue called out of the murky water.

The sky ahead filled with smoke and orange sparks, and Yonie could hear the snapping roar of the conflagration. Her hands clenched on the wood of her paddle and on the copper tube of the kaleidoscope. Her shoes scuffed over weeds and mud. Orange chips of glass whirled like leaping flames in the kaleidoscope's view.

At the end of the Bitterway, the cottage was barely an outline inside a billowing cape of fire. An acrid wind whipped Yonie's face. The rushing of the fire was deafening, and behind that were the crashes of roof beams collapsing and timbers exploding.

"Yonie! Get back!"

A hand grabbed at the stern rope of her canoe, and in the crazy orange light she saw Aunt Elisa, hair down around her shoulders, hauling the *Dragonfly* back from the inferno. Gustave sat shirtless at the oars of their boat, hair drenched with sweat, rowing furiously until he had towed the *Dragonfly* well up the shadowy tunnel of the Bitterway.

Aunt Elisa nearly capsized the canoe as she scrambled over and crushed Yonie to her nightgowned chest. "Thank 'eaven, thank 'eaven," she moaned, "at least *you* got out —"

"Where are they?" Yonie screamed. "Are they still inside? We 'ave to go back!"

"It's no use," said Gustave. His eyes were like stones. "No one could survive in there."

Yonie felt LaRue against her ankles, a shuddering bundle behind her skirt.

"Maybe they got out the backdoor into the water meadow —"

"Nay," said Aunt Elisa, her voice breaking, "they didn't."

"You don't know that!"

"I do." She looked at Yonie with wet eyes. "And I'll be

giving thanks for the rest of my life that you didn't 'ave to 'ear it."

"It's not true!" Yonie wailed. "Let me go. I 'ave to go back!" She struggled against Aunt Elisa's embrace, kicking herself loose to tumble out of the canoe, down into the water of the Bitterway. Her arms ached from paddling, but maybe if she swam fast enough, far enough, deep enough, she could get back — back to a time when Mama and Papa were still sleeping safely in their bed.

Yonie's shoes skidded on the muddy slope. She stumbled forward and pitched off the steep side of the canal bank into the water below.

Her dress soaked up the canal water, the wet skirt tangling around her legs. Her stockings and shoes were anchors dragging her down. Her arms remained motionless, still clamping the kaleidoscope to her eye.

The flame-orange was gone now, and the blue. There was only the silent black of nighttime under water.

CHAPTER TWENTY

SOMETHING DRAGGED Yonie upward. She found herself lying, profoundly disoriented, on the bottom of a rowboat, with the seamed face of an aged woman peering down at her. The kaleidoscope was gone.

"Hmmm. Should I be taking you 'ome with me, I'm a-wondering?"

The old woman spoke in the thickest bayou dialect Yonie had ever heard. She wore a sleeveless, much-mended dress of no particular color, and her arms were wiry with muscle under the wrinkled skin.

"I got a mighty fine pot o' gumbo on the fire. Every kind o' fish you can think of."

Yonie struggled to sit up. Her head was resting on something damp and lumpy. A pile of knotted rope.

"Aye, I use me a net sometimes," the old woman said. "But mostly, I like the line." She grinned down at Yonie with gapped brown teeth. Above her the sky between the tree branches was purple with twilight.

Hadn't it been full dark when Yonie left the Starry Plough?

"What time is it?" she asked fuzzily.

"I couldn't rightly say, granddaughter. But it's the perfect time for fishing."

Those giant, moss-swagged boughs overhead — where in the city could you find trees that age?

Yonie strained up onto her elbows. Around them were cypress trees with boles thicker than the boat, their knobby knees poking out of the inky water like bones. Huge fallen logs lay melting into black mud. No insects whirred, no birds trilled, no frogs croaked.

Yonie stared up at the face of the old woman, its wrinkles like water-carved channels, and she felt suddenly very cold.

"Grandmother," she stammered, "do I have to go home with you?"

"Don't you want to, child? My gumbo's been cooking for a long, long time, and it's got a deep rich flavor, with all those little fishes stirred in together."

"Not yet," Yonie pleaded.

The old woman pursed her lips. "Hmf," she said. "It's not common — but I do sometimes throw one back."

Yonie was coughing and gasping, and there were shrill city voices around her, and the sharp scent of trampled grass, and a lantern hurting her eyes.

It was just as confusing as the bottom of Granny Pitchers's rowboat, but considerably more noisy and unpleasant, with the vomiting and the wet hair in her eyes, and all the people's hands trying to make her stand up.

At last Yonie did lurch to her feet. Finding the kaleidoscope still gripped in one hand, she staggered over and smashed the glass end of it against the brick canal-path. Only then did she let it drop to the ground, where someone quickly made off with it.

A burly officer of the guard arrived, causing the more unsavory members of the crowd to disperse. No one, it turned out, had seen Yonie fall in, and she was forced to explain between coughs that no one had pushed her.

The gendarme asked her some questions clearly meant to assess her level of intoxication and her emotional stability. Yonie's wits had returned enough that she avoided mention of the kaleidoscope. The evening had been eventful enough already without spending the night at the police station.

"Well, ma'am," the officer finally said, "please watch your footing in the future, 'specially at night when no one's

around. It's lucky for you these folks even heard you screaming."

"There was really no missing it," said one of the more
solicitous men, who, judging by his sopping clothes, must
be her rescuer. "I say, have you had voice training, ma'am?"

Yonie supposed that she had, from her mother, though
she had no memory of crying out or, in fact, of anything
much she'd done in the real world after lifting the kaleidoscope to her eye.

"You saved my life," Yonie wheezed. "Thank you, from
the bottom of my 'eart."

"Oh, sugar, stop bothering the poor girl." The man's
companion put her hand on his wet sleeve, then threaded
her other arm up to squeeze his biceps. "She's in good hands
now."

"I suppose—" With one last glance at Yonie's clinging
dress, the man allowed himself to be pulled away.

Yonie heard his companion purring, "Ever so brave
. . ." as they walked away, arms entwined.

It was not until Yonie was trudging back down Swallow
Street that Luc caught up with her.

"There you are—" he started off angrily. Then he
noticed her bedraggled dress dripping onto the wooden
sidewalk. He reached forward and felt her wet braid, in
what Yonie thought was a far too intimate gesture. "Floods,
you're soaked! What happened to you?"

"Your gift nearly drowned me, that's what," she growled,

knocking his hand away. "It was wily as anything. Made me pitch right into the Rose Canal."

Even in the dimness between streetlights, she saw his face go pale. "That flooding bastard. If I'd known, I never would've — I mean —"

Yonie's eyes narrowed. "Would have what?"

"I — uh —" He looked away.

"Luc, where did you get that kaleidoscope? Whose idea was it, to give it to me?" Yonie grabbed his smooth chin in one strong hand, forcing him to look at her. "Tell me," she snarled.

Luc's eyes darted. "He said he needed to know what a pearly would make of it, but he didn't want you to have any preconceptions, so he thought, if it came from someone you trusted —"

"And that didn't sound *strange* to you? It sounds like he wanted me to look into the thing without doing a Seeing first."

"I swear, I didn't know it was dangerous!"

Yonie released Luc's chin and wiped her hand on her dress. "You didn't know anything about it, did you? You'd never even seen inside that box." She gave a sharp laugh. "You even asked me what it was! Who gave it to you, Luc? Will you tell me that much?"

"A — a fellow at the pub, he said his name was Max. He was asking after you, and I said I knew you. But he didn't seem rich, so I think the thing must've come from somebody higher up —"

"Because you got paid so much, you mean?" Yonie flicked a searing glance down at Luc's new alligator-skin boots.

"Yonie, you know I would never want to hurt you! I hold you in the highest regard, and —"

"I don't even know which is worse," Yonie burst out. "That you would deceive me like that, or that you could be so stupid!"

She glared at Luc, and suddenly he bolted.

Yonie swiped her face with her damp sleeve. She had not realized until then just how much the canal water had affected her eyes.

She stumbled along the sidewalk, regretting many things. High on the list was accepting Luc's boat ride to the ballroom. Now she was stranded in High Town without her canoe.

Yonie slumped down onto a cold brick doorstep and put her face in her hands. The shop fronts around her were closed up for the night. The faint shouts of High Town partygoers sounded very far away. Even the mosquitoes seemed to have forgotten her.

Then something small and soft brushed up against her ankles.

Yonie gave a hoarse cry and swept LaRue up onto her lap. "You came back," she sobbed, voice muffled by the cat's fur. "I'm so sorry for what I said. I'm so, so sorry —"

"Never mind that now," LaRue said gruffly. "You've had quite a harrowing experience, and we should get you home and into a nice warm bed. What that young officer was thinking, letting you walk home by yourself, I simply don't know."

"You saw that? Did you see me fall in?"

"Oh, yes."

Yonie stroked the cat's back. "It was you that screamed for help, wasn't it? I don't remember doing it myself."

"Of course it was me. Drowning people don't scream. They're far too busy trying to breathe."

"Then you saved my life, LaRue. Every bit as much as that man who pulled me out."

LaRue fixed her eyes on Yonie's. Her cat pupils were caves in the darkness. "Do you know what went through my mind when I saw you go down? I thought, *I lost five siblings to drowning. I'm not going to lose another.*"

LaRue's claws clenched through the ruined fabric of Yonie's dress. "You were right, you know. I'm not your mama, and I've got no business trying to replace her. I'd be glad to be your sister, though. For as long as you want me."

Yonie hugged the cat's small body to her. It was some time before she could speak. "You don't have to look after me at all," she said raggedly. "It's not your job. Even if the guile in you makes you think so."

The next moment, Yonie was aghast that she had even voiced that thought. LaRue had never been open to any sort of discussion about what she called her Nature.

But the cat didn't take offense. "I considered that, while we were apart," she said slowly. "Those evenings hunting mice down at the cannery and the paper mill, and daytimes sleeping on rooftops and in the chapels along Gleese Avenue. *I could live on my own like this,* I thought. Why did I keep checking on you and worrying about you? Was it just my guile making me act that way?"

LaRue gazed up at Yonie. "I finally reached a conclusion, and here it is: it doesn't matter if the guile makes me care about you, because I'd feel the same way without it. I look back over what we've been through together, and I just know — even if there weren't a drop of guile in me, I would be a fool not to love you, Yonie." She licked a paw. "And one thing I know for certain about myself is that I'm no fool."

Yonie smoothed her hand again and again over LaRue's fur. The cat's tail had picked up some burrs which she had evidently not been able to remove. Yonie suspected that LaRue's last few days had been harder than she was willing to admit.

Could LaRue actually lead a life on her own? She could feed herself, but what would she do for companionship? Other cats typically shunned her. Most humans would do worse. Any prolonged contact would betray her true nature, even if LaRue didn't speak. And realistically, how long could LaRue go without speaking?

Suddenly Yonie's shrewd, competent companion seemed terribly vulnerable.

Yonie managed to clear her throat. "So I suppose you followed me and Luc tonight? Even after I specifically told you not to?"

"Yonie, please. I'm not a dog. I don't take *orders.*" LaRue jumped down and gave Yonie a commanding look. "Now, up you get. I know you're exhausted, but there's a long walk ahead of us."

Yonie's sinuses felt raw, her legs were weak, and her stomach still churned, but looking at the fluffy form at her feet, suddenly she smiled. "No, there's not," she said, putting a hand on her belt. Her purse was still securely closed, the stiff buckle having withstood its dunking. "We're only walking as far as LeClerc Bridge, and then we're taking a water taxi."

"All the way? You poor thing, I wish we could, but we can't afford to spend that kind of money."

"LaRue," Yonie said, "we have a lot of catching up to do."

Yonie's story was delayed. There were pedestrians on the way to the bridge, then the oarsman in the water taxi, and then Yonie's utter exhaustion upon arriving home. She awoke the next morning to find LaRue pacing along the edge of her bed.

"At last! You can't imagine the restraint I've exercised, letting you sleep so late. You simply must tell me everything, starting with how you handled that DesMaray man. How on earth did he end up paying you?"

The cat listened avidly as Yonie described her experience with DesMaray, interjecting tart comments about the man's character. When Yonie came to the actual revelation, however, LaRue was uncharacteristically speechless for almost fifteen seconds.

"That will take some getting used to," she said eventually. "I look forward to meeting the man, though I hardly approve of how he deceived you." Her ears flicked. "Speaking of which, I found out something that might interest you about your friend Luc Lazard —"

"He's not my friend anymore."

"Oh? What a pity — just when I was starting to loathe him slightly less." The cat sleeked back her whiskers with one paw.

Yonie reflected that if LaRue intended to scale back her role from a maternal to a sisterly one, it was certainly a sarcastic, bossy sister that she was destined to play.

"I followed him down to Road-end for a couple of nights," the cat continued, "and it turns out he's not a professional gambler at all. He waits tables at the Last Chance Saloon and does odd jobs around the neighborhood. Why he thinks that should impress girls less than gambling, I can't imagine."

"One of his odd jobs nearly killed me," Yonie spat. She recounted her last conversation with Luc.

"What?" The cat's hackles rose. "Yonie, I know you were just half drowned, but haven't you thought about what that *means?*"

"It means you were right about him, LaRue. He's willing to lie to his friends for money. You know what? He never even apologized to me."

"I'm glad we're in agreement about the young man's character, but right now that's the least of our concerns. Consider — someone sent you that thing deliberately."

Yonie's eyes widened. "It's like the locket and the shop sign! But worse." She clutched Aunt Elisa's quilt to her, breathing in its comforting scent. "There *is* a guilemonger behind all this, and he doesn't like me interfering. He tried to get me drowned! What are we going to do?"

She sprang up and began to dress hurriedly. But as she was transferring her belt and purse back onto her everyday skirt, the tension drained out of her body, to be replaced by the same warm, giddy feeling of safety that had visited her regularly over the past few days.

"It's all right. I'll go talk to M'sir DesMaray. If anyone can protect us, it's him. Maybe he can even help find the guilemonger." Yonie picked up LaRue and twirled around.

Then she noticed how tense LaRue's body had become and how her claws had emerged even more than this sort of indignity would usually warrant. Yonie apologized and set LaRue down on the pallet.

LaRue wrapped her tail around her paws without a trace of her usual flair. "Yonie," she said softly, "it occurs to me that it might not be the guilemonger himself who tried to kill you."

"What — you think someone *purchased* that thing to use on me? That doesn't make sense, LaRue. I help people! I don't have *enemies!* And even if I did, they'd be Low Town folks. They couldn't afford to go to an expensive dealer." She paused and frowned uncertainly. "There is M'sir Turcoat — I'm sure he's still angry at me — but I just can't imagine —"

"No, no. He's neither wealthy nor ruthless enough to be our man. But I know someone who is." The cat gazed up at Yonie. "Someone whose fondest plans may be endangered by your very existence. Someone who recently took steps to verify the threat and to keep you quiet until he could arrange a more permanent silence —"

"LaRue! That's insane!"

The cat winced. "Is it?" she said apologetically. "I know this is hard for you, Yonie — but we have to consider Felix DesMaray."

CHAPTER TWENTY-ONE

THE *DRAGONFLY* felt scarcely heavier than usual as Yonie yanked it down the Petty Canal under a hazy morning sun. Four treasured books, the largest one holding the sketch of her mother between its pages, lay carefully wrapped in Yonie's raincoat. Her spare set of clothes, plus one hopelessly mud-stained dress, were stuffed into a string shopping bag. An apple, a piece of smoked fish, and a bottle of water waited for noon in her knapsack, and the sun and stars quilt lay folded on the bow seat underneath LaRue.

The air above the Petty Canal was as moist as a dog's

breath and smelled far less pleasant. The sky was a bright white over the wide sheet of the Ford.

Yonie still could not quite imagine DesMaray as a villain. But as LaRue pointed out, *someone* meant her harm, and whoever it was might not be so subtle the next time. Yonie had been doing business out of her garret for two years now, and anyone willing to ask around would eventually be able to find her home.

Surely no city assassins could find her in the Sloughs. And though it was galling to ask for help from the relatives who had pushed her out, at least Aunt Elisa and Gustave and his wife would give her shelter, not to mention copious advice.

Yonie cast a regretful look at the sun and stars pattern under LaRue's orange fluff. She would miss that quilt. She had washed out the algae stains long ago, but she hadn't had the heart to wash the whole thing. It smelled like cypress smoke and baked bread and a whole mix of indefinable but deeply reassuring scents that she thought of as simply the smell of home. On certain nights of late, that smell had brought her great comfort.

Yonie planned to ask Aunt Elisa to return the quilt to Gilbert, thus avoiding another awkward encounter. He would prefer it that way too. Certainly he hadn't seemed eager for her company.

Should she be worried about Gilbert? In the Bad Bayous, people tended toward the extremes. They could be

energetically social, enjoying extended visits or long hunting trips with friends, gossiping insatiably about their
neighbors, and traveling many miles to attend all-night
parties. Papa, with his fiddling always in demand, was the
social kind, and he had carried Mama and Yonie along in
his wake.

Other folks isolated themselves: outlaws of varying
degree, religious hermits, or those who, for whatever reason,
simply preferred to be alone. The Sloughs were noted for
their proportion of eccentrics; "twisty waters, twisty people," the saying went.

Annette Sansoucie, who ran the trading post at Smoky
Mouth, shook her head about the rusty-voiced bachelors she
saw once or twice a year. "They come in with a raft full o'
furs, and they buy flour and salt and some fishhooks and
razor blades. Sooner or later, they stop buying the razor
blades."

Gilbert, separated from his brothers, might well be
floating down that same stream. She was just as glad not to
be visiting him again, Yonie thought guiltily.

It took Yonie several hours to fully rue that decision.

Gilbert could have given her directions to Aunt Elisa's
new home. Knowing that it was "down near Charwater"
was not nearly enough.

Of the dozens of boaters Yonie had hailed in the course
of the day, more than half had heard of the DuRoy boy from

up the Bitterway who'd married that nice Rowbear girl. Several people had even given descriptions of how Lydie's pregnancy was going, with more details than Yonie (and probably Lydie) would have wished.

Folks had provided long lists of turnings, laced with dubious landmarks and unfamiliar channel names. Since almost all swamp folk were illiterate, any signs Yonie encountered were cryptic at best. Was that board nailed to a tree supposed to depict a goat's head, or could it be a hammer? Was that tangle of rope just a piece of trash, or was it meant to indicate Spider Inlet? It was a challenge to remember all the details people told her, and Yonie had not packed her pencil or notebook.

Gilbert could have given her written directions. The DuRoy cousins could all read and write — Mama had seen to that.

When a pair of massive, fire-blackened trees came into sight, Yonie let out a moan.

"We've come all the way round to the Charwater again," she told LaRue. "I'm going to have to ask Gilbert for directions if we want to get to Aunt Elisa's before dark."

LaRue, who had slept away most of the day, opened one eye. "It's a bit dark already," she said dubiously. "I don't like the look of those clouds."

Yonie glanced up at the sky, then down at her books. Would they survive a downpour, even with the oilcloth raincoat bundled around them? Was it even worth trying to save them? She could tolerate a soaking, but poor LaRue would be miserable without her usual shelter underneath Yonie's coat.

The day grew darker. Fewer and fewer folk were out in boats. No one was sitting out on the porch or working in a kitchen garden. By the time Yonie neared the Bitterway, she had not passed another craft for over an hour, and in that time the only person she had seen was a worried-looking man with a hammer in his hand, up inspecting the shingles on his shack.

The air was tense with moisture, and the trees seemed to be flinching already at the prospect of the beating they would receive. Preoccupied with her troubles, and dreading the coming storm, Yonie did not see the stranger until he was quite close.

He was rowing a dilapidated swamp skiff, and as he approached in the steely half-light, the first thing Yonie noticed about him was the pale scars across the knuckles of both his enormous hands. His clothing was rank with spilled alcohol.

"'Ey, there, girl," he called to Yonie in a slurred voice.

Yonie inwardly cursed her carelessness. She should never have let this man get so near. She backpaddled, but the man's hand had already come down over the side of the *Dragonfly* like a grappling hook.

"Got some nice things in that there canoe," the man said. The direction of his gaze revealed that what really interested him was Yonie herself.

Yonie considered chopping at the stranger's hand with her canoe paddle, but he looked as if even a blow to the head might not faze him. Her heart pounded. Within moments, one of those hands could be locked around her wrist like a shackle.

The man grinned sloppily and shifted one long, burly arm.

Yonie could see LaRue gathering herself for some sort of heroic and possibly suicidal attack. Her stomach roiled, and if she'd already eaten her lunch, it would have come back up.

Her lunch . . . An idea bloomed in Yonie's head. She reached into her knapsack and pulled out her apple, a plump Southern Gold that looked eerie white in the storm clouds' glow.

"I've got a *tasty* apple here," she told the man, smiling savagely. "And I'd love to share it with you — if you would only lend me your *knife.*"

She pulled out her own belt knife just as a whip of lightning lashed up from behind the black claws of the trees. "You see?" she crooned as she held the blade up beside the apple. "Mine isn't nearly sharp enough for what I need . . ."

The whites of the man's eyes were visible all the way around his irises as he yanked his hand back from the *Dragonfly's* side. With a whimper, he drove his oars into the dark water and shot off past Yonie, down the way she had come.

A sudden boom of thunder almost made Yonie upset

the canoe. She emitted a slightly hysterical laugh. Then, as the thunder rolled on, she raised the apple and tore out a gigantic bite.

"Oh, my Elders," said Gilbert involuntarily as he opened the door. His black hair was tousled, his shirt was off, and he was hitching up his pants as if he'd just pulled them on.

Yonie shouldered past him into the room and laid the sopping bundle in her arms down onto the stone hearth before the remnants of a fire.

The top layer of the bundle stood up, moved closer to the warmth of the coals, and began to briskly lick the fur that was plastered to her body. Yonie wished that she were alone with LaRue, so that she could properly thank the cat for her sacrifice. The top of the oilcloth was actually still dry where she had stretched herself, and the books inside were unharmed.

"So, you finally brought back that quilt," said Gilbert from behind her. He had pulled on a shirt, and Yonie noticed belatedly that since she had last seen him, he had reduced his shaggy beard to a passable goatee.

"Yes," said Yonie breezily. She unfolded the quilt, which promptly trailed water all over the hearth and floor. "I wanted to wash it before I brought it back."

"Yonie, you look like a dead rat picked up on the end of an oar. Let me find you some dry clothes. I'll turn my back and everything."

"I don't think so." Yonie turned abruptly. "I'm going to go flip my canoe. No, you stay in where it's dry." You too, she almost said to LaRue, but the cat had already slipped out ahead of her.

"You really should accept that change of clothes if you don't want to catch cold," LaRue hissed as they hurried to the dock.

Yonie grunted as she heaved the *Dragonfly* up out of the water. "Remember that time I was taking a bath up at Bitter Springs, and Gilbert and Gregory stole my clothes, and dipped them in mud, and hung them way up in a gum tree like a scarecrow? With a bird's nest for a *head?*" Yonie plucked her knapsack out of the canoe, and with more effort dragged out the sodden mass in the string bag. "It was horrible. Do you have any idea what it's like to climb a tree in the nude?"

"I'm actually not sure if my answer should be yes or no," LaRue said pensively. "But in any case, Yonie, that was ages ago! I was only a kitten, which would make you what, six or seven?"

"I don't care, the idea of undressing anywhere around Gilbert makes me *extremely* uncomfortable." She overturned the canoe, sending a gush of water over the dock.

"I see," said LaRue. "On that subject, though, Yonie? The next time a man opens his door to you in a state of partial dishabille, you might want to make sure he doesn't have company before you go barging in."

"What?" Yonie's face colored. "Oh, for goodness' sake, LaRue! It's *Gilbert!* He was taking a nap!"

"Just a thought," the cat said airily. "But do consider the dry clothes. The ones you have on are sticking to your body in a way that's not quite modest."

A short while later, Yonie's entire wardrobe was draped over a line strung across the room. She was wearing Gilbert's spare trousers (which were the right length, but had needed the addition of Yonie's wet belt) and his brown sweater, which was warming up her chilled arms nicely.

Yonie settled down in front of the fire, which Gilbert had refreshed while she was outside. Gilbert pulled up a chair, turned it around, and sat down facing Yonie with his arms resting across the back.

"So," he said. "It couldn't 'ave been just that old quilt that brought you for a visit. Did you come to apologize for last time? Because you don't 'ave to. I thought about it a lot afterward, and —"

"What? No! I wasn't planning to come here at all. I left Wicked Ford because my life was in danger."

Gilbert nearly toppled forward. "Elders! What 'appened?"

"Somebody tried to kill me — or actually, paid someone to arrange it, in an exotic kind of way. It's a long story. But anyway, I thought I'd better go somewhere else for a while. Though I must say, the Sloughs haven't turned out to be so safe either . . ."

She recounted her run-in with the gigantic drunken stranger, and by the end, she was shaking with laughter. "All I can say is, it's a good thing swamp folk are so superstitious. I can't picture many city folk getting spooked by that old Apple Sharer story."

Gilbert's face had taken on a peculiar expression. "Yonie, that story? That was one of the ones I made up. No one outside our family's ever 'eard it."

"Oh."

There was a thoughtful silence.

"I'm surprised you didn't just 'op in the water. You can outswim anyone in the Sloughs."

Not anymore, Yonie thought bitterly. Now, after the kaleidoscope, even the thought of swimming made her feel the water closing over her head and filling her lungs.

"Which other stories did you make up?" she asked.

He listed a half dozen.

"But those were the scariest ones!"

Gilbert looked gratified. Then he cleared his throat. "You're welcome to stay 'ere if you want, till things blow over back in the city," he said, with the air of someone putting his weight on a rotten plank.

"Actually, I was planning to go visit your mother for a while. I just stopped to get directions, and I'll be getting along as soon as the rain lets up."

"I don't think that's a good idea. You'd be safer 'ere.

It's pretty far away from anywhere else, and so long as you didn't go out much —"

"Oh, come on, Gilbert, are you really that lonely?"

"Nay, that's not why — I mean —"

He got up and used the poker on the fire, stabbing a perfectly good ember until it crumbled away.

"There's something you ought to know," he said abruptly. "They didn't want to tell you. They never told me, either, but I figured it out. Little things people said, when they thought I wasn't listening."

"Who do you mean, they?"

"My mama, and the aunts and uncles. And I think Gustave knew too, because 'e was there."

"Where?" said Yonie, a horrible foreboding growing in her. The fire crackled behind her, throwing out sparks.

"At your old 'ouse," Gilbert said in a rough voice. "The night somebody burned it down."

CHAPTER TWENTY-TWO

T HAT CAN'T be," Yonie whispered, even as the memories, recently refreshed via kaleidoscope, came rushing back. That sharp stench as she paddled toward the blaze — wasn't it a chemical smell?

LaRue, still damp, crept under her hand. The cat's ears were laid back flat.

"I asked Mama 'ow she knew for sure. She didn't want to talk about it, but I kept after 'er and finally she told me. She'd gone back to your kitchen garden to see if she could save anything, she said. I bet really she wanted to do some crying, off by 'erself. Anyhow, she was digging up the potatoes, and she found a whole mess of empty kerosene cans pushed down into the middle of the patch. Not rusted, either.

"I'd wondered why your parents didn't get out in time. Oftentimes with a fire, folks can run outside and jump in the water. But now I know. Someone didn't want them to get out."

Yonie closed her eyes and saw the dark outline of the cottage, like an eyeless face with whipping fiery hair. Why eyeless? Why weren't the windows showing the yellow flames inside? It was summertime, and there should have been nothing more than mosquito-cloth over the frames. Unless the wooden storm shutters had been closed, maybe even nailed shut — or screwed shut, since that could be done stealthily. They would have had to seal the door as well . . .

"It doesn't make sense! Why would anybody want to kill my parents?"

"None of us could figure it, either," Gilbert said gruffly. "We don't even know if it was your papa or your mama they were after, or both, or maybe all three of you together. That's 'ow come the family thought you should go live in the city for a while. If your parents 'ad got caught up in some kind of feud, that would keep you well out of it."

"And nobody even thought about warning me?"

"Aw, Yonie, you know what would've 'appened. You never would've left the Sloughs. You would've gone poking around asking questions and making trouble, and maybe getting yourself killed. You know you would've."

Yonie gave a grudging nod.

"As it was, most folks 'ereabouts assumed you were dead too, and we thought it'd be safest to leave it that way."

"So that's why no one wanted me to visit?"

"Aye, o' course. None of us wanted to risk it."

Yonie gave what she hoped was an inaudible sniff. "I was starting to wonder if anyone even remembered me."

"'Oo could forget *you?*" said Gilbert, in a way that might or might not have been a compliment. "Yonie, I know it must 'ave been rough. It wasn't easy for us, either. Mama cried a lot. But she said it was a comfort, knowing you were safe with your mother's folks."

Yonie straightened up and stared. "Why in the great green deeps would she think that?"

"Floods — I forgot, you almost got killed. I guess it wasn't so safe after all."

"That's not what I meant! Gilbert, you all must have known that Mama and her parents weren't on speaking terms."

"Well, we knew they didn't get along, but family's family, right? They'd 'ave to take you in . . . Yonie, what's the matter?"

Yonie wiped angrily at her eyes. Gilbert had spoken with such conviction, as if family loyalty were a law of nature. And evidently the other relatives had felt the same way.

"It's different in the city," she said sharply. "I've been living on my own."

"Aye?" said Gilbert, somewhat taken aback. "So 'ow've you been earning a living, then?"

She avoided his eyes. "I cleaned fish for a while, but I, er, couldn't keep up. Then I got a job at a cannery, but I got sacked for talking back to the floor boss. I waited tables, but that didn't last long — one day there was a customer who was acting like a spoiled child, and I told her so."

"Wish I'd 'eard it."

"I almost got hired as a children's governess, for a wealthy family. Because of my accent, you know? It would have been good money. But it was a live-in position, and they wouldn't let me keep a cat. Can you imagine?"

"Ah." Gilbert eyed the straggly tuft of fur still huddled against Yonie's side. "So what did you end up doing?"

How would Gilbert react if she told him she was a pearly? Feelings against slyfolk ran high in the bayou country. But telling him she was a *fake* pearly would sound even worse.

She shrugged. "This and that."

"And somehow you made a bad enemy. I don't s'pose you know 'oo it is?"

"It might be some sort of underworld dealer in cunning weapons. I call him the guilemonger."

Gilbert raised his eyebrows. "Great name."

"Thank you. Or" — she paused dramatically — "it could be *Felix DesMaray*."

"'Oo's that?"

"You mean you — oh, never mind. He's the wealthiest man in the Bayous."

"Drowning waters, Yonie. And they say I used to get in trouble! 'Ow'd you get on their bad side?"

"I messed up some business deals for the guilemonger."

"And the rich fellow?"

"I know something he might want to keep secret." It would remain secret from her bayou kin, too, Yonie vowed. Mama had wanted it that way.

Gilbert ran a hand over his beard. "And then there's the fire-setter on top of that. Good thing you came 'ere before you went to visit my mama. At least nobody knows you're back."

"But I didn't. I spent most of the day trying to find her place. I must have talked to two dozen people."

"Sink it! Did you tell 'em your name?"

"Of course. I'm not rude!" She thought a moment. "Come to think of it, some of them did look rather surprised."

Gilbert ran his hands through his hair. "You should 'ave come 'ere first! You could be in bad trouble now, all because you didn't want to ask me for 'elp. Is talking to me really that awful?"

Yonie didn't answer.

"Well, you can't go down there now." As if in agreement, the wind raised its voice another degree and dashed a bucketful of water and twigs against the side of the house. "I know you 'ate the idea, but you'll 'ave to stay 'ere tonight."

* * *

Yonie turned over yet again under the unfamiliar blanket. Gilbert had given her his mother's old bed and was sprawled under his coat on the rag rug by the last glow of the fire. Yonie suspected that was his usual sleeping arrangement — the DuRoy boys had been accustomed to bedding down on the rug like a litter of puppies. Did Gilbert miss having his brothers crowded around him?

LaRue's motionless weight pressed down the blanket near Yonie's feet, but for all she knew, the cat might have been just as wakeful as she was. What they had learned from Gilbert would have been just as shocking to LaRue as it was to Yonie herself.

In some ways, the news had actually relieved Yonie's mind. For the last two years, she had agonized over what would have happened if she'd been where she was supposed to be on the night of the fire. Could she have woken up in time to warn her parents? Now she knew there was nothing she could have done, except die along with them.

It also helped to have an explanation for the strange behavior of her relatives afterward, which had hurt more than she had wanted to admit.

But in other ways the news was deeply disturbing. Yonie had always believed that her parents were widely liked. Papa, with his fiddle and his funny stories, and Mama, with her ability to sing harmony, had always been welcome at parties. But now Yonie revisited every petty dispute and affront. The time at that fish fry when Papa had punched Charles Drapeau in the mouth? That woman from Fever Creek who had taken it as a deep insult when Mama offered to teach her son to read? A person would have to be seriously unbalanced to make that kind of thing the grounds for murder.

But: twisty waters, twisty people.

The most appalling thing was the feelings Yonie found rising up in herself. After her parents had died, Yonie had raged against the world, against fortune, against the Elders themselves. Eventually her anger had cooled into a numb acceptance.

Now the anger was back, and it was very hot and very specific. Yonie's temper usually just flared and went out, but she suspected this might burn for a long, long time. When Yonie discovered who had killed her parents, she didn't know what she might be capable of.

The clouds drenched the land unrelentingly for the next four days. The series of storms was violent enough to make canoe travel impossible, or at least dangerous, though by the fourth day, Yonie was almost willing to give it a try.

She desperately missed talking to LaRue but had curtailed her trips outside after the first day, when Gilbert (making the obvious assumption about her destination) had delicately expressed concern about her health.

"I can't take it anymore!" she muttered. "Just sitting around doing nothing!"

Somehow Gilbert heard her over the pounding of the rain. "You 'aven't been sitting," he objected from his seat by the hearth. "Pacing, more like — you've near worn a path through the rug. And you've been doing plenty. We must've played a dozen games of chess. And you've been catching up on sleep and eating about five meals a day."

"Do you really consider smoked meat and water a meal, Gilbert? I'm surprised you've stayed as healthy as you are, with your mother's kitchen garden gone to ruin."

"You just 'ave to eat the right parts of the animal. Take that sausage we 'ad last night. When I was cutting up the possum —"

"I don't want to hear about it!" Yonie said loudly, and then bit her lip. "Sorry. I just have no idea what to do next. I need advice. From someone older," she said, pointedly looking at LaRue. "And wiser," she added, in case Gilbert might suppose he qualified.

"You could always ask the Elders."

Yonie glanced at the memory alcove near the door, with its wooden figurines of departed family members. She wasn't sure how serious Gilbert was.

Though city folk and bayou folk both venerated their ancestors, they did so in very different ways. City folk paid homage to a set group of ancient admirables, whose histories and qualities had been highly mythologized over time.

Bayou folk were more clannish. Yonie could still remember Granny Charlotta's matter-of-fact voice: *If you 'ave to revere somebody, then it surely ought to be your own kin.* And though Yonie was not among those who believed that their dead relatives actually spoke to them, she had to admit that it seemed more likely than getting a reply from a complete stranger.

Her feet had brought her up to the memory alcove. There they were, Granny Charlotta and the other grands she barely remembered, and Uncle Stephan, who probably only Gustave was old enough to clearly recall.

She reached for the two newest carvings and cupped them in her hands. The one of Mama showed her smiling serenely, holding a book to her heart. The one of Papa showed him with his fiddle, wearing an impish grin. What would they advise her to do?

"You can 'ave those, if you want." Gilbert's voice came from behind her. "I can always make more. I know the fire didn't leave you anything to remember them by."

"Thank you," said Yonie quietly. Then a thought struck her. "I do have one thing, actually. Would you like to see?"

The charcoal sketch was still dry, safe under the front cover of *The Unlucky Prince*. Gilbert studied the evocative lines and the deft, swooping smudges.

"'Oo drew this, then?"

"Some old schoolmate of Mama's."

"She was good." Gilbert touched a callused finger to

the lettering that said *V. Bruneau*. "So that was 'er birth name . . . Looks like this book was 'ers, too." He pointed to the front flyleaf, where one corner was inscribed in faded blue ink: 'To Valery on her tenth birthday. May you always follow your dreams. Love from Aunt Nettie."

"It's the only one that survived the fire," Yonie said. "It happened to be in my canoe."

"'Oo's this Aunt Nettie? Could she 'elp you?"

Yonie automatically shook her head. "I don't know her. Mama never would talk about any of her city relatives . . ."

Yonie stopped. Something nagged at her about the name. She had seen it in the front of many of her mother's old books, so often that the inscription had become all but invisible to her. Why did she get the feeling it should be somewhere else as well?

Then she had it. *Bellamy's Social Roster.*

"That's odd," she said. "I looked up Mama's side of the family just a few weeks ago, but there wasn't any Nettie listed."

"Listed?"

"Their names are published. In a book."

Gilbert gave a disbelieving snort.

"It's true! Not just the Bruneaus. A lot of other families too."

Gilbert absorbed this. "Are you sure? Do you even know what Nettie's short for?"

Yonie shook her head. "I suppose it could be a lot of names. Nanette?"

"Or Minette."

"Fanette? Antoinette?"

"Bernette," Gilbert put in. "Jeanette."

Yonie gasped. "Gilbert! *There's a Jeanette Canal in my neighborhood!*"

He gave her a strange look.

"You see a lot of Bruneau first names around that area," she explained.

"This family names their children after *canals?*"

"No, after previous Bruneaus—" Yonie's eyes got wide. "Deep waters. I think I might be named after my grand-aunt Nettie. Yonetta is really just Jeanette put into bayou dialect."

Yonie remembered her Bruneau grandfather's indignation: *She named her* Yonetta? Was it the dialect or the name-sake that had upset him so?

"Maybe Nettie was disinherited, like Mama, and that's why she wasn't in the roster!"

"Or else—I 'ate to say it, Yonie, but she might've died."

"But she wouldn't have been that old—and also, do you remember how Mama used to go up to Wicked Ford a few times a year, all by herself?"

"Course. She'd come back with dozens of books."

"I always took it for granted, but that was before I knew how much new books cost. Now I don't know how we could have afforded them all. Look at this one. It's even got color plates."

"You think they were gifts from this Nettie?"

"They weren't from Mama's parents, that's for sure." Yonie passed her hand along the furry back of LaRue, who had materialized in her lap the second she sat down. "But why didn't Mama ever take me to meet her aunt, if they were still close?"

"I reckon she wanted to keep you away from Wicked Ford," said Gilbert. "She 'ad strong feelings about that place, remember."

"She could have at least told me who she was visiting."

"You'd 'ave wanted to meet 'er, right?"

"My namesake? Of course!"

"That's why, then. Once you get curious about something, Yonie, there's no use standing in your way."

"Well, I'm glad you feel that way, Gilbert, because I'm curious now." Yonie stood up, arms cradling the small orange cat. "If I can't go see Aunt Elisa, I'm going back to Wicked Ford and try to find my grand-aunt Nettie. Whoever my enemies are, they won't be expecting that."

Gilbert winced. "I sure 'ope you're not planning to go in this rain."

"It's better than staying cooped up here. What are you groaning about? I'd think that after four days, you'd be glad to get rid of me."

"I'm groaning because I 'ave to go with you. You've got people trying to kill you, there and 'ere. You shouldn't 'ave to face that all by yourself."

"Do you honestly think you'd be any use?"

Gilbert glowered at her from under his black eyebrows. "I've got my eyes. I've got my wits. And if it comes to a fight, I'll be at least as much 'elp as a flooding apple."

CHAPTER TWENTY-THREE

THEIR RAINCOAT hoods made Yonie and Gilbert anonymous, but Gilbert pointed out that the matte-black *Dragonfly* with its grotesque gong in the stern might be recognized once they reached the city. Though Yonie had refused to consider taking any other craft, she consented to draping the gong with a piece of canvas. The hunched silhouette this produced made the *Dragonfly* appear, if anything, even more sinister.

Already Yonie could feel moisture through the seams of her raincoat. She was glad she'd left her books, the sketch, and the figurines of her parents safe and dry under Gilbert's roof. LaRue traveled in relative luxury underneath Yonie's seat in the blanket-lined bottom half of a tin box, covered with a decrepit oilcloth hat Gilbert had unearthed.

The landscape had changed over the last three days. Sleepy streams had become eerie lakes, and bushes that had lined the waterways now lurked below the surface, clawing at the hull of the canoe. A tree had fallen across Hanged Man's Throat, forcing a squishy portage over the adjoining bank. Many landmarks were completely submerged.

When they reached the Ford late that afternoon, no lines of wagons crossed the great expanse, and the ferries rode low, packed with travelers. The freight barges hurrying to dock were draped in tarpaulins, like old ladies with their shawls pulled over their heads.

"It's bigger than I remembered," said Gilbert in a subdued voice as they entered the Petty Canal. He looked around at the warehouses and inns and houseboats that lined the banks, and at the buildings of High Town rising up in the distance. "'Ow are we ever going to find your grand-aunt in a place this size?"

"I've got some ideas," Yonie told him.

Gilbert objected at first. He had come along to protect Yonie and didn't like the idea of splitting up. But Yonie knew that he had wits as well as brawn. He would be capable of questioning people in an intelligent way, maybe even a subtle and devious way. He could ask after Jeanette

Bruneau, and it wouldn't be tied to Yonie. And LaRue would make sure that he didn't get lost.

Of course, Yonie didn't know that her grand-aunt's name *was* Bruneau — or even Jeanette. That was why she had to go to the library.

Yonie had wondered if Bellflower Academy would be open in such extraordinary weather. But Mama had skipped Yonie's lessons only in the most extreme of circumstances, and it turned out that her school held to the same spirit.

Yonie burst through the library door and stopped short in front of the main desk, pinned by the horrified gaze of Adele Pierpond, who today was looking regal in a sea-green dress with foamy lace collar.

Yonie was so used to thinking of the library as a haven, she had forgotten that she was in disrepute with the librarian. The warmth and light of the library seemed like a fabulous dream that was about to dissolve.

Pierpond rose from her chair with the speed and power of a wave breaking on a beach. "Yonie Watereye, my word! What are you thinking, coming in here like this?"

Yonie's throat closed up painfully.

"You're sopping! You can't possibly handle books in that condition."

The librarian peeled Yonie out of her oilcloth and hung it on a peg by the door, next to a row of lily-pad-colored ponchos. "Over by the stove, now, and just maybe you can get dry enough to go near paper."

Unable to speak, Yonie nodded and sidled her way between shelves until she reached the round iron stove in the back of the room. Like its mistress, it proved to be fearsomely efficient.

A little later, Pierpond came by.

"Honey, I was a bit cold to you the last time we met. I think you know why? But I talked to M'sir Cordell recently, and he said you had helped him again."

Yonie's letter to the headmaster about the locket and the guilemonger seemed so long ago now, it might have been a childhood storybook.

"Anyway, he was very appreciative. If there's anything I can help you find—"

Yonie smiled hesitantly. "Ma'am, have you ever heard of a woman named Jeanette Bruneau? She probably went to Bellflower. She would be in her fifties or sixties now."

Pierpond's salt-and-pepper braids rustled as she shook her head. "I'm afraid not, honey, but that was before my time. You could always check the social roster."

Once again, Yonie faced the rows of blue spines. Low Town canal names were all very well, but what if she was wrong? "Aunt" could have been a courtesy title for a close family friend — in which case she might never find the mysterious Nettie.

Clinging to the rolling ladder with one hand, Yonie

plucked out a volume from the time of her mother's childhood.

There was indeed a Jeanette Bruneau! She was the older sister of Yonie's grandfather Jacques, who had thrown Yonie out of his house.

Yonie made trips up and down the ladder until she was sitting on the floor inside a ring of rosters. She found no other "-nette" relatives, and very little about Jeanette Bruneau. Jeanette had won first prize in a citywide essay contest when she was fifteen. She had graduated from Bellflower at age seventeen with high honors. Other than that, Jeanette's name appeared in the Bruneau entry without details — up until the year she would have been nineteen, when it vanished.

There was no notice of death, however.

Yonie trudged along the walkway, the wind shaking clots of cold water down from the blue gum leaves onto her head. She wasn't looking forward to telling LaRue — and Gilbert — how little she'd found out.

"Yonie! Is that you?"

Yonie turned. She was able to identify the green-cloaked figure by its bounce even before the girl threw back her hood.

"Chloe said she saw you heading this way, or at least someone with your same coat, and who else could it be?" Justine said in one breath. "I haven't seen you in ages! What have you been up to? All sorts of exciting things, I'm sure!"

Yonie considered all the events of the past week and feared that her friend might explode if given the full account. Anything she said, Yonie sensed, would be instantly translated in Justine's head into phrases like "tried to slay her most foully by the use of guile" and "fled the city to escape the murderous fiend."

Feeling like a traitor, Yonie opted for the most boring possible truth. "I've been trying to locate a relative of mine. A grand-aunt. I was just up at the library looking in the social roster, but the trouble is, she's only in there up to the age of nineteen, so I've got no way of finding her current address."

Justine flipped her hood back on and pondered. "Is she estranged from her family? Nineteen years old — did she elope with a mysterious stranger?"

Yonie thought of the books Mama had brought home only months before the fire. "I'm pretty sure she's still living in Wicked Ford. At least, as of a few years ago."

"It could still have been a marriage," Justine said darkly. "There are plenty of inappropriate men right here in the city. I'd check marriage registers if I were you."

"Thank you," said Yonie, and meant it. "How've you been, and your family?"

"Oh, Father's in a state." Justine's eyes glowed. "He found out who sent him that locket! It was Prue Barzilay's father, can you believe it? The other day he was talking to Father in his office, or shouting at him, more likely — he's a horrible bully, no question where Prue gets it from — and he was staring at Father's neck in a very peculiar way, like he was disappointed. So Father confronted him courageously, and the scoundrel sneered and admitted his guilt, and said Father could never hope to respond in kind. As if Father would ever stoop so low! But according to Prue's father, only the most important people ever get a letter offering them such 'unique custom merchandise.' That's how he found out the locket was for sale — by anonymous letter! Evidently it's the newest thing among a certain set. Anyway, there's nothing Father can do legally, but he's still getting Prue kicked out of Bellflower, which I think is very brave. For disciplinary reasons," she concluded breathlessly.

Justine shot a look down the walkway, where a pair of non-green coats were approaching. "Teachers!" she whispered, at a volume that would have been appropriate on the stage. "Sorry — I still mustn't be seen with you, or they'll have a conniption. I must fly!" She wrapped her poncho around her and swooped away.

That night, with Gilbert asleep at the far end of the garret, Yonie recounted the news to LaRue.

"So I wasn't quite right about the guilemonger," she finished. "People don't seek him out to buy wily objects — he approaches them."

"Hmm. I suppose it is easier to shield one's identity that way," LaRue mused. "And there's a certain mystique, isn't there, in making the customers feel like part of an exclusive club? But that means that he must already have an intimate knowledge of his clientele. The feuds and tensions and so forth."

Yonie shivered. "Which would imply — the guilemonger doesn't just sell to High Town folk. He *is* High Town folk."

"Ah, Yonie." The cat sighed. "I still can't say if it's DesMaray or this guilemonger who's after you. For all we know, they could be one and the same! But one thing's certain: you have a high class of enemy."

In the morning, Yonie was alarmed to see that the dock outside the Mole-in-'Ole was wholly submerged, with only two steps of the wooden stairway showing above the surface. Clusters of boats trailed like giant wooden tassels from the single possible mooring spot at the top of the railing.

Inside, the air was steamy with the smell of scrambled eggs and wet coats. Although it was daytime, it was so overcast that Molyneaux had lit the two kerosene lanterns that hung at the ends of the bar.

"Nice place," said Gilbert, stopping inside the door. "Wish I'd found it yesterday. I might've 'ad more luck."

"You did fine. In this weather, I'm surprised there was anyone at the fish market, let alone three Jeanettes."

"I'd feel finer if one of them 'ad been yours. But at least I didn't get lost like you thought I would."

"I was never worried," Yonie said truthfully.

"I did get turned around one time. But then I 'appened to see your little cat, and I thought, 'ey, it's near dinnertime. I can just follow 'er 'ome!"

"Clever."

Gilbert surveyed the room. "We should ask around 'ere, after you talk to your friend."

Yonie had just caught a glimpse of familiar chestnut hair at a corner table. "I don't think so," she said tightly.

She hurried toward the bar, with Gilbert sauntering along behind. They passed through several conversations, all about flooding, all in worried tones.

"M'dam Watereye! Something for you and your friend?" Molyneaux eyed Gilbert amiably.

"No thank you, sir, just some advice. I'm trying to find a city relative of mine, and I want to look up marriage records. Where should I go for that kind of thing?"

Molyneaux picked up a grubby towel and rubbed it over his huge hands. "Hmm. Most folks around here say their vows in a chapel, and the clerk records it afterward. Do you know where they held the wedding?"

Yonie's face fell as she thought of the hundreds of chapels speckling Wicked Ford. "I have no idea." She noticed peripherally that Luc had risen from his seat. "Thanks for your help, sir," she told Molyneaux, and grabbed Gilbert's arm. "Let's go," she told him in a low voice. "There's someone I want to avoid."

She had just set her knapsack down into the *Dragonfly,* wet wind licking at her face, when Luc's rangy form appeared in the doorway. He peered out, trying to shield his vest from the rain.

"Yonie!"

"I don't want to talk to you!"

"It's important!"

"Then come out here and tell me!"

Coatless and shivering, Luc emerged. Yonie was startled to see that both his eyes were purple and swollen, one nearly shut. His lip had bled in two places, and he limped as he walked, which rather took away from the splendor of his gator-hide boots.

Luc didn't spare a glance for Gilbert, who was holding the canoe against the side of the steps. "Yonie, that fellow Max came to see me. The one who gave me the kalidy-whatsit. He was—upset. He wanted to know where you lived." He licked his lip and winced. "I didn't tell him. But still, I think you should leave town."

Yonie narrowed her eyes. "Did this Max pay you to tell me that?"

"Yonie, please!" Luc laid his fingers on her arm. She brushed them away with a snort of disgust.

"You leave 'er alone," Gilbert said menacingly.

Luc shot him an amazed look. "Stay out of it, taxi boy! This is private."

"I'm no taxi boy."

"Yeah? Who are you, then?"

"None of your business," Yonie cut in.

"But maybe it is!" Luc turned his eyes back to her. "I care about you, Yonie, and I'll venture to say that you still have feelings for me. I would hate to see you wasting your time with the wrong man." Luc attempted a charming smile. The effect was ghastly.

"Are you trying to *flirt* with me?" Yonie said incredulously. "Don't waste your *own* time, M'sir Lazard." She swung herself down into the *Dragonfly,* followed a moment later by Gilbert.

Just before they pushed off, the pub's door swung open, and Molyneaux's busboy poked out his head.

"M'dam Watereye!" he shouted. "The boss wanted to tell you, try the Shrine of Sophie-of-the-Threshold, up on Chandler Street. They say it's the best place in the city for weddings. Oh, and he says best of luck!"

"Thanks," Yonie called.

As they paddled away, she glanced over her shoulder and saw that Luc's mouth was hanging open, his gaze moving back and forth from Yonie to Gilbert. He took a step as if to follow them down the stairs and planted one of his magnificent boots in ten inches of water.

CHAPTER TWENTY-FOUR

S O , D O you?" asked Gilbert as the pub receded from sight.

"Do I what?"

"'Ave 'feeeelings' for that city fellow."

"Only bad ones, at this point," Yonie snapped. "I don't wish to discuss it." Seeing Luc all beaten up had been disturbing, and not just because of what it showed about her unknown enemy. It had completely taken the zest out of imagining doing it herself.

Yonie and Gilbert entered the Shrine and were greeted by a sleepy-looking man in formal clothing.

"Hello, my friends. Are you here for the Rosse-Kjellberg wedding? I'm afraid it's been postponed. Due to weather," he added hastily.

"Actually —" Yonie began.

"Ah, you're here to reserve, then? Congratulations." He beamed at them. "When were you hoping to schedule the event?"

Yonie flushed. She expected Gilbert to snicker, but he was busy studying the fine woodwork on the ceremonial arch that formed the focal point of the room.

"No, I'm just hoping to do some family research. Could we trouble you for a look at the marriage records?"

Some time later, Yonie and Gilbert had combed through all the ledgers in the shrine's back room for the year Jeanette Bruneau turned nineteen, and the adjacent years as well.

"Do you think you might have missed it?"

Gilbert scowled. "I may not read as fast as you, Yonie, but I'm just as careful. She didn't get married 'ere, is all."

Yonie turned to the shrine attendant, who was ensconced in an armchair nearby. "Excuse me, sir? I've heard this is the most popular place in the city for weddings, but what would be the next choice?"

The attendant lowered his newspaper. "Mmm, Holy Theodore's, over by Westbridge. Or Maurice-Michel, for those who like that sort of thing . . ." He yawned and listed several other possibilities. Yonie wrote them down and thanked him for his help.

"You're welcome, young lady." He favored Yonie and Gilbert with a paternal smile. "May Blessed Sophie smile on you, and I hope that when the time comes, we may be seeing you two back here again." Yonie cringed, and Gilbert looked down at the floor.

Holy Theodore's was a more colorful but less tasteful building in a cheaper part of town. Its hall stank of spiced candles, and its records were in such disarray that it took half an hour to find the correct volumes. Jeanette Bruneau's name was not in them.

The chapel of Maurice-Michel was full of lush murals on the theme of physical love. Much skin-toned paint had been used, running the gamut through all humanly possible shades and then some. The artist had also fully displayed his knack for painting folds of drapery, though in Yonie's opinion, not always strategically enough. She was grateful for the torrential rain — she didn't know if she would have been up to witnessing a wedding ceremony there.

The attendant requested cash upfront to see the record books, which Yonie considered rather crass. Then they found that some entries had been deliberately defaced.

"What if her name is one of these scratched-out ones?" Yonie moaned. "It really could be! Her parents could have done it. I'm sorry to waste your time like this, Gilbert."

Gilbert rubbed his goatee. "Maybe we ought to stop looking and start thinking," he said at last. "From what you know about your grand-aunt, if she was going to get married, would she 'ave chosen a place like this?"

"I don't know, I never met her. All I know about her is she gave books to Mama."

"Aye, but what kind?"

"Adventures. Travel to far-off lands. War memoirs. Legends of strange magical creatures. Romances — usually doomed, or with noble sacrifice involved." Yonie looked around. "No, she probably wouldn't have come here."

"We could stay longer if you want to make sure." Gilbert grinned as he imitated the attendant's voice. "Remember, they're open aaaall night."

Yonie whipped out her list of chapels.

It was in the House of Roland the Wayfarer that they finally found it, down in the very shadow of Wycke's Pillar where the Grand Canal opened into Lake Leery. The shrine was a pinched storefront that gave no hint from the outside of the strange paintings that danced on its plastered ceiling or the dozens of alcoves in which travelers had left tokens of hope for a safe journey or thanks for a safe return.

Yonie could have spent hours examining the peculiar coins and trinkets and dried nosegays of exotic flowers, but the daylight was fading. She walked down the length of the deserted room, head tilted back to follow a shadowy painting of the Elder Roland striding with what looked like ships instead of shoes on his mystic feet.

Gilbert finished searching a shelf on the rear wall. "These're all maps, or else they're in some other language. Eh, well. This was a long shot anyway."

"But she did love travel. I know it." Yonie looked up once more at the ceiling, and drew in her breath. "Wait — look at that!"

Gilbert craned his neck. "What? The slice of bread?"

"It's *supposed* to be a page in a book. Or maybe a sacred pool," she said, somewhat less sure of herself. "Anyway — it's full of names! And they're all in pairs."

Gilbert squinted up at the ceiling. "With dates alongside! They could be marriages, at that. I can 'ardly read them, though." The light from the front window had grown dim.

"Lift me up!" Yonie demanded.

"Uh — all right." Gilbert laced his fingers together to make a stirrup, and Yonie stepped up into it. She scanned the names, which were written in a medley of hands, obviously by the couples themselves and not any official witness.

And there it was! "Jeanette Nicole Bruneau wed Duncan Osgar McKnee."

Jeanette's name was written in the same loopy cursive that Yonie had learned from her mother. Duncan's was in a spikier script with a foreign flavor. Yonie felt a thrill.

Perhaps her grand-aunt *had* married a mysterious stranger after all.

"It's here!" she shouted.

Gilbert grunted. "I'll be putting you down now, all right?" His voice was muffled, and Yonie realized with a surge of embarrassment that her hands were gripping Gilbert's hair, and her belly was pressing into his face in a most unseemly manner. Quickly she slithered back down to the floor.

They both hastily left the shrine, emerging into a street whose dockside bustle was only halfway subdued by the heavy rain.

"So, what did it say?" Gilbert asked brusquely.

Yonie told him. "There's something familiar about that name," she mused. Where had she heard it before?

No, not heard — read. The names floated up into her mind's eye, stamped in gold on the leather spines of a line of volumes. D. & J. McKnee. Coauthors of almost a dozen books in the archaeology section of the Bellflower library.

Those books had been inscribed, hadn't they? Personal gifts from the authors to the library — as one might expect, if Nettie had been a graduate of the school. And Yonie suspected that schools did not lose the addresses of alumni donors if they could help it.

To think that Yonie was actually related to these people! She could hardly wait to meet them. Her shoes and stockings had soaked through hours ago, but her steps suddenly felt light.

* * *

They returned to find a refugee in the garret.

"I beg your pardon," Two-Hats Shambly told Yonie, an embarrassed smile wrinkling his leathery face. "My own place's a mite damp now, you might've seen. I'll be getting along now, and give you two back your privacy."

Damp? It had to be knee-deep. Yonie's building, which usually resembled a wading heron, now looked more like a floating duck.

"I couldn't hear of you leaving, sir," Yonie exclaimed. "You're welcome to sleep here until the water goes down and things dry out. No privacy necessary," she added primly. "This is my cousin."

"Thank you, ma'am. That is a relief to me," Shambly said ambiguously. He tipped his uppermost hat, a well-oiled leather affair, revealing the gray knitted cap beneath.

Shambly had brought with him a bundle of firewood and a stockpile of food. After a day in wet clothes, it was indescribably good to be dry and comfortable, and once Yonie retired behind her bed-curtain, she had no trouble falling into a deep sleep. It was not broken until the small hours, when a loud soldier's oath erupted from M'sir Shambly near the door.

Fuzzy from sleep, Yonie wondered what Gilbert had done to set her neighbor off. Then she catapulted upright as she heard a stranger's snarling yell — followed by Gilbert shouting furiously, the high-pitched *yerow* of a cat, and the eerie sound of Shambly cackling with glee.

"Get to Under Town, you devil, or I'll dish you more of the same," Shambly bellowed into the night from the balcony.

The next sound Yonie heard was the slam of her door, then a scraping as someone poked up the fire. Yonie peered around her bed-curtain. A glow emerged from the stove to reveal Shambly pulling the woolen cap back down onto his head. "Looters," he growled. "Drown 'em! A little rain, and they think they can do what they like. Guess that one didn't expect two big men to be sleeping in front of the door!"

Gilbert, his face lit red by the shine of the embers, turned from the stove to look at Yonie.

"Do *you* think 'e was a looter?"

"I'd prefer to think it was someone who got rained out, looking for a place to sleep."

"Then I don't know why 'e 'ad 'is knife out," Gilbert said. He took his hand away from his shirt sleeve.

His palm was dark with blood.

CHAPTER TWENTY-FIVE

I T'S ONLY a scratch," Gilbert said.

Yonie, who had read war dramas in which those were a soldier's final words, shot forward and nearly burned herself fumbling a candle-stub alight in the embers of the fire.

"Aw, Yonie, it's not much. I've gotten worse from a blackberry bush."

Yonie lifted the sliced cloth away from the cut on his forearm. It did look shallow. She let out her breath. "Those must have been some blackberries."

"Big as your fist," Gilbert said, grinning.

Yonie retrieved her bottle of brandy from its hiding

place. "Still, we'd better keep it clean. You'll have to get out of that shirt — do you need some help?"

"Well, maybe —"

Shambly appeared at their side. "I'll take care of it," he boomed, unbuttoning Gilbert's cuffs and peeling the shirt deftly off him. "I was a medic back in the war. M'dam Watereye, if you'd just get me a clean rag, some rainwater, and that brandy? And more light to work by, if you please. We don't want any bits of thread left in the wound."

Tasks done, Yonie retreated to a corner, averting her eyes from her cousin's muscular, rather shaggy chest. Gilbert submitted to Shambly's genial care with more ill temper than Yonie had expected.

This was all her fault, Yonie berated herself. It was time she faced the truth: this quest to find Nettie was as much about her own curiosity as about the need for a safe haven. After all, Nettie had been a part of Mama's life, a part she never knew.

But now she had brought Gilbert into danger. If they failed to find Grand-aunt Nettie the next day, Yonie vowed, they would return to the Sloughs.

"The McKnees? Oh, honey, of course I know them," said Pierpond, adjusting a small rope of hair that had strayed from its designated area. "Well, not personally. But they're brilliant scholars, and M'dam McKnee went to Bellflower, so we like to hold her up as an example to the girls. How lovely for you, to be related to them!"

"So they're still alive?"

The librarian smoothed her golden-yellow dress. "I'm sorry, but the husband passed away some years ago. He was quite a bit older, you know. The wife — I couldn't say. She became rather reclusive after that. Health troubles, I think."

Yonie took a deep breath. "What else can you tell me about them?"

"Oh, it's a colorful story. Jeanette was a standout student at Bellflower, and she asked her parents to send her to the University. But they refused. It was almost unheard of for women back then, and they thought it would be a bad influence on her character, which was already on the strong side, you understand.

"But she audited classes anyway. Sat in as a guest," the librarian explained at Yonie's confused look. "That's how she met her husband. He was a visiting professor. I suppose when she got married — to a foreigner, no less! — her parents felt that all their fears were justified. But it turned out to be a happy marriage, so far as I know. He joined the faculty permanently, and they spent years puttering up and down the river, collecting artifacts and folklore and coming back to Wicked Ford to lecture and write up the results.

"And every book they published, we have here," Pierpond concluded proudly. "I do hope you can visit the University library someday, honey — all their journals are housed there. M'dam McKnee donated them after her husband died. Of course they'd been donating artifacts to the University museum all along."

Yonie instantly added the museum to her mental list of attractions to visit.

"Er—would you happen to have M'dam McKnee's address?"

"It would be in my files." Pierpond fixed Yonie with a hard stare. "If I give it to you, though, you have to promise me you won't do anything unseemly. I don't want you barging in on an ailing retired lady and making a shameful display, the way you did at Bowdown Hall."

Yonie's face felt hot. "I'm very sorry for that, ma'am. I still don't know what came over me," she said. "I intend to treat M'dam McKnee with the greatest respect. She's family, and she was very kind to my mother."

The librarian looked at Yonie a moment longer, then nodded.

Grand-aunt Nettie's home was in Skulkside, a motley assembly of stilt-houses that studded the bank of the river just before it widened into the Ford. The wind was much stronger on the Skulk than in the sheltered canals, and it drove blades of rain across the open river as if it wanted to scrape their canoe off.

At one point the *Dragonfly* almost overturned, and Yonie felt a tremor up her spine as the memories of her near drowning came surging back. She hoped LaRue was not too frightened in her box under the seat.

When Yonie finally reached out and caught the corner of the cottage, her arms were shaking, and she imagined Gilbert's had to be as well.

It was a narrow, flat-roofed dwelling, stepping upward to two stories in the back. A neatly railed half circle of porch extended in front. The house number was painted in bold white on the door, or Yonie might not have seen it in the darkness of the rainclouds and the approaching evening.

Someone was home. The checked curtains showed light behind the windows, and the wind tore shreds of smoke from the tall stovepipe on the roof.

It looked as if the cottage normally sat much higher on its pilings. Yonie moored the canoe to one of the front stair railings, next to a sedate-looking skiff, and scrambled up the few unsubmerged steps to the front porch.

She straightened her coat and tucked wet strings of hair back under her kerchief, feeling like something that had crawled up from the river bottom. She would be lucky if Nettie didn't slam the door in her face.

"Yonie? You all right?"

She smiled wanly. "I tried looking up my mother's parents a while back, and they treated me like I was nothing to them. Less important than a speck of dirt. I just hope this time it'll be different." She knocked loudly with her frozen knuckles.

Yonie's mother answered the door.

"Hello?" Her brows pulled down, and she held up the kerosene lantern in her hand, looking suspiciously at Yonie with familiar brown eyes. She wore a neat housecoat, slippers, and white gloves.

Of course it wasn't Mama. This woman was a shade taller, and her face was thinner. Her mouth was pinched, and there were more wrinkles on her forehead and fewer around the eyes. But still, the resemblance was amazing.

Yonie mustered a smile. "Good evening, ma'am. I'm Yonetta DuRoy, and this is my cousin Gilbert. I'm looking for Jeanette McKnee."

The woman looked almost as shocked as Yonie. "You're —" Her face twisted with emotion, and she pulled at a mended spot on the fingertip of her glove. Yonie was afraid for a moment that she was about to turn them away. But then she gave Yonie a shaky smile. "I think you'd better come in."

She fastened the door behind them with three separate bolts and set the lamp on a table. It cast a golden glow over walls lined with shelves, which contained books, intriguing knickknacks, and mysterious tools. There were no chairs in the room, only window seats and padded benches with cabinets built in below. The wall across from the front door had a doorway leading back and was decorated with framed art.

By the time they had hung up their wet coats and found a spot to stow Yonie's knapsack and LaRue's box, their hostess had recovered her composure.

"Miss DuRoy, I'm terribly sorry to tell you, but Jeanette McKnee is dead." The woman lowered her voice. "Her — you know — *ailment*. It finally got too much for her body to take."

Yonie's face was too stiff to let her speak. She had been looking forward to meeting her grand-aunt more and more with each new thing she learned. She remembered all of the thoughtfully chosen books that had brightened her childhood. She'd never even gotten to thank Nettie for them. Why in fortune's name hadn't Mama ever taken Yonie to visit?

Then Yonie saw the evasive expression on their hostess's face and understood. Nettie had spent much of her life digging in sunken ruins. She must have been severely disfigured by guile.

Perhaps Mama thought the sight would be too upsetting for a child, or too humiliating for Grand-aunt Nettie. Or perhaps she simply considered the effects of guile too improper to display to her young daughter.

"When did she pass away?" Yonie managed.

"A couple of years ago — although the poor soul barely left the house these last ten years. She had no children, so she left this house to me, her favorite niece." The woman gave Yonie a strained smile. "Yes, I'm your aunt, dear: Vedette Bruneau. I'm your mother's older sister." She approached Yonie, and after a moment of hesitation, gave her a stiff formal hug.

So this was one of the Bruneaus that Yonie's grandparents had so shrilly warned her off of. And yet Vedette wasn't throwing her out. Yonie squeezed her aunt back and offered her a tremulous smile.

"I'm very glad to meet you, ma'am. I hope we can get to know each other. I'm surprised you even know who I am."

Vedette laughed awkwardly. "Frankly, I'd never *heard* of you up until about two weeks ago, when you were in the news."

That *Bugle* article! Would it follow her forever?

"And you haven't met our side of the family at *all*, have you? Growing up in the, er, *outskirts* as you did."

"I've met your parents, actually. But it didn't go well."

"Bitter old vultures," Vedette muttered.

Although Yonie agreed, it seemed rude to say so. "I'm sorry I never got to meet your aunt Nettie and her husband," she said. "They must have had a fascinating life." She looked around the room. "I suppose this is their collection?"

"Oh, no, their *important* finds are all in the University museum. These are just a few funny old things they kept back for themselves. But maybe you'd enjoy seeing them, after you've had a cup of tea?"

"Very much," said Yonie. "I'm interested in old things."

"I'm interested in 'ot tea," said Gilbert. "You're an angel, ma'am."

They followed Vedette toward the doorway at the back

of the parlor, but Yonie paused to look at a watercolor on the wall there. It showed a boy running along a wharf, scaring a seagull into flight. "What a lovely painting," Yonie remarked. "He looks like he'd be happy to follow that bird right up into the sky."

"That's one of mine," Vedette said shyly.

For a moment, Yonie didn't take her meaning, but then she saw the lettering in the corner of the painting: *V. Bruneau.* Just like on the sketch of her mother.

That hadn't been a label. It had been the artist's signature.

When Yonie spoke, her voice was ragged. "Ma'am — Aunt Vedette. I have an old sketch you made of my mother, for a school assignment. It means a lot to me. I —"

There was a clatter from the parlor behind them, where LaRue had leapt up onto a narrow shelf to peruse its contents.

Vedette whipped her head around. "My *things!* Young lady, could you please control your animal?"

"I'm so sorry!" Yonie strode over and tried to lift LaRue down, but the cat hooked her claws over the shallow rim fronting the shelf.

"Come on, LaRue!" Yonie whispered. Now was not the time for LaRue to indulge her curiosity, not when Yonie was on the verge of gaining her aunt's trust.

Reluctantly, the cat let Yonie detach her and pour her down onto the floor.

The kitchen was a peculiar room with a strangely designed, barrel-shaped stove and countertops that seemed to have been built around and over some sort of mysterious apparatus. Disused archaeological equipment? Yonie hoped she could examine it later.

Vedette opened the door of the stove and clucked irritably. "Bother. The fire's nearly out, and the only wood I have left is in the crawlspace downstairs." She crossed the kitchen, slid back a bolt on the floor, and hauled open a trapdoor. Then she winced and laid a hand on her back. "Ohh, I've got to stop doing that . . ."

"Don't worry, ma'am. I'll get it," Gilbert said reflexively.

Vedette looked pleased. "You'll need a light," she said, and handed Yonie the lantern.

Yonie descended a short iron stepladder into a dank space just tall enough to crouch in. The walls were hidden behind a layer of crates and loosely stacked firewood, and the floor didn't show at all. It bounced back a reflection of the lantern like a black mirror. The water was less than knee-deep, but she could see why Vedette had been eager to avoid this task.

Gilbert splashed down behind her and scooped an armful of logs and kindling from the dry top of the pile. In a painful-looking crab walk, he followed Yonie back to the steps.

Yonie passed the lantern up to Vedette's outstretched hand. "I guess you know about the flooding down here?" she said. "It's —"

But both her sentence and the view of her aunt were cut off as the trapdoor suddenly crashed down onto her head. Her feet slid off the bottom rung and she fell backwards into Gilbert.

Yonie pushed herself up into darkness, gasping. Water streamed down her face. The blow on the head had dazed her, but her garret's rafters had made her enough of a connoisseur to know that she was not seriously hurt. She knew where she was. This was not a canal, and she was not going to drown, she told herself, and the panic receded.

Part of the floor moved out from under her hand, and she heard Gilbert snorting water out of his nose. "Sunken 'ell! You all right, Yonie?"

"Yes — I'm sorry. I must have fallen right on top of you."

"Felt better than the firewood."

Yonie looked up toward the slivers of light around the trapdoor. "Aunt Vedette, what happened? Is it your back? Do you need help?" She got to her knees and felt for the iron ladder.

"Don't call me that." The woman's voice slid through the cracks like a snake returning to dark water. "And I don't need any help from you, *Yonie Watereye.* You've been *far* too helpful already."

Yonie felt Gilbert crowd up next to her. He tensed, and she heard a heavy *thunk* from the trapdoor above.

"She's bolted it," he said quietly.

CHAPTER TWENTY-SIX

"AUNT VEDETTE, what are you doing?" Yonie cried. "What do you want?"

"I've never *wanted* much," Vedette said in an aggrieved tone. "Just my own home and a few little *luxuries,* the kind I never had growing up. It didn't seem like too much to ask. But it took years and years of waiting, and *suffering,* before I finally got them.

"And then what happened? I got a little slyboots poking her nose into my business. I was sure you were going to take it all away — my livelihood, and my home, and all the precious things inside. I was living in *fear*, I was crying every night, all because of *you*, young lady.

"But you'll definitely drown *this* time. The water's still rising, and all the wiles in the world won't save you." She paused. "Sorry about your cousin, though. He had nice shoulders."

Yonie's mind whirled. "Aunt Vedette," she said, straining to sound reasonable through her tight throat, "you're not a killer, I can tell —"

"Gracious, I'm not *killing* anyone! What a horrible thing to say. I'm just going to go stay a few days with friends in a higher part of town — *quite* understandable, what with the flooding. And when I get home, I'll find that some *looters* or *vagrants* broke in and got caught by the rising water. Most likely they were passed out from drink."

Vedette seemed to have already discounted Yonie and Gilbert and was thinking out loud as she continued in a dreamy voice, "Then I'll find Duncan's map, even if it *does* mean taking this house apart. Go up to that lake he wrote about. I hope it's not far. Travel is *so* hideous . . . but if I can get that kind of power into my hands, it will *all* be worthwhile. Delphine and her friends won't be laughing then. No, they will not . . ."

She trailed off into mutters about what clothes to pack, and her slippered feet shuffled away.

The light from around the trapdoor went away with Vedette. The only sound was the rain outside, and Yonie and Gilbert's clothes dripping into the dark water.

"Well," said Gilbert, "you shouldn't 'ave worried. Turns out your aunt *does* think you're important."

Yonie gave a strangled laugh. "Right now I'd rather be a speck of dirt."

"Trying to drown 'er own kin." Gilbert's voice sounded hollow. "Least, I don't s'pose she could be lying about being your aunt? Not with that face on 'er."

Yonie pictured Vedette again, her mouth like Mama's but with frown lines etched in, her eyebrows like Mama's but plucked and pinched together. "No — though it's hard to believe she could have turned out so different. How can someone even think like that?"

Gilbert lowered his voice. "Lucky for us she *doesn't* think straight. There's no way the river's going to rise more than maybe another foot. We've got plenty of air. We've got our knives. We can saw our way out of 'ere if we 'ave to. Might even be a 'atchet down 'ere for making kindling. And if we wait till Vedette leaves the 'ouse, there won't even be a fight. See? No cause to panic."

But actually, Yonie thought, there was.

She pictured LaRue in the kitchen above. The cat had to be rigid with fury — yet she had not lashed out at Vedette. LaRue must be waiting, just as they were, for Vedette to leave. That bolt was heavy, but LaRue was probably capable of pawing it back.

That would reveal her to Gilbert as a slybeast. Yonie desperately hoped the cat had heard their murmured conversation and would not take action.

"So, while we're waiting," Gilbert said, "what did your aunt mean about you wrecking 'er business? Is she this, uh, guilemonger you told me about?"

"She must be," said Yonie, still badly shaken. She'd thought no relative could be worse than her city grandparents. No wonder Mama had tried to keep her away from them all. "And she's the one who tried to drown me before. You heard her admit it." Yonie apologized mentally to DesMaray for ever having suspected him.

"'Ow'd she do it? She doesn't seem like the type to get 'er 'ands dirty."

"She arranged to deliver a wily thing to me, a really dangerous one." Yonie thought a moment. "And now I know where she got it. Those things Grand-aunt Nettie and her husband left in this house — they must be ancient relics. It stands to reason they would have soaked up a lot of guile. I guess Vedette's a pearly and can sense it."

And so could LaRue. No wonder the cat had been so riveted by the objects on the shelves.

"'Ow about that man 'oo broke into the garret last night? Think she sent 'im, too?"

"Possibly. She did seem surprised to see me tonight."

"What in the great green deeps did you do to make 'er 'ate you so much? You'd never even met 'er, right?"

"I just helped some people out."

"But —" Gilbert paused. "It sounded like she thinks *you're* wily."

Yonie steeled herself and said, "To tell the truth, Gilbert, I am. I've been making a living as a pearly these last two years." She waited for his exclamation of disgust.

He snickered. "Sorry, I'm not biting that 'ook. I've known you your 'ole life, Yonie. You never say 'to tell the truth' except when you're telling a whopper. And you're way too young to be a pearly."

"B-but—" Yonie sputtered. "How else do you think I figured out Vedette's wily weapons, so I could help those people? Why do you think I've been going by Yonie Watereye?"

"It isn't like you to make empty promises to folks," Gilbert admitted. "You're serious, Yonie? I guess it would explain some things about you."

Gilbert's foot scraped against the ladder, and for a terrified second, Yonie was sure it was the bolt sliding back, pushed by LaRue.

"I think we've waited long enough," she said abruptly. "I don't hear—"

Vedette's feet, now in hard-soled shoes, came clacking across the kitchen floor above them. The footsteps continued through the parlor and out the front door.

A few moments later Yonie heard the yowl of an enraged cat, followed by human shrieks. LaRue must have decided that her façade of normality would not be harmed by getting in a parting shot with her claws.

Yonie's grin vanished as she heard an agonized feline cry.

"LaRue!" she screamed. She set her foot on the ladder and rammed her shoulder against the trapdoor, to no effect. She whipped out her knife and slid the blade into the crack, whacking it against the bolt.

There came a sharp blow from the front of the house. It sounded just like the chop of a hatchet.

Yonie half fell from the ladder. The cold water splashed up around her legs as she scrabbled her way toward the front of the house, tripping over ridges in the floor and crashing against boxes, guided by the continuing hatchet strokes from above. The knife was still in her hand, and she struck upward where Vedette might be standing.

The blow jarred her wrist so hard that the knife jumped from her hand into the darkness.

Even if she had managed to poke through and wound Vedette in the foot, Yonie knew, it would have been nothing. Not compared to what that woman might have just done to Yonie's closest friend, whose meows she could no longer hear at all.

Wet and weeping as she was, Yonie did not recognize immediately that a spray of water was now bathing the side of her face. It was not until an especially loud whack from the hatchet sounded next to her that the spray turned into a gush.

Yonie stumbled back as the gush turned into a small torrent, spilling in from just below the ceiling and crashing down into the standing water on the floor.

"What's 'appening?" shouted Gilbert.

"This room is below water level," Yonie said numbly. "From the flooding. I should have remembered, from how low the house was sitting. It's kept most of the water out till now — but Vedette just chopped a hole in the wall.

"It looks like she might drown us after all."

CHAPTER TWENTY-SEVEN

MERCIFUL ELDERS," said Gilbert softly. "I'll go at the trapdoor with my knife, and you search for tools. Not much 'ope of finding a second 'atchet, but you never know."

Yonie assented, and there began an eternity of running her cold fingers over unseen walls.

"Find anything?" Gilbert was panting with effort.

"No. We could start opening crates, but I'd need your knife for that. I lost mine." Yonie could not keep her voice from wavering. "How's it going?"

"Slow." His voice sounded gray. "This old oak is like rock."

The waterfall noise made it hard to think, and the cold water had now crept up to Yonie's knees. She finally had to admit to herself that LaRue was not coming. The cat had to be injured or even dead — as Yonie and Gilbert soon would be.

"Gilbert." Yonie's voice broke. "I'm so sorry." She turned and wrapped her arms around him.

He hugged her back. It was more comforting than Yonie had expected and had an unexpected flavor of familiarity to it. As the hug went on, Yonie tried to figure out why, and froze when she discovered the answer. The scent of the sun and stars quilt, that reassuring smell of home that had helped her to sleep on many a troubled night, was in large part composed of the personal smell of Gilbert.

Well, Yonie thought, *how extremely disturbing.*

She began to pull back just as Gilbert yanked himself away. "None o' that, now," he said gruffly. "I don't care if we are about to die, we're still cousins."

"*What?*"

"I mean it, Yonie. No matter 'ow much we might want to, some things are just wrong."

Yonie's outrage flared as hot as her face. "Gilbert, you are *unbelievable!* Did you think I was hugging you out of *attraction?*"

Water continued to pour into the room.

"Is that so impossible?"

"Aaagh!" Yonie squeezed her hands into fists and beat

them against her legs. "Only you, *only you,* could take a situation like this and make it *more* tense!"

"I'm sorry," he said humbly. "I guess I can tell you now —I've always been kind of fascinated by you, Yonie. But you never wanted anything to do with me. You just wanted to be off by yourself with your books. I swear, I thought you cared more about that cat than you did about me."

"So that's why you decided to torture me for years on end?"

"Aye, well, at least when I was pestering you, you couldn't ignore me."

"You think that *excuses* you?" Yonie spat. "You just say, 'Oh, all along it was just because I *liked* you!' And then I say, 'Oh, poor thing, how sweet?' Gilbert, you didn't *pester* me. Mosquitoes are pesky. You were cruel. You and your brothers made me miserable for years. For your own entertainment. And you were the worst!"

Yonie was nearly screaming. "You played tricks on me, and when I cried, you laughed. You stole my things and destroyed them. You called me names; you made up horrible songs to taunt me with. You were even mean to my *cat!*"

Thinking about LaRue, not knowing her fate, Yonie began to sob.

She would not have been surprised if Gilbert had backed away, but when he finally spoke, he had not moved. "I know it doesn't excuse me," he said. "Not by 'alf. I was awful to you, Yonie. I know I can't ever apologize enough, but for what it's worth, I'm sorry."

His voice shook slightly as he went on. "I was a 'orrible boy. But I'm trying to be a better man. I 'ope that someday, maybe you can forgive me."

"Not yet."

Yonie's whole body itched with mortification. How many people had noticed Gilbert mooning after her? Had Mama and Papa known? Aunt Elisa had, she was willing to bet. That was probably one more reason she hadn't wanted Yonie living under her roof.

It belatedly occurred to Yonie that, given what she had recently learned from DesMaray, Gilbert was *not* actually a blood relation. Thank fortune that Gilbert didn't know — that would have made things even more awkward between them in the future.

Except that they weren't going to have any future, either of them, if they couldn't get out of this room.

"Let's open some crates," Yonie said tightly. "Maybe we'll find a ceremonial ax or something."

"Like as not, we'd cut off our own fingers on it, if we did."

"Keep your chin up! It's not over yet."

In the darkness, they pried the lids off crate after crate. The objects inside felt unfamiliar and intriguing, and Yonie was intensely frustrated that she couldn't see them — might not ever see them.

"What do you think 'appens when you die?" Gilbert asked.

"You're not keeping your chin up," Yonie scolded. "Maybe we could go back to talking about my deranged aunt? What kind of person puts a bolt on a crawlspace, anyway?"

"The same kind that puts three bolts on 'er front door, I reckon. Nay, really, Yonie — will we get to see the Elders, or what? What do you believe, deep down?"

Yonie recalled her vision of Granny Pitchers. "Apparently, deep down I believe that our spirits get stirred in with those of all the other living things that have ever existed. Like gumbo," she added.

"Gumbo."

"Yes."

"Well, thanks, Yonie. I was already cold and tired and scared out of my wits, and now I'm 'ungry too."

"At least you're not bored."

"Aye, that's one advantage of being around you. Though I 'ave to admit, looking through those marriage records was boring enough."

Had that been only yesterday? Yonie felt almost nostalgic, recalling the hours she and Gilbert had spent tediously scanning names and dates, until —

"Stop looking, and start thinking," she muttered to herself, remembering Gilbert's words as she ran her fingers over something that resembled a gravy boat.

"Hmm?" Gilbert peeled off another lid with a screak of nails.

"Gilbert," Yonie said, "why isn't this room already full of water?"

"'Ow do you mean?"

"The way the river's been rising, this room must've been below the waterline for days. But when we came down here, there was only a foot of water on the floor. Doesn't that seem odd? Why would anyone bother to make a little storage area that watertight?"

"I 'ave no idea," Gilbert said. "If they were that worried about flooding, they could've just built the 'ouse on taller stilts."

"Exactly! So I'm wondering . . . well, remember the parlor? No chairs, just benches and cabinets. And the shelves all had a little lip on the front, to keep things from sliding out."

"Oh, wrecks! You're thinking —"

"This isn't a house at all," Yonie declared. "It's a houseboat."

It seemed obvious now. The stacks of crates had concealed the curve of the hull, but the "crawlspace" smelled faintly of tar, as ships tended to do, and the ridge running down the center had to be the keel beam. Upstairs, the half-circle balcony outside the front door even looked like the bow of a riverboat, if you ignored the added-on steps.

Gilbert whistled. "Yonie, I never will understand 'ow

you do that. You start with three tail 'airs, four legs, and a scrap of 'arness leather, and end up with a full-size 'orse."

"Except every once in a while, I get a horsehair sofa instead," Yonie demurred. But since it was dark, she allowed herself a small, satisfied smile.

"So, I guess when your grand-aunt and -uncle went traveling to foreign parts, they brought their 'ome along. Must've been 'andy."

It must have been terribly romantic, Yonie thought. "Yes, and then after they retired, they felt like having a solid floor underfoot, so they raised their boat up out of the water. Or maybe Vedette did that. I wonder how many houses in Skulkside started out that way?"

"The real question is, how's the boat fastened to those stilts? The way the water is now, the 'ull must *want* to rise. Are there nails? Screws? Bolts?"

"And can we get them out?"

It turned out to be nails: slapdash clusters of them, in four locations on the flat-bottomed hull. Whoever had raised the houseboat seemed to have relied mostly on its weight to keep it in place on its posts.

After that, it was a matter of teasing out the nails, using Gilbert's knife and, more effectively, an object from one of the crates that resembled a claw hammer without the hammerhead. It was probably a priceless antique.

It was painstaking work, done underwater with cold clumsy fingers. But as she pried out each nail, Yonie imagined the boat lifting minutely, shifting restlessly on its supports. By the time three of the posts were free, the boat was slewing beneath their feet, fighting to bob upward.

"One left," Gilbert said breathlessly. "Just have to get under it —"

But then the floor heaved, and with a tremendous lurch, the houseboat ripped free of the last piling and surged upward. Tumbled and bashed in the lightless space, for a moment Yonie lost her sense of up and down. She flailed wildly until she once again felt the floor of the hold beneath her hands and feet.

She raised her face out of the water into near silence. The cascade of water had stopped. The chopped hole was now above the waterline, and the boat was wallowing on the surface of the River Skulk.

"We did it!" Yonie whooped. "We're safe!"

From across the hold came a burst of strangled laughter. "We're trapped in the 'old of a waterlogged boat, and it feels like we're 'eaded down the river. Which is in flood. We've got no running lights and no way to steer. Aye, we're safe all right."

"We will be." The boat rocked, and a bucket's worth of river slopped in through the hole in the hull. "So long as we bail."

There followed what felt like hours of dipping up water and pouring it out through Vedette's hatchet hole. The scoop Yonie had found felt as if it had been made from the long, sawed-open skull of some large animal, and the teeth seemed to champ her hand resentfully every time she shifted her grip.

Twice the houseboat collided heart-stoppingly with a floating log or other debris, but at last it ran aground, leaving the hole, thankfully, well above water level. Yonie and Gilbert collapsed onto the piled crates to endure until morning.

Yonie woke to a jagged piece of gray daylight, framed by the hole that Vedette had chopped. She waded over and looked out onto oak trees and rain.

Something nosed her leg, and she looked down to find the bailing scoop floating there. It was not in fact a sawed-open animal skull, but a wooden replica of one, crafted with great care. Somehow this struck Yonie as particularly macabre, and she was glad when a groan from behind her signaled that Gilbert was awake.

Escape was simple in the daylight. Half an hour later, Gilbert boosted Yonie through a gap they'd made by hammering up two kitchen floorboards. She spared a second to slam open the bolt on the trapdoor before she shot out of the kitchen, wet skirt dragging at her calves.

She hurtled onto the front porch — no, the bow deck — and stood with the drizzle hitting her face. "LaRue!"

The houseboat had lodged against a muddy bank infested with scourge oak and overhung with mossy, crooked trees. Off to the side, Yonie could see open water under a clouded sky. They must have floated clear across the Ford and right down into Lake Leery, that noxious puddle at the end of the Skulk from which dozens of shallow waterways tendriled out. No docks or buildings were in sight.

"LaRue?" Yonie peered over the edge of the deck, which now rode a good two feet above the water. The *Dragonfly* was still tethered to the deck rail, though it had been hoisted upward by the boat's rising. No small feline body was anywhere in the canoe.

There was no trace of blood on the deck — but then, it had been raining. And Vedette wouldn't have needed the hatchet. A single kick could have crushed LaRue's little body, or sent it flying into the flood-maddened river.

Yonie shuddered in her wet clothes, and wrapped her arms around herself as she watched the rain mist down.

Oak leaves had blown onto the boat's deck during the night, and they were drifted along the front of the house. It took a moment for Yonie to notice the sodden orange fur in one of the heaps.

Her knees banged down onto the wet deck. With trembling fingers, she brushed the leaves away from a small, still form. Not knowing had been torture. This was worse.

LaRue had been only ten years old. That wasn't young for a cat, but who knew how long LaRue, with all her differences, could have lived?

Around Yonie, rain sifted down past wet black tree trunks. Everything was utterly silent.

CHAPTER TWENTY-EIGHT

T HEN LARUE blinked her eyes.

"Yonie?" she said in a thready voice. "Dearest, you're alive . . ."

Yonie's hands flew out to touch the cat's matted fur. "Oh, LaRue!" She scooped LaRue's wet body into her arms. "Your poor paws, they're like ice! — I was so worried — when you never came back in the house —"

LaRue let out a sound like a door creaking, and Yonie loosened her grip.

"I do apologize, love," the cat rasped. "I saw your aunt pick up that hatchet, and I got curious, so I followed her out the door. When I understood what she was up to—well, I'm sorry to say, I lost control."

Yonie tried to imagine the bundle of fluff that was LaRue hurling herself at an opponent twenty times her weight. LaRue did not have any combat skills to speak of and had been known to evade hostile dogs by barking at them and escaping in the moment of confusion.

"She threw me down and kicked me into the water. It wasn't easy climbing back aboard, and by then, she was gone. And she had closed the door." LaRue, to her great frustration, had never mastered doorknobs.

"And then I failed you again. The windows were too strong to break. And I was so tired, and so very cold . . ."

Yonie glowered at the door, a flimsy construction considering all the locks lavished upon it. Her foot drew back. Although the door, regrettably, was not Vedette, it still helped a little to smash out one of the bottom panels with a few well-aimed kicks.

"There! You'll never get shut out again."

"Merciful waters, darling, it's enough for me that you survived, by some miracle. And Gilbert too, I assume? Then *she* failed, as well. I can take comfort in that."

LaRue shivered. "But before we go in, you should know—this boat is positively reeking with guile. Those objects on the parlor shelves are so wily, I'm surprised they don't slither away. And there's more guile somewhere nearby, a large concentration."

"The hold's chock-full of boxes," Yonie said.

"That will be it, then — more finds that the McKnees kept back from the University museum. But not because the things were too *dull,* as that Vedette person implied." The cat sniffed. "No, I'd guess your relatives judged them too *dangerous* to expose to the public. You must promise me, Yonie, that neither you nor your cousin will touch any of those items, unless I've checked it first."

Yonie thought of the night she and Gilbert had just spent, sloshing around in a soup of relics and river water, and swallowed hard. "All right."

LaRue gave a shuddering sigh. "Promise me this as well. Those things — they must *never* fall back into Vedette's hands."

LaRue, after laboriously licking herself dry and lapping some warm broth, fell into an exhausted sleep in her box by the stove.

"She's bound to catch cold," Yonie fretted. "Out in the rain all night like that. And her side's all tender from where Vedette kicked her. I only hope she didn't crack a rib."

Gilbert scowled. His goatee was losing definition as dark stubble filled in at the sides. "That Vedette is a waste of drinking water. 'Asn't she 'urt enough people already, without picking on a little pussycat?"

"At least we have all her wily things, so she can't hurt

anyone else that way." Yonie had already cautioned Gilbert about handling the items.

"Aye, I reckon she wasn't expecting that." Gilbert gave a sudden bark of laughter. "Can you picture 'er *face?* When she comes back in a few days, like she said, all ready to find our corpses . . . and 'er 'ole *'ouse* is gone?"

Yonie snorted. Then she sobered. "She'll report us to the gendarmes is what she'll do. Maybe even the River Authority. We're boat thieves, taking advantage of the storm — that's how it'll look."

"Oh." Gilbert glanced out the stern window, which had four big glass panes just like a window in a High Town house. "And 'ere we sit, like a tick on a short-'aired dog. We should get in the *Dragonfly* and light out."

"No! We can't let Vedette get those artifacts back. We know what she'd do with them."

"So, we toss 'em over the side before we go."

"They'd float, or wash up on the bank, or get pulled up in someone's fishing net. I'm not going to dump this kind of poison right next to my home, for children to step on when they go wading!"

Gilbert rose to his feet and leaned forward to meet Yonie's glare. Their noses were almost touching. "What *do* you want to do, then? This boat's too big for bayou channels. Only reason it got over the Ford into Lake Leery is the flooding. Once the water goes down, it'll be stuck 'ere for good."

"Then the sooner we move it, the better. We'll take it upriver a few miles, find a nice deep spot somewhere out of the way, and sink it, wily things and all."

"You think the two of us can paddle this washtub up the Skulk, against the current?" Gilbert smirked. "I am pretty strong, but—"

"Of course not," Yonie scoffed. She pointed at the peculiar stove and its surrounding apparatus. "We'll use the engine."

"What? Oh. Is that what it is?" Gilbert suddenly seemed to realize how close his face was to Yonie's, and stepped back.

"Obviously," Yonie said airily, though it had only just occurred to her.

"It likely 'asn't run in twenty years! It might not even 'ave its, uh—" He made a vague whirling motion with his hand.

"Propeller," Yonie supplied. "I am aware of the difficulties. But we have a day or two before Vedette discovers we're gone."

Gilbert stared at the stove. "You know 'ow steam engines work?"

"I've studied illustrations." Yonie didn't mention that they had been in *Wanda Takes to the Water* and had included a squirrel wearing a kerchief. "The boat needs carpentry work—like fixing that hole Vedette made and plugging the nail holes in the bottom. And it would be smart to disguise the boat a bit, too. Think you're up to it? Or is that too much to get done?"

"Nay, I can manage that in under a day," Gilbert protested reflexively. "I saw some tools down in the 'old. Course, we'll 'ave to bail that out before anything . . ."

Gilbert lunged for the trapdoor, leaving Yonie to figure out the boat's propulsion system on her own. She smiled as she pushed through the back door of the houseboat onto the stern deck.

"Morning, ma'am!"

Yonie whipped her head around and spied a wiry older man paddling a pirogue. His head was wet as an otter's, and he wore no coat, just a faded shirt with the sleeves rolled up. He glided up and displayed a catfish, plainly offering it for sale.

"And 'ow are you faring this morning? Which I won't call fine, eh, but it's a sight better than what we've been 'aving, true?"

Yonie returned him a level look. She was not tempted by any fish from Lake Leery, catch basin for all the effluvia of Wicked Ford.

He waved an arm in her direction and grinned slyly. "Could do with a little more of the 'usband lately, eh?" Again he waggled the catfish, in what Yonie could not help but construe as a suggestive manner.

"No, thank you," said Yonie frostily. She slid out her belt knife and began to groom her nails. She wished there were direct sun on her, so she could bounce a shard of light off her blade into the man's eyes.

He didn't look especially menaced, only puzzled and mildly affronted, but at least he went away.

Yonie was now even more determined to get underway. What if the next person to float by was a busybody with questions about the boat?

Her view of the propeller was blocked by three tiers of planter boxes rising upward from the stern of the boat: kitchen herbs, beans and greens, tomatoes and peppers. All looked lovingly tended, if somewhat rain-battered.

Yonie started back around the boat to the landward side, so she could jump down into the muddy water and locate the propeller. Halfway there, she stopped. She hurried back to the stern and stared at the kitchen garden in horror. Vedette hadn't!

But she had.

The houseboat was not, in fact, a propeller-driven craft. The plantings were growing in earth packed between the blades of a small paddlewheel. It would be a wonder if the wood hadn't rotted away.

Dreading what she might find, Yonie yanked up a fistful of greens. She let out her breath. The wood was still sound.

The paddlewheel had to be cleared, of course, but it would be a pity to waste all this food.

Yonie had just dumped a skirtful of freshly picked

produce onto the kitchen table when Gilbert emerged from the trapdoor, lugging a cask of wine. He watched, bemused, as a tomato rolled off the table and bounced to a stop near his foot.

"Uh — Yonie? What does picking tomatoes 'ave to do with working on the engine?"

"Trust me, it's all part of the process," Yonie said primly. "I personally can't imagine what you're doing with that wine."

"I guess you'll just 'ave to trust *me*." Gilbert grinned, put the cask on his shoulder, and tromped off toward the front door.

Yonie and Gilbert succeeded in starting the engine late that night just before the kerosene in the lantern ran out. They engaged the paddlewheel just long enough to determine that it would rotate, despite its years of neglect. But would it actually move the boat?

At dawn, Yonie opened the stove door and added another stick to the fire. She let steam into the engine, and the kitchen filled with an industrious *putt-putt*. She could feel the houseboat thrum as the paddlewheel turned, but the side of the boat was still lodged on the bank. She opened the throttle a little more.

The boat lurched as if a large creature had leapt onto it. This soon proved to be the case, as Gilbert hurried into the kitchen. Despite his horror of the nearby scourge oak, he had ventured ashore to push off the boat.

"We're afloat!" he shouted.

Yonie pelted up the stairs.

The upper level of the house was an airy room that had once served as the pilothouse, judging by the wraparound windows front and back and the steering wheel Yonie had discovered under a paint-stained table. More recently it had been a combination bedroom and art studio. One wall was lined with cabinets of art supplies, the other with a built-in wardrobe that Yonie had raided for dry, atrociously ill-fitting clothes, much to Gilbert's amusement.

The only major furniture besides the table was a large double bed. In the gray morning light, LaRue was an indistinct mound of fur atop the molasses-colored coverlet.

Victoriously, Yonie planted her rump on the wooden stool in front of the steering wheel seconds before Gilbert reached the top of the steps. The wheel turned easily under her hands.

She had spent many afternoons watching the majestic riverboats stop at Wycke's Landing to let off and pick up passengers, and she had dreamed of the day when she could afford to travel upriver. She had never imagined that when it happened, she herself would be at the wheel.

The pilots on the big riverboats had to learn every mile of the Skulk and the Stride, all the way up to Stone Head. They could spot a snag or a sandbar just from the ripples on the surface. Lacking their skill, Yonie was lucky that the river was so high at the moment. And, she reminded herself regretfully, that they wouldn't be traveling far.

"Give me a turn," Gilbert begged.

"It's *my* aunt's boat."

"'Ey, I stole it just as much as you."

"All right! After we pass the city."

Grumbling, Gilbert flopped down on the bed. LaRue groaned in protest and then went quiet again.

Yonie frowned. LaRue would normally be up on the windowsill peering out, but since the previous morning, she hadn't budged from her blanket nest.

Yonie maneuvered past an early ferry and sucked in a breath as the houseboat's hull lightly grooved the silt of the shallows.

They were out of Lake Leery. They had crossed back over the Ford.

So far, no one was pointing or chasing after them. Gilbert had taken some pains to disguise the boat. He had transferred the gong from the stern of the *Dragonfly* to the bow of the houseboat, where it seemed to feel equally at home. He had changed the boat's profile by rigging up a canvas awning over the front door. Vedette's hatchet hole was now a tarred blotch above the waterline, and the kicked-in panel on the front door added to the overall scruffy look. The houseboat no longer looked homey, but rather rakish and piratical.

Gilbert had also mopped down the entire portside wall with the wine from the hold, turning the whitewashed boards a dingy lilac gray. Yonie felt they might have been better off watering down the wine further to cover both sides. But if anyone in Wicked Ford was scanning the river traffic for the houseboat, the gray side was what they would see.

The city slipped by with magical ease and speed. Soon even the wharves and cottages of the outskirts had dwindled to the occasional shack and ramshackle dock clinging to the sides of the twisting river.

By nightfall the houseboat was tied up in a secluded spot a little way up one of the side branches that joined the Skulk. Gilbert was already collapsed in a makeshift bedroll on the parlor floor downstairs, and Yonie and LaRue had the bedroom to themselves.

"LaRue," Yonie said sleepily, "right after Vedette shut us in the hold, did you hear what she was saying about a map hidden in the house?"

The cat raised her head. "Probably better than you did, considering I wasn't underneath a trapdoor at the time." She misted Yonie's face with a sneeze. "It sounds suspiciously romantic. A hidden map? To a secret lake with mysterious powers? It's probably a pool of sludge with near-lethal concentrations of guile. One more thing we don't want your aunt to have, and one more reason to sink this boat. Not that she's had any luck finding the map, after searching for years. You shouldn't hope to find it yourself, you know — if such a thing does exist, it's very well concealed."

Sometimes LaRue was just no fun at all.

Although, Yonie thought as LaRue produced a short, hacking cough, the cat's recent crankiness was probably due to the cold she had caught the night of the storm.

Yonie wished she could consult *Nesbitt's Housecat Handbook,* which was back in her garret. She did recall that cats were more delicate than humans where respiratory illness was concerned, and that a cold in a cat could turn quite serious.

CHAPTER TWENTY-NINE

THE NEXT morning, Yonie was sitting slumped in a kitchen chair, cradling a cup of tea, when Gilbert poked his head out of the trapdoor. "'Ey, guess what? I found a map."

"*What?*" Yonie shoved her cup away, slopping tea onto the table. "Let me see it!"

Gilbert produced an accordion-folded rectangle of paper. It was a mass-printed copy of *Berjay Brothers' River Guide,* sold in every bookstore and hotel in Wicked Ford. Not a navigational chart with depths, or even a proper map — just a fat, stylized line with the labeled dots of towns along it and humorous cartoons and slogans alongside each one.

Gilbert looked at her face and chortled in glee.

"You thought it was that map your aunt was spouting off about? Right after she locked us up, when she started sounding like a complete loony? *Once I get that power into my hands, they won't be laughing anymore!*" His falsetto imitation of Vedette brought back unpleasant memories of how he and his brothers had often mocked Yonie's speech.

Stonefaced, Yonie stared down at a droll illustration next to Selbyville, Home of Barbecued-Bat-on-a-Stick. She hoped the river would continue shallow for quite some time so she could search the houseboat top to bottom before they sank it.

Yonie had always assumed that the hamlet of Shoe Tree, like so many places in the Delta, drew its name from a corruption of some more sensible name in the Old Language. Soon it became clear that the comical picture of a shoe-bedecked tree on the Berjays' guide was nothing but the truth. On rickety jetties sprouting from the riverbanks, children jounced worn-out shoes by their laces and chanted, "Luck for the tree? Luck for the tree?"

As Gilbert piloted the houseboat around a bend, the tree itself was announced by the presence of a gigantic, gleaming paddle wheeler, holding position underneath the overhanging branches.

Yonie ran out onto the bow deck. Due to Gilbert's lack of steering skill (or possibly his excess of curiosity), the houseboat was passing nearer to the riverboat than Yonie thought wise.

The Shoe Tree was a dead oak of landmark proportions, whose skeletal branches bore a bizarre crop of dangling footwear. There were bargemen's boots, rough rope sandals, and winter moccasins, as well as dressier shoes much the worse for wear. Young people on the top deck of the riverboat were flinging tied-together pairs of shoes upward while laughing dementedly.

Then the party atop the riverboat ran out of ammunition. There were cries of disappointment, and Yonie heard someone wail, "Oh, Jamie, why didn't you get more?"

Inspiration struck. Yonie dashed inside and up to the pilothouse, yelling to Gilbert to slow down. She yanked open a cabinet and pawed Vedette's collection of shoes out onto the floor.

Vedette's shoes were more aggressively feminine and less practical than anything Yonie had ever owned. Some of them, such as the beaded dancing slippers, were quite beautiful, and the fact that they were much too small for Yonie had pricked at her ever since she'd discovered them.

"Uh, Yonie?" Gilbert said from the pilot's seat. "Elders know we could use some luck, but we're way too low and too far away to land any o' those in the tree."

"I know that!" Yonie snapped. "Just keep us near that other boat." She collected an assortment of the lace-up varieties into her skirt, pelted back downstairs, and started lobbing shoes onto the lower deck of the great paddle wheeler.

Shouts of joy went up. Soon a young man in a stylish striped suit hurried down to gather up the bounty and, as Yonie had hoped, toss a few coins across the gap between his boat and hers.

"Thanks!" Yonie called.

"Thank *you,* Your Highness!" he answered, before running back up to his companions.

Yonie, down on her knees slapping at the coins before they could roll away, thought indignantly that she had just done that man a favor, and there was absolutely no need to make fun of her ragged appearance.

Gilbert was jubilant. "Good thinking, Yonie! Now we can stop somewhere and buy some real food. Something besides tomatoes."

"And we can find out if anyone's looking for us." Yonie's gaze flicked to LaRue at the head of the bed to see if she approved, but the cat returned only a glazed look out of gummy eyes.

Yonie returned to examining the back of the parlor bookshelves for secret compartments. She discovered a cabinet with a leaf that folded out into a small desk and a lower portion that rotated out, equally cleverly, into a seat. She was delighted by the craftsmanship, if slightly disturbed by the needlepoint on the seat cushion, which depicted a limpid-eyed bunny with an abnormally large head.

Had Vedette perpetrated that needlepoint herself? Surely not. Yonie's gaze went to the expert oil paintings on the rear wall of the parlor, and suddenly she realized who must have produced the miniature of M'dam Cordell to put inside that locket.

What was it M'sir Bassompierre had said? *Any fellow this good, even an amateur — I would know him.* What if it wasn't a fellow at all, but a spinster lady whose talent was unknown outside a small circle? Maybe Vedette even knew the headmaster's wife well enough to paint her face from memory.

Yonie sat down at the fold-out desk and searched the neighboring cabinet for hidden drawers. Then she rose and studied the cushion, which was far less comfortable than it should have been. She unbuttoned the cover and inserted her hand into the horsehair.

There was something inside.

It was not a map. It was a battered leather-bound note-book. *Third C'thovan Expedition* was inked on the front, in the same foreign-looking, angular handwriting Yonie had seen on the ceiling of the House of Roland the Wayfarer.

The first page began, *Moon-day, 5/30. Made Shoe Tree by sunset. Nettie insisted on continuing to Selbyville.*

Yonie's fingers tightened on the covers. This had to be the journal of Duncan McKnee. But where were the other volumes? He and Nettie had made dozens of expeditions.

Donated to the University — M'dam Pierpond had said

as much. But why had Nettie kept this one back? And why had Vedette hidden it?

Yonie paged through the notebook. There were small sketches: a thatched hut with a chicken on the roof, a child in a coracle, a toothless woman grinning as she plaited a sun hat out of reeds.

After the travelers passed Gabel Town, where the River Stride fed into the Skulk, the sketches became less peopled. Instead of turning up the straight thoroughfare of the Stride with the rest of the boat traffic, the McKnees had continued along the snaking Skulk into the Shunned Lands, a region known for its ruins and its ghosts. Duncan's sketches were of crooked pillars and time-ravaged walls. Yonie looked forward to reading this section at her leisure.

Now she noted that a number of pages had been removed toward the end of the book — not torn out, but neatly cut away. After that gap came only a few more pages of text.

If a village elder had related to me the events of the last few days, I would have smiled and recorded it as folklore. My own reputation, however, denies me the luxury of the telling — for I just might be believed.

I have used the last eighteen pages as kindling for our cook fire, and I will let no record of our route survive (save for that in the boat, which I cannot bring myself to destroy). Nettie and I must never publish our recent discoveries, and although that is bitter to scientists like ourselves, thoughts of what such exposure might unleash are enough to seal our lips. Hordes of people seeking miracle cures would be the least of it.

Our secrets should be reasonably safe. Given the desolation of the area, few people will ever stumble upon what Nettie has ironically dubbed Bonegarden Lake. Even if they do, none but an avid archaeologist would linger there for long.

So I will write no more about our experience at the lake, trusting that even in old age I will never forget the insights I received there, nor my grati— tude for a shattered leg made sound.

The expedition, I will be forced to say, was a failure.

A small whine of frustration escaped Yonie's lips. Duncan McKnee's writing, even in his private journal, displayed the same qualities that had made his books so popular with the public. Even while concealing information, he had been unable to resist making it as tantalizing as possible. No wonder Vedette had been fixated on finding the map he described.

And no wonder Grand-aunt Nettie had withheld it from the University collection. Otherwise she might have had glinty-eyed students breaking into her home on a weekly basis to hunt for the hidden map. As it was, Yonie herself could hardly wait to get back to the search.

Later that day, Yonie moored the *Dragonfly* at Harkene Village while Gilbert kept the houseboat out of sight downstream.

Harkene Village was one of the plumper dots on their river map. Its immigrant settlers had built their houses with complete disregard for local climatic conditions, immediately gaining it status as a quaint tourist getaway. Yonie felt comfortably inconspicuous as she strolled among the visitors craning their necks at the sharply peaked roofs, generous eaves to shed the nonexistent snow, and chimneys bearing artificial birds' nests complete with wooden storks.

Yonie made a few small purchases and then found a newspaper vendor who sold her a *Wicked Ford Keen Observer* bearing yesterday's date. She returned to the *Dragonfly* and skimmed through the paper. The crime reports featured a few incidents of flood-related looting and several stolen boats, but no houseboats.

Feeling cautiously optimistic, Yonie turned to the classified advertisements.

LOST HOUSEBOAT.

25gal reward for information leading to recovery of the 30' steamer *Moon Princess*. White walls, open deck, stairs at bow, garden at stern. May be partially submerged. Contact V. Bruneau c/o this newspaper.

Yonie seized her paddle and shot off down the river.

Within minutes, though, the rhythm of the paddling calmed her. There was no crime report, and the advertisement said "LOST HOUSEBOAT." Vedette must have assumed that the boat had broken loose in the storm. And thanks to Gilbert's efforts at disguise, her description was no longer accurate.

Yonie took a deep breath. The sun was out, and the river level was finally down to normal. Yonie felt almost lighthearted as she approached the houseboat.

That feeling did not last long.

When Yonie had put the *Dragonfly* into the water, she had lowered it on the landward side of the houseboat. Now she decided to pass along the river-facing side so she could inspect the paddlewheel for waterweed.

Painted on the hull between the deck and the waterline, in white letters as big as Yonie's head, was the name *Moon Princess.* Next to it showed the upper half of a painted face, with its crescent headdress plain to see.

Gilbert groaned. "'Ow the drowning 'ell did I miss *that?*"

Yonie shrugged. "The first time we saw the house, it was dark, and we came at it from the front. Then after that, we just never got out on that side."

"Wonder 'ow many people noticed it so far."

Yonie remembered the Shoe Tree paddle wheeler and the young man shouting, *Thank you, Your Highness!*

"The passengers at the Shoe Tree, at least." She thought another moment. "And there was that fisherman, back in Lake Leery . . . I didn't understand him at the time." *Could do with a little more of the 'usband, eh?* And he'd gestured — not toward her, as she'd assumed, but toward the boat. In all the old stories, the Sun was the husband of the Moon. It had been an innocent remark about the weather.

"We'll sink 'er, next good place we come to." Gilbert ducked into the kitchen and fetched the Berjays' guide. "'Ow about Sully's Branch?" He poked a finger at an upcoming fork which, according to the map, had no towns for miles.

"I suppose." Yonie spoke past the knot in her throat. "It's got this bayou here, Devil's Pie-hole. I can't imagine that's much of a picnic spot."

"Sounds good. Want to take the wheel for a while?"

"So we've been showing her name to everyone for days," Yonie concluded glumly. She gave the steering wheel an unnecessarily hard twist. "Even a picture, for folks who can't read. LaRue, are you listening?"

"What? No. Not *hers*," LaRue said vaguely from her pillow. "Not the *Moon*."

"Yes, really! I thought about scraping it off — it looks like that's been done a few times already — but we just don't have the time. So we're going to leave the Skulk soon and turn up a fork called Sully's Branch. Then tonight after dark, we'll sink the boat, and hopefully no one will ever come across the wreck."

The cat's voice sounded dull and distant. "Won't like that."

"I know, and I'm so sorry to move you when you're not feeling well. I'll bring lots of blankets and make a nest in the *Dragonfly* for you."

"Wasn't talking — about me."

"Oh. You're right, I won't like it either. I really wanted to find that map. And I've gotten rather fond of this boat."

The cat seemed on the verge of speaking again, but a spell of coughing left her too spent to do more than lay her head back down.

Yonie left the wheel and stroked her hand along LaRue's bony spine. For just a moment, her fingers felt the vibration of a heartbreakingly thready purr.

Hurrying back to the pilot's seat, Yonie admitted to herself the main reason she now wanted the map. LaRue's health had continued to decline. If there was some location with extraordinary healing powers, as the journal had implied, she feared that LaRue might be in need of it very soon.

It wasn't just the map Yonie would regret. She had always loved clever artifacts and marvelous constructions. Sinking the houseboat would be excruciating. But the boat was just too visible, and the wily things had to be put beyond Vedette's grasp.

* * *

Gilbert stormed into the pilothouse. "Yonie, that was Sully's Branch we just went by! 'Ow could you miss it? There was even a sign!"

"I saw it!" Yonie's cheeks were hot. "But there's something wrong with the steering. I just couldn't make the turn."

"I'll believe that when trout fly. We *agreed,* Yonie. Sink 'er as soon as we could. 'Ere, if you can't do it, I will." He shouldered her aside and took the wheel.

Yonie watched with great satisfaction as the houseboat made a 180-degree turn, then glided downstream right past the mouth of Sully's Branch.

"What the sunken 'ell?"

Gilbert's next attempt, heading upstream this time, was just as unsuccessful.

"Must be a funny current, round about there," he mumbled. "Guess we'll 'ave to wait for the next fork."

As soon as Gilbert had slunk away down the stairs, Yonie whipped around on the stool.

"LaRue, that was no current. This boat must be like the *Dragonfly*! There was probably a snag blocking that channel, and the *Moon Princess* didn't want to bash her hull into it. Am I right? I want to be sure before I tell Gilbert."

The cat gazed out unfocused. Finally she croaked, "No."

"Are you sure? It would explain why we haven't crashed into any other boats yet."

"Not — a snag," LaRue rasped. "And not — like the *Dragonfly*." The cat fixed Yonie with a feverish look. "The boat knows, Yonie. Knows — you want to sink him. And he doesn't like it one bit."

CHAPTER THIRTY

L ET ME get this straight, LaRue. You're saying this boat, the *Moon Princess* — she can understand what we're saying?"

"Not *she*." LaRue's panting breaths stirred the orange silk of her paws. "Real name is — *Jack-of-the-Mire*."

Jack-of-the-Mire! Yonie had grown up on stories of that bawdy trickster and his trusty shape-shifting dog, Curly. It made sense that two archaeologists would name their boat after the leading character in Delta mythology — and that Vedette would paint over the name with something more ladylike.

"Felt his wiles—from the first day," LaRue continued in a faraway voice. "Thought it was—crates in the hold." She let out a wheeze that might normally have been a laugh. "The hull, Yonie. The hull itself. Can't imagine—what sort of brew this boat has been swimming in. I've had dreams—" LaRue stopped to cough at length. "He hears us, Yonie. Sees, feels, moves—everything."

"That's hard to believe," Yonie protested. "Even if the boat heard us talking, how would it know that particular fork was Sully's Branch? I went a little way up that other creek earlier, and the boat let me do it. How could it know the difference?"

As soon as the words were out of her mouth, the steering wheel jerked under her hand, and the houseboat spun a tight circle on the smooth brown water of the Skulk. The movement was remarkably nimble and also, Yonie could not help but feel, rather smug.

Yonie yanked her hands off the steering wheel and then cautiously set them back.

"Boat? Er—M'sir Of-the-Mire? Can you hear me?"

The boat swerved sharply to the right, then returned to its original course.

"I'll take that as a yes," Yonie said, a little shakily. "Might I suggest, perhaps, a small twitch to the left or right would be adequate for communication? Starboard for yes, port for no?"

The boat's wheel turned slightly under Yonie's hands, to the right and then back.

"Sir, am I correct in believing that you know the river well?"

A violent yank to the right.

"LaRue," Yonie breathed. "I think I've found the map."

That had to be it. The McKnees had carefully eliminated all records of the way to the hidden lake, *save for that in the boat, which I cannot bring myself to destroy.*

It was the *boat* that Duncan couldn't bear to destroy. And now that Yonie knew the truth, she couldn't imagine destroying it either.

Not it — *him.*

Yonie let out a slightly hysterical snicker. The time Vedette must have wasted, searching for a map that didn't exist! The route to the lake resided solely in the memory of this wondrously wily boat.

Yonie's palms were sweaty. She had been dealing with wily things for years, but this houseboat had to be the most powerful one she'd ever encountered. Now here she was, sitting inside it. And she had threatened its life.

Yonie left the stool and slid onto the bed next to LaRue. She put her lips right up to the cat's ear.

"LaRue," she said in a faint whisper, "what should I do now?"

LaRue's chest rose as she took a scraping breath. "Take care," she said huskily. "Dangerous —"

Then the little cat's body was racked by a series of terrible coughs.

Yonie, her face down near the pillow, sucked in a sharp breath. The dark brown fabric around LaRue's face was flecked with blood — some fresh, some dry. How had she not seen that before?

Yonie rested her hand against LaRue's side, feeling the ribs under the downy fur. The cat had not really answered her question, but Yonie knew exactly what she was going to do.

Gilbert's feet thumped on the stairway, and he burst into the pilothouse.

"Drown it all, Yonie, what do you think you're doing? Running us round in circles, yanking us back and forth!"

"I'm glad you're here, Gilbert. You need to hear this." Yonie resumed her pilot's seat but didn't take the wheel. "M'sir Of-the-Mire," she said clearly, "I have a bargain to offer you. Will you listen?"

Gilbert goggled as the wheel jinked right, then back.

"You're aware that we were planning to sink you. How do you feel about that?"

The wheel swung wildly to the left, and the gentle chug of the engine from the kitchen below increased to a frantic tattoo.

"Left means no," Yonie told Gilbert. He was staring at the steering wheel as if it were a basket of scorpions.

"We will not harm you, sir," she announced loudly.

The houseboat's engine stuttered and then returned to its normal tempo.

"We will not harm you," repeated Yonie, "if you take us with all possible speed to Bonegarden Lake, where my Grand-uncle Duncan's leg was healed during his third C'thovan expedition."

The houseboat's engine fell silent for a moment. Yonie could even hear the sound of Gilbert opening and shutting his mouth several times.

Then the *putt-putt* resumed at a more eager pace, and the paddlewheel churned. The *Jack-of-the-Mire* had accepted the bargain.

Gilbert stared at Yonie with haunted eyes. "We've been living in a—" He pulled in a breath. "'Ow long 'ave you known?"

"I figured it out just before you came in."

"Most people, they'd call this boat an abomination. They'd put a dozen 'oles in it the moment they found out."

"Gilbert, please! He can hear you."

"But you—you're all backwards and upside down! You wanted to sink it before, and now you don't!"

Yonie crossed her arms. "LaRue's getting worse every day. If Bonegarden Lake could fix Duncan's leg, maybe it can help her."

Gilbert scowled. "This boat likely 'ates us now for planning to sink it. And you want to ride it out into the middle of nowhere? For the sake of a sick *cat?*"

"Gilbert, she might die!" It was the first time Yonie had

wholly admitted this to herself. "You can take the *Dragonfly* if you want to go home."

"Aggh! What sort o' fellow do you take me for, anyway? I'm coming with you."

"I don't need your protection!" Yonie yelled. "And I can live without your company!"

"That's not what I meant," said Gilbert, sounding insulted. "You showed me that part in the journal! 'Ow could I just turn tail and go 'ome, and let you go see that lake without me? Like as not, you'd come back and never tell me a thing. You're not the only one in the world to get curious, Yonie DuRoy!"

Yonie gaped.

"So you *are* going to take me. And you just might be glad to 'ave me along."

The Skulk slithered north. The hamlets they docked at were a blur of hastily struck bargains and staring faces as they bartered away Vedette's possessions.

Yonie and Gilbert purchased paint and brushes to obliterate the *Moon Princess* name and face on the boat's side, kerosene for the lantern, lengths of rope for mooring, and a small spyglass to scan for possible pursuit. After that, they stopped only to replenish their food supplies.

Yonie spent most of her hours up in the pilothouse next to LaRue. She read through much of the houseboat's library, desperately gobbling books up before she was forced to sell them.

She learned to tell by the sound of the engine when the boiler needed more water or the stove needed more fuel. Gilbert supplied the firewood, halting the boat when he spotted a dead tree and leaping ashore to hack it apart.

After they passed the mushroom-cap roofs of Gabel Town and chose the sleepy curves of the diminished Skulk over the rush of the Stride, towns grew sparse. On the Berjay Brothers' map, the Skulk vanished altogether, covered by a border of coupons for Rostock & Sons Boat Rentals and a "Family Breakfast Delight" at the Blackmire Inn.

Swamp oaks and thickets gave way to grasslands and then to tall, silent conifers with handsome crows wheeling among their branches. There came a day when they did not pass a town, and then one when they passed no other boat.

That was not to say that there were no signs of settlement. Square edges of foundations showed among the ferny shadows of the trees, and in places the riverbank was unnaturally straight. Hundred-year-old pines clutched slabs of pink stone in their knuckles, revealing glimpses of unfamiliar lettering. They had entered the Shunned Lands.

Yonie was accustomed to the Delta summer, whose weather grew increasingly sticky until dramatic thundershowers brought relief. But here a dreary drizzle persisted for days. Yonie cocooned LaRue in blankets and brought dishes of warm fish broth for her to lap at.

One afternoon the *Jack-of-the-Mire* left the Skulk and turned up an unremarkable fork. The duckweed that coated its surface undulated gently with their passage and closed around the houseboat's wake, leaving a raised seam like a scar. Now they were completely at the mercy of the *Jack*. Since the houseboat ran all night, there was no way they could hope to map every turn.

On the third morning, a sudden lurch shook Yonie awake. She heard a shouted curse from Gilbert downstairs as she staggered up and stared out the front window of the pilothouse.

In the bleak light of an overcast dawn, four pairs of towering stone piers reared out of the river ahead. They had been fashioned in the shape of human arms with fists upraised and clearly had been supports for a bridge, though the bridge itself was long gone. Each arm was a single piece of sculpted stone, with no cracks or mortar, and Yonie wondered if she was seeing her first chiridou relic. She imagined a battalion of ancient C'thovan soldiers marching across the bridge on one of their endless campaigns against the nation of Gry.

Only when Yonie had dressed and hurried down to the bow deck did she understand why the *Jack* had stopped.

"I don't flooding believe it!" Gilbert shouted. Rain had plastered down his black hair and stuck the shirt to his back.

The top part of the bridge had evidently been stone as well, and had remained in large sections even after it collapsed. The river poured smoothly over the edges of the slabs, forming a waterfall about four feet high.

CHAPTER THIRTY-ONE

T HAT PART must not have fallen yet when the McKnees came through," Yonie said in a numb voice.

"Elders!" Gilbert swore. "To come all this way and just 'ave to turn round again and go 'ome —"

"We're not going home."

"Oh, aye? You think you can portage this boat like a sinking canoe?"

"These channels are all knotted together. There's probably an alternate route." Yonie, who had already raised her voice over the rush of the rain and the waterfall, raised it again. "Jack, am I right? Is there a way around?" She and the houseboat were now on a first-name basis.

The *Jack-of-the-Mire* rocked from side to side. Its version of a shrug, she supposed.

"'E isn't a map, Yonie," Gilbert interrupted, in his most irritating I'm-being-patient voice. "'E remembers where 'e's been, that's all. But if we go off that path, 'ow's 'e supposed to know where we'll fetch up? The way these channels wind around, we could go a 'undred miles in the wrong direction before we even know it. Maybe with a compass we'd 'ave a chance, but as it is, we're sunk."

"We can use celestial navigation — there's a book about it in the parlor."

Gilbert lifted his gaze toward the solid gray sky. "If it clears up. But that could take weeks."

"I don't think LaRue has that long," Yonie said in a hollow voice. "I guess I'll have to go on ahead in the *Dragonfly*. The *Jack* can tell me the way — can't you, Jack? I'll write down the directions very carefully. And I'll take plenty of jars, to bring back lake water for LaRue."

"You want to go off in the *canoe?* By yourself?"

"Well, obviously I can't take LaRue — she'd get chilled to the bone! And she's going to need someone to look after her."

"Yonie, you must be out of your sinking mind. I'm not about to let you go off alone through strange country, with 'oo knows what living in it, while I stay 'ere babysitting a cat!"

"Somebody has to go, and I don't hear you volunteering. So much for your being curious to see Bonegarden Lake! That was a complete lie, wasn't it? This whole time, you just came along to protect me!"

"So what if I did? You're doing all this to save your cat. You can't blame me for wanting to save *you*."

"I do *not* need saving!"

"You drowning well do, 'cause you're not thinking straight right now." Gilbert took her by the shoulders and pinned her with an intense brown gaze. "Yonie — *it's just a cat.*"

"Don't you *ever* say that again!" Yonie wrenched her shoulders free from his grip, stumbled backwards, and banged her elbow hard on the rain-streaked brass of the boat-gong.

The sound shivered in Yonie's skull, and suddenly homesickness pressed in around her like rising floodwater. Yonie didn't want to be here, in this gloomy forest with its sharp-needled branches. She didn't want to be in the Shunned Lands, with their sad clutter of ruins and weeping sky.

Standing in her damp clothes with the rain trickling through her hair, Yonie could feel Wicked Ford beckoning her like a warm hearth. Maybe Gilbert was right. Maybe it was time to head home.

She wanted to be back in her city, paddling down to the water market in the sunshine, or admiring the statues along Gleese Avenue, or sitting on her steps of an evening listening to M'sir Shambly's war stories. She wanted to visit Bellflower and bounce along on the sun-speckled walkways, talking history with M'dam Pierpond or laughing with Justine and the others. She wanted to stop in at the Mole-in-'Ole to chat with M'sir Molyneaux, and maybe even give the ruby ale another chance.

But if she turned back now, she would probably have to do every one of those things without the weight of LaRue on her shoulder.

The gong's voice wasn't nearly as persuasive as it had been before LaRue reasoned with it. It offered a homeward suggestion, not a compulsion. And it was a suggestion Yonie intended to ignore.

Yonie would never forget emerging from Bowdown Hall and finding she'd left LaRue behind. That time, she'd gotten her back. This time, if Yonie lost her, it would be forever.

She recalled how the cat had cleverly found her way home in the dark through a maze of unfamiliar streets. *Once I rang it,* LaRue had said, *I could actually feel the garret pulling me like a fish on the line. It was as good as a compass for keeping my bearings.*

Yonie's eyes snapped open wide.

The gong's note still throbbed in her head. And far to the south, Wicked Ford still tugged at her heart. It didn't matter that she couldn't see the sun or stars. The gong would keep her oriented while the *Jack* searched for an alternate route.

Yonie turned to Gilbert, who was also gazing southward with a yearning look. "Gilbert," she said, "remember how you said that with a compass, we'd have a chance?"

It took most of a week to find a way around the waterfall. They were helped by a slim volume entitled *Charting Your Course: A Primer for the Geographically Inept.* Judging by the humorous inscription on the flyleaf and the splashes of wine that had stained several pages, the book had been a joke gift for Duncan McKnee, but alongside the illustrations of comically befuddled sailors, there was genuine navigational advice.

It also didn't hurt that the *Jack-of-the-Mire,* having once traversed a stretch of waterway, could flawlessly retrace its route.

Then one evening the *Jack-of-the-Mire* shimmied like a wet dog, sending Yonie's and Gilbert's dinner plates skating across the kitchen table.

A volley of questions from Yonie determined that they were back in familiar waters, upriver of the fallen bridge and only a day or two from their goal. The houseboat's motion had been a victory dance.

"We did it!" Yonie whooped.

It was going to be all right. Soon LaRue would be eating down in the kitchen with them, lapping up healing lake water along with her dinner.

Gilbert cracked a grin. "Guess now we get to find out what's so special about that lake."

"Gilbert! For a moment there, you almost sounded curious."

His teeth shone white in the midst of his black beard. "A little. I 'ave no idea what to expect. Unless you figured out something else from that journal?"

Yonie shrugged. "There's a Bonegarden Park back in Wicked Ford — probably it used to be 'good garden,' in the Old Language. Nettie might have had that place in mind when she named the lake. But my grand-uncle said the name was ironic."

"Heh. Sounds like we better brace ourselves for a mighty ugly lake."

Early next evening, the *Jack-of-the-Mire* bulled its way through a tunnel roofed with pine boughs and emerged with a flourish onto what looked like a table covered in green felt.

The fetid, weed-choked surface of the lake stretched ahead for some distance before it was broken by a forest of pale stumps. The *Jack-of-the-Mire* slowed as it approached the stumps and coasted to a stop.

Gripping the front railing in both hands, Yonie stared. The "stumps" were white stone pillars, capped with wide, double-domed finials that made them resemble the ends of bones — a vast field of giants' femurs, growing crookedly from a smooth green lawn.

"Sink it! There must be thousands of 'em," Gilbert whispered.

Yonie nodded slowly. "Bonegarden Lake, indeed."

The *Dragonfly*'s bow incised a neat line through the carpet of duckweed as Yonie paddled toward the shallows where the houseboat could not go. If this water had guile enough to cure LaRue, she would not settle for anything less than the strongest, most stagnant sampling she could find. And if that meant going among these ancient monuments, she would do it, no matter how forbidding they looked in the shade of the great dark pines.

She darted a look behind her, where Gilbert was tying up the houseboat along the wooded bank.

Yonie glided into the shadowed water where the nearest row of pillars stood. The bleached stone was incised with a ponderous script, and although the letters were unknown to her, their arrangement, along with the motif of human skulls carved above, confirmed what she had already suspected. This lake was a vast flooded cemetery, unspeakably old.

Wicked Ford had a cemetery—a half-acre of crypts and family mausoleums, with statues of Holy Elders to watch over them. It was as crowded as a storeroom full of boxes, and overgrown with roses and bougainvillea. Every Sun-day it was swarmed with visitors and incense hawkers and itinerant florists.

It was nothing like this desolate lake, with its half-drowned gravestones and its multitude of unremembered dead.

The *Dragonfly*'s bow struck something with a jolt that nearly knocked Yonie off her seat, and for a horrible moment, it was vivid in her mind: how the canoe would overturn, toppling her into the hidden water, how the duckweed would close over her head, leaving only a rippled mark. How she would gasp, and the cold would snake into her lungs —

Yonie sucked in breaths until she felt almost normal again.

She reached down for the glass jar rolling around her feet and shakily dipped up a measure of murky water from the base of the nearest stone. The cloudy gray-green liquid didn't look much like a healing elixir. Flecks of matter swirled in its depths, and it carried the same penetrating odor as the rest of the lake. But if it could help LaRue mend, then Yonie was prepared to call it beautiful.

Yonie padded into the bedroom, holding a bowl of lake water with both hands. She had strained it through one of Vedette's embroidered dishtowels, but even with the specks removed, it did not look terribly wholesome.

The little cat lay on her side, eyes half closed.

"LaRue, we finally made it. To Bonegarden Lake."

Yonie's hands shook slightly as she slid the bowl under LaRue's nose.

The cat's eyes flew open and she recoiled. A hiss escaped her throat, sending her into a paroxysm of coughing. If it hadn't been so unthinkable, Yonie might have believed she heard uncouth words mixed in with the hacking.

She snatched up the bowl. "I'm so sorry. I thought you were awake! It does have a rather strong smell —"

"The smell's the least of it! Take it away, and for mercy's sake, don't get any on your skin." The cat's eyes, already feverishly bright, became slightly unfocused. "That stuff's guile syrup, Yonie," she hissed. "Pure poison."

CHAPTER THIRTY-TWO

"I APOLOGIZE FOR my language," the cat rasped. "But if I'd drunk that water, there'd be something worse than indelicate words coming out of my mouth. You haven't *bathed* in the lake, I hope? No, I can tell you haven't, thank fortune. What about your cousin?"

"There hasn't been time," said Yonie in a small voice. "I went and got the water first thing." Her throat felt tight as she stared down at the bowl of water she had traveled so far to find.

She shivered, thinking of how she had almost capsized the canoe. There had been several more terrifying collisions on the way back before she figured out that each monument had a shorter submerged pillar at its foot. "I did get my hand wet, collecting it," she added.

"Then you need to wash that hand well — don't lick it, use fresh water from the rain barrel and soap. Don't stint. And make sure Gilbert understands too: that water is not to be touched. Bad enough that you're breathing in its vapors, without getting it on your skin and fur! And for goodness' sake, don't even think about washing clothes or dishes with it, or eating any fish you might catch. Or birds, for that matter." The cat sighed and dropped her head back onto the blanket.

Yonie concentrated on not tripping as she went downstairs to dispose of the tainted water. After the jar, bowl, and dishtowel had vanished overboard, and she had made her hands pink with scrubbing, Yonie laid her forehead on the rail of the boat.

She did not like the rapid, heedless way LaRue had spoken, or the way she had referred to Yonie's having fur and catching birds. Had she forgotten that Yonie was not another cat? LaRue was feverish again, worse than before. And yet, Yonie did not doubt her Seeing.

Gilbert hurried up from the bow. "Any luck?"

"It's no use," she forced out. "The water's poison." She gave him a fierce look. "Don't drink it, Gilbert! Don't even touch it! Did you wade in it, when you moored the boat?"

"Nay, I just 'opped across . . . 'Ey, come sit down." Gilbert led Yonie to the bench in the stern.

"I was so sure," Yonie said brokenly. "All this time, I've been telling myself, one sip of lake water and she'd be cured. I dragged you all this way for nothing."

Gilbert awkwardly patted her back. "Yonie. Your kitty cat's still 'anging on." He paused. "And as I recollect, that journal never said anything in particular about drinking the water. Did it?"

Yonie raised her head. "It said that the healing happened at the lake. I just assumed—"

"Well, there you 'ave it. For all we know, your granduncle found some herb or mushroom or such in these woods that fixed 'is leg. 'Oo knows what strange things might grow in a place like this? We can't think about leaving till we've at least 'ad a look ashore."

"Gilbert, I *am* glad you came along." Yonie gave him an impulsive hug before jumping to her feet. "Will you take care of LaRue while I go look?"

Gilbert cleared his throat. "Getting kind of dark," he said gruffly.

The long shadows of the pines had enveloped the entire lake, and the darkness beneath their branches was now impenetrable. The ropes leading from the houseboat's bow and stern vanished into dim sketch marks before they reached the mooring trees.

Reluctantly, Yonie inclined her head. "I'll wait till dawn."

* * *

In the depths of the night, Yonie awoke to the sound of LaRue's voice.

"Dogs," LaRue moaned. "An Under Town of dogs . . ."

LaRue had never talked in her sleep before — it would have been fatal to a slybeast accustomed to napping in public, and even unconscious, she never let that control slip. That she had done so now showed just how sick she was.

Yonie laid a hand against LaRue's back. She hesitated to wake her — what if she cried out, and Gilbert heard? What if he came upstairs to find LaRue raving in a human voice?

Yonie wandered to the windows, rubbing at her eyes.

The waters of Bonegarden Lake did not mirror the moon. They were like black velvet, sequined here and there with water lilies. The funerary monuments were silver shadows against the shore.

The wooden floor felt suddenly cold against Yonie's soles as she saw a distant humped shape sliding through the water.

Gilbert's words came back to her: *Who knows what strange things might grow in a place like this?*

"Gilbert?" Yonie whispered.

The blanket-draped form on the parlor rug did not stir. One muscular shoulder showed in the moonlight next to a tousled head. Yonie hesitated, then pulled the blanket up to cover Gilbert's shoulder before she tapped it. "Gilbert!"

"Mhhm?"

"There's something swimming around, out in the lake. Something big."

Gilbert's face heaved into view, eyes still half shut. "Aw, Yonie. Don't be scared," he mumbled. A warm hand fumbled out of the blanket and patted her randomly on the knee. "I doubt it's big enough to eat the boat. We can bolt the doors, if it'll 'elp you sleep."

"I'm not looking for *comfort*," she said stiffly. "I'm just wondering what it is. Er — would you like to go out on the deck with me to look at it?"

After a short silence, Gilbert said, "Aye, all right. Turn your back."

They stepped out onto the deck, Gilbert now clad in threadbare trousers and a sleeveless, mostly buttoned shirt; she in Vedette's nightgown, which was six inches too short. The night air was cool around them, and if one could ignore the stench of the lake, the moonlit scene had an eerie beauty.

If she had had any change of heart about Gilbert, Yonie suddenly realized, inviting him out here would have been a perfect way to contrive a romantic situation. She knew that this would soon occur to Gilbert as well. If it hadn't already.

Mortified, she hurried to the rail, fervently hoping that the lake monster had not passed out of sight. "There, do you see —"

Gilbert saw. "Yonie, that's no animal, that's a boat."

"I can see *that!* It's closer than it was."

"What's that thing sticking up in the middle? A smokestack? Do steamboats come that small?"

"It could be a small steam launch. I've seen them in Lake Leery."

"Well, it's drifting now. And there's somebody in it, looks like."

"Some secret lake! I thought there was no one for a hundred miles." Yonie squinted. "He's all slumped over," she said, in quite a different voice. "I think he's in trouble."

Gilbert rubbed his head. "Maybe 'e just fell asleep. It 'appens. 'Specially if nothing was biting and 'e brought a bottle along."

"The water's poison, remember? He shouldn't be fishing in it." Already Yonie was hurrying to the bow and swinging herself over the side.

"Sink it, Yonie, it's the middle of the night!"

Yonie's bare feet touched down in the *Dragonfly*. "If there *are* people living around here, they might know about healing plants. Before we go tromping around collecting random weeds, don't you think we should at least ask?"

"What if 'e doesn't want to 'elp? Could be it's a secret lake for a reason. Maybe somebody wants it to stay that way."

"What if he's hurt?" Yonie countered. "Or sick from the water? What if he dies in the night and we could have saved him?"

Gilbert groaned and thunked down onto the rear seat of the canoe. They cast off and soon were dipping their paddles in rhythm, flicking up pats of vegetation as they skimmed toward the dark outline of the strange boat.

"I'll be drowned. You were right, Yonie," Gilbert murmured as they neared the craft. "Look 'ow 'is arm is dragging in the water."

"Hello!" Yonie called gently, as they brought the canoe up alongside the launch. "Are you all right?"

The figure looked up, and the moonlight fell full on a small, startled face. For a moment all Yonie could see was the expression of complete outrage that contorted it.

"Will you *never* be done tormenting me?" Vedette Bruneau howled.

Vedette's face still looked like an elegant version of Mama's, but more gaunt and bleary-eyed than before. Her hair straggled down over the shoulders of a traveling dress that even in the moonlight showed smudges of mud.

"You meddled in my business," Vedette said in a choked voice. "You *stole* my *home*. And you painted over my beautiful *Moon Princess*!"

"At least we didn't try to drown you," Yonie retorted. But Vedette was not listening.

"You sold my most precious possessions! Can you imagine the *pain* it caused me, seeing my New Year's sandals dangling from a *tree?* My best spring frock spread out to dry on a riverbank? You even sold my books! I saw one in the hands of a *fishmonger!*

"*Honestly!* These last two days, after I dismissed my boatman, I thought I would go insane, staring at trails in pond-scum all day and night to track your turnings. And no one to talk to at *all!* The only thing that made it *bearable* was the hope that you were leading me to Uncle's secret lake. Elders only know how you found his map, but that's what you *do,* isn't it? Pry into things that aren't yours!"

Vedette leaned toward Yonie. "And now I'm here at last, and you try to prevent me from healing my poor *hands?*"

Yonie stared at what had been hidden in shadow before. The hand that Vedette had been trailing through the water was pebbled with scales, and its loosely webbed fingers were tipped with thick blunt claws, like those of a mud turtle.

Gilbert let out a strangled sound. Only then did Yonie notice Vedette's other hand, equally scaly, which she had brought up to rest in her lap.

It was holding a pistol.

CHAPTER THIRTY-THREE

Don't stand in my way," Vedette said ominously, raising the barrel of the gun to point at Yonie's frozen face. "Least of all you, young lady, since it was your own mother who did this to me."

"What? You're in —" Just in time, it occurred to Yonie that telling a gun-wielding woman she was insane would not be wise. "In error," she finished. "It's the guile in the lake that's affected your hands."

"But it hasn't." Vedette lifted her turtle claw off the side of the launch and inspected it sadly. "I was hoping the healing would be faster, but I've been soaking them for hours now and they're still the same. Disfigured and ugly, the way they've been for most of my life."

A memory came back to Yonie: Vedette, opening the door of her trim little nailed-down house back in Skulkside, wearing a pair of white gloves.

"I'm so sorry," said Yonie, in a genuine burst of sympathy. "How did it happen?"

Vedette smiled mirthlessly. "Did your mother ever tell you how we used to jiggle open the lock on the staircase door at night and sneak down to the flooded level to play?"

Yonie shook her head. It didn't seem prudent to admit that Mama had never even mentioned Vedette's existence.

"We waded and played find-the-spoon with our toes. The light from our candle stubs looked *so* pretty on the water."

"It does sound pleasant," Yonie said carefully. Vedette's face had taken on a dreamy look, and she had lowered her hand so that the pistol rested on her knee, though it was still pointed in Yonie's direction.

Did the woman actually intend to shoot them? Vedette had proved more than once that she wanted Yonie dead. What else did Yonie know about her? She liked to feel sorry for herself—and she liked to talk, to the extent that a few days of her own company had been a torment to her.

Yonie resolved to be the best audience Vedette had ever had. She hoped Gilbert would do the same. He was so quiet, Vedette seemed to have forgotten he was there.

"As time went on, it got deep enough to swim," Vedette rattled on, "and sometimes we did, though we knew it wasn't at *all* proper. We were careful not to leave anything out of place — the servants sometimes went down there to draw wash-water when the barrels were running low.

"But then Valery spoiled it all. One night a rotten floorboard gave way under her foot, and she got stuck. She wasn't in any danger *whatsoever,* but she started to scream. Even at that age, she had a strong voice."

"What did you do?" Yonie asked, her fascinated tone not entirely feigned.

"Well, I was simply *frantic.* I started diving down and trying to dig her foot free. My poor fingers got all torn up on the splinters, and I swallowed a good deal of water too. All I could think about was stopping that awful screaming.

"It was all for nothing — our parents heard the noise, and when they discovered us, they were *appalled.* They boarded up the stairway, and they punished us both severely. I got a heavier punishment because I was older, which I still think was terribly unfair."

Yonie nodded understandingly.

"I cried for days, and I told Valery I would never forgive her. But I didn't really mean it — not until my hands began to change."

She tilted the gun, casting a hateful look at the scaling on her knuckles and the turtle claws.

"Nothing ever went right for me after that. The other

girls were so *cruel!* The whispering, and the catty little gifts. Gloves and skin creams and *manicure sets.*"

Yonie felt an unwelcome surge of empathy. She remembered Vedette's rambling, back in Wicked Ford, her voice coming down through the trapdoor: *If I can get that kind of power into my hands . . . Delphine and her friends won't be laughing then . . .*

"Mother tried everything — ointments, pumice, a barrel's worth of Aloette's Tincture — but finally she told me that it was hopeless. I would always be flawed.

"It was all Valery's fault. Still, I didn't truly hate her until she took Felix away from me."

"Who?" Yonie croaked.

"Felix DesMaray, the most eligible young man in all of Wicked Ford! He wouldn't give me a single look when Valery was around, even though I was the elder sister. She hadn't even made her debut — it was *shocking!* All he saw was her pretty exterior. If it hadn't been for my hands, I could have shown him the beauty, the *art,* that I have in my soul.

"Of course Mother and Father were *livid* that Valery turned down such a good match. After she left, they started saying she was dead. And I wished it were true."

"Did you make it true, then?" Yonie asked in a hoarse voice. "Did you kill 'er? Are you the one 'oo burned down my 'ouse with my parents inside?"

"No," said Vedette, and Yonie heard true regret in her voice. "Though I do wish I'd been there to watch."

Yonie gripped the sides of the *Dragonfly* so tightly that the muscles in her arms bunched. Otherwise she might have launched herself at Vedette, regardless of the gun.

Vedette went on, oblivious. "I tried to comfort Felix after Valery ran off, but of course she had ruined things for everybody else. Only now has that poor man finally found happiness with another — something *I* seem destined never to do."

"Unless you can cure your hands?" Yonie said, carefully if a little raggedly. "I should warn you, it's not going to happen by dangling them in the lake. The water here's toxic with guile. It'll do you more harm than good."

Vedette looked suspicious.

"I'm sure if you look harder you'll see it for yourself," Yonie said. "I know you must be a pearly —"

"*Please!*" Vedette straightened her spine. "I have a sensitivity to certain *emanations.* I like to think that even before my immersion, I possessed perceptions that others do not."

The sad thing was, there was a shred of truth there, judging from the paintings of Vedette's that Yonie had seen.

"Well, naturally," Yonie managed. "But in any case, the cure can't be the water itself. It must be something affected by the water — probably something growing along the shore."

Vedette narrowed her eyes. "Like what?"

"I wish I knew. Some root, maybe? Believe me, I want to find it just as much as you."

"You couldn't possibly," Vedette sneered. "Look at you! You've got no problems that could *ever* compare to mine."

It showed a lot about Vedette, Yonie thought, that it never occurred to her that Yonie might be trying to heal somebody else.

"You poor thing," Yonie said, trying for the intimate schoolgirl tone she'd heard among Justine and her friends. "Are your hands really that bad? I can barely see them in this light."

Vedette's face glowed from even this imitation kindness. "The nails are the worst," she confided.

The gun lay forgotten in her lap as she reached out both hands to display her clawed fingertips.

Yonie grabbed Vedette's wrists, hollering for Gilbert. He was already diving for the pistol tangled in Vedette's skirts.

"How *dare* you!" Vedette screeched. She twisted her hands, and Yonie felt scaly skin slipping in her grip.

Gilbert came up with the barrel of the gun in his fist just as Vedette managed to free her hands. Shrieking, she scrabbled for the weapon, while Yonie tried to capture her flailing arms. The *Dragonfly* rocked alarmingly. The pistol sploshed into the water between the steam launch and the canoe.

"Look what you've done!" Vedette wailed. "That was Uncle Duncan's! It was *valuable!* Why do you *treat* me this way?"

"You were going to shoot us!" Yonie sputtered.

"I never was! What a crude mind you have. A hole in your canoe would have done *just* as well."

Gilbert picked up his paddle and roughly shoved the *Dragonfly* off from the steam launch. "You keep clear of us," he snarled at Vedette. "Or you'll wish you 'ad."

Yonie glanced back at him. Black whiskers shadowed half his face, and his hair stood up like brambles. His ragged shirt revealed the hard shoulder muscles that came from chopping and hauling wood every day. The knife scar was a ghostly stripe along his forearm. At that moment, he looked every bit as menacing as the surly bargemen in the saloons down at Road-end.

"Don't worry, I've got more important business!" Vedette shrilled as Gilbert backed the canoe away from her. "I'm going to fix my hands. I swear to the Elders of my line, when I go home to Wicked Ford, I will *not* be mocked!"

CHAPTER THIRTY-FOUR

N EXT MORNING, Gilbert braced his elbows on the
bow railing and set the spyglass to his eye. "Your aunt'll
make more trouble for us if she can," he said darkly.

"You think so? She swore to her family's Elders that
she'd keep searching till she cured her hands. That's the
strongest oath there is."

"I 'ave to admit, she does seem busy at the moment."

"What's she up to?" Across the lake on the western
shore, the smokestack of the steam launch gleamed in the
early morning sun, and if Yonie squinted she could see a
small figure moving on the bank.

"Grubbing round in the mud. I guess she figures the cure's a root now. She must put a lot o' stock in your opinion."

"I would hope so! I'm a much better pearly than she is," Yonie lied.

The only genuine pearly on the *Jack-of-the-Mire* was still dozing fitfully on the bed in the pilothouse when Yonie went up. The cat had not taken water in many hours, and it had been over a day since she'd lapped a little broth. In a brief period of lucidity, she'd dismissed the herbs and mushrooms Yonie had collected that dawn as "about as cunning as a bowl of potpourri."

"LaRue, I'm going out again to look for medicine. I'm going farther this time."

The cat did not stir.

Forehead creased so hard it hurt, Yonie hurried down the stairs with her knapsack bumping on her shoulders. As she crossed the deck, Gilbert intercepted her.

"I'm coming too. The search'll go faster with me 'elping," he said firmly.

Yonie wondered if it was safe to leave LaRue alone. What if Vedette showed up at the houseboat? She had hurt LaRue before.

Then again, LaRue would hardly be attacking her this time, and as far as Yonie knew, Vedette had nothing against cats. In fact, most of the plates in her kitchen had kittens painted on them. Leaving LaRue might be a risk, but not finding a cure soon would be a bigger one.

The pine woods around the lake were much like the country they had been chugging through for the past week, floored with ferns and great cushions of moss. Yonie's shoes left bare scrapes as she scrambled over green-carpeted boulders and the flanks of collapsing logs.

Yonie had sent Gilbert off gathering in the opposite direction, but now she was finding the solitude surprisingly oppressive. She looked toward the lake, trying to calm herself. The tiny plants that covered the surface flickered as the rain tapped their leaves.

When she turned back, two strangers were looking down at her.

Yonie's foot skidded, and she almost fell. The men had arrived so silently, it was as if they had materialized out of the gloom beneath the pines. They were big and rugged, with smoke-colored hair and beards bristling out wildly and deep creases on their foreheads and along the sides of their mouths. They wore identical canvas trousers, jackets, and boots.

One of them moved his lips for a moment without speaking, and Yonie realized he was almost incoherent with rage.

"She's been diggin'," he forced out. "There's mud on her hands."

"Just a few roots and things — I'm sorry if—"

The man lunged forward and seized her knapsack. Her braid caught in a buckle as he ripped it off her back, and a clump of her hair tore away.

He fumbled with the pack, seeming baffled by the mechanism. "Open it!" he barked.

Blood pounding, Yonie crouched down and loosened the drawstring. She spilled out hours' worth of collected odds and ends onto the wet ground.

The man looked nonplussed. He stirred the pile with one well-worn boot. "Roots and twigs and such litter? What for?"

"I'm looking for medicine for — for my sister." That sounded better than *my cat*. "I apologize if I'm trespassing, sir — I had no idea anyone lived around here."

The forest men were as tall as DesMaray, and as light-complexioned. Those traits were more common the farther north you went. Could these be actual descendants of the ancient C'thovans? Yonie had been taught that they all perished in the Speckled Plague.

"What're you hopin' to brew up out of this lot?" the second man asked. His harsh voice with its slight accent sounded identical to the first's. Their features, as far as Yonie could tell under the beards, marked them as brothers or even twins.

"I don't know." Yonie swallowed down what would have been a humiliating sob. "But I have to try. She's so ill.

It would take something really powerful to cure her — but maybe I can find it, my grand-uncle Duncan did —"

"Duncan McKnee? He sent you here?" the man demanded.

"Did you know him?" Yonie's eager expression died under the man's fierce look. "No — he's been dead for years, I'm afraid. I only figured out how to get here from a few hints he left behind. But please, sir — do you know how he treated his hurt leg? It might save my sister's life."

"Truth is, we don't much care what happens to your kind," the man said brusquely.

"You do know," Yonie breathed, staring into his face. "You told Duncan your secret — why not me?"

"And now we see how well he kept it," the man's companion growled. "Only one safe way to deal with outsiders." With unexpected speed the big man grabbed Yonie's arm and bent it up behind her.

Yonie screamed in pain, wondering if Gilbert would hear. The two men and a wall of tree roots hemmed her in. Fear throbbed in the very air around her.

And then it eased.

It was as if the rain had suddenly stopped. Yonie was still afraid, but the feeling no longer beat on her from all sides.

The man holding her arm loosened his grip, as though the pressure had lifted from him too.

"What *was* that?" Yonie gasped.

The two men exchanged puzzled looks.

"Leave her," the other man said abruptly. "She doesn't have them, and she's no threat, so long as we don't keep on talkin' to her."

The first man sighed and released Yonie's arm.

"Sirs, please," Yonie appealed, rubbing her shoulder, "if Duncan was your friend, why won't you help me?"

"You could never match what Duncan did for us," the man said with scorn. He pointed to the monument-studded lake glittering between the trees. "Can you read the letters on those gravestones? No traveler ever could, until Duncan. He taught us, and now we can swim down and find our ancestors' names."

Yonie's nape prickled at the thought of anyone submerging themselves voluntarily in Bonegarden Lake.

"So, when you do us a favor that big," the first man said dismissively, "that's when we'll help you with a healin'. Till then, don't waste your time with weeds and berries."

Yonie stumbled after them. "Wait! Is there a town around here? Other people who could help me?"

"There's only us. And we've got more important things to be lookin' for."

The two men vanished into the shadows under the trees. For a few minutes, Yonie tried to follow them, but their woodcraft was astonishing. It was as if they had simply melted away.

Yonie turned back to get her knapsack, and with cold, muddy hands, scraped up her pathetic collection of wilted leaves and squashed berries and mushrooms. They might be completely useless, but they were all she had.

An hour later, drenched with rain and almost drained of hope, Yonie met up with Gilbert and told him about her encounter.

"Let's pick up some deadwood for a fire, and 'ead back to the boat," he urged. "I think we've got enough potatoes left for soup."

When they rounded a curve in the shore, Yonie was grateful to spot the gray outline of the houseboat ahead. Arms full of damp branches, she strode up to the *Jack-of-the-Mire*. She was about to toss the wood onto the bow deck when she stopped short, nearly making Gilbert collide with her.

Incredulously she said, "LaRue?"

The cat was not, as she had for an instant hoped, miraculously cured. Huddled beside the front door, her fur crushed down by the rain, LaRue looked even more pitiful than she had after her night out in the storm. Yonie couldn't imagine what could have induced the cat to leave her warm bed on such a day, even if she hadn't been dreadfully ill. Was she delirious?

Yonie tossed her firewood aside, but before she could

even step up onto the deck, LaRue dragged herself forward and stood there swaying. Her mucus-crusted eyes lingered on Yonie's face, then traveled to Gilbert's.

"You mustn't go in there," LaRue said. Her voice was raw and husky, but completely intelligible.

Behind her, Yonie heard all of Gilbert's firewood cascading to the ground.

CHAPTER THIRTY-FIVE

LARUE'S LEGS were trembling, but she remained upright as she faced Yonie and the stricken Gilbert.

"Vedette's inside," she rasped. "I woke up when she came into the bedroom. I — couldn't move. Too frightened. She went straight to the cupboard and rummaged around. Couldn't see what she took out."

LaRue paused to wheeze for breath.

"She went down to the kitchen, and after a while — I suddenly got my courage back. I came out here to warn you," the cat finished hoarsely.

Yonie shuddered to think of the ordeal it must have

been for LaRue to descend the stairs, much less squeeze through the splintery gap in the door and wait out in the rain.

"Vedette's been trying—to start the engine. I could hear her complaining all the way out here."

The cat's legs buckled under her, and her belly fur stuck to the rain-washed deck. "Yonie, my dear, sweet sister," she choked out, voice barely audible over the whisper of the rain. "Don't trust that woman an inch. Not a whisker. She meant to abandon you both."

"She can talk," Gilbert said blankly.

Yonie hopped across to the deck and scooped LaRue into her arms. "Gilbert, whatever you're thinking, just put it away for later, do you hear me? Vedette's our problem now."

Gilbert passed a hand over his face. He stepped across to the deck, averting his eyes from LaRue. "Think it was another gun she took out of that cupboard?" he managed to say.

"I never saw anything like that in there."

"Aye, but remember 'ow you found that journal? There could be dozens of 'idey-'oles all over the boat. The safest thing to do is wait till after dark. Sneak in while she's asleep and take control."

LaRue was breathing shallowly, and her body felt as light in Yonie's hands as a tiny wicker basket.

"But what if she gets the engine going? Maybe she ran

into those strangers and got scared enough to leave the lake, oath or no oath. And anyway, I don't think LaRue can stand much more cold and wet."

Gilbert's mouth twisted. "You'd risk your life for a sly-beast?"

When Yonie replied, it was in a low, deadly voice. "She's been a better friend to me than you ever were, Gilbert DuRoy. She's loyal and kind and wise. She's saved my life before this, and she might have killed herself just now trying to warn us both. Well, I'm warned. And I'm going in." Yonie set her hand on the doorknob.

"Drown it all," Gilbert burst out. He roughed his hand back through his hair, sending raindrops splattering to the deck. "Maybe I'm crazy as you, but I'm sick of running and 'iding from that ol' crabapple. There's two of us, right? And either one alone could take 'er in a fight."

The parlor was dim, windows streaked with drizzle, and the kitchen door a rectangle of lamplight. Yonie felt a peculiar sense of anticipation as she approached the doorway, LaRue still cradled in her arms. Last time, Vedette had threatened them, true, but she had also been willing — in fact eager — to talk about her younger sister . . .

Perhaps LaRue was right, and Yonie's curiosity really would be the death of her.

Yonie stepped through the kitchen door and blinked in the light from the hanging lantern. Vedette stood by the stove, already turned to face them.

"I *wondered* when you'd be back." Vedette carefully replaced a strand of hair behind her ear, as if the rest of her head were not one huge birds' nest. "I suppose I should say 'make yourselves at home,' but it's *quite* clear you've already done so. I hope you don't *mind* that I've seen fit to enter my own home?"

It was eerie to hear Vedette, who had recently aimed a pistol at them, now using the tones of a hostess who was slightly peeved at tardy guests.

"Can't blame you for getting out of the rain," Gilbert said brusquely. "Taking a break from the search, eh?"

Vedette tittered. "Oh, that's all over with, young man. I'll be going home very soon now."

"You found a cure?" Yonie demanded. Vedette's hands looked unchanged, mud-colored scales rasping against the wicker handle of the teakettle as she adjusted it on the stove.

"No."

Gilbert looked genuinely shocked. "But 'ow about that oath? Don't know about your Elders, but I'd sure 'ate to disappoint mine."

"I never promised them I'd find a *cure*." Vedette gave a giddy smile. "I only said — and I recall this *very* precisely — that when I returned to Wicked Ford, I would not be mocked. And that's true. What I found in those woods will make me more famous than Wycke the Founder and richer than a dozen DesMarays. No one will *dare* ridicule me, ever again."

Vedette rubbed her mud-crusted claws. "And I realized, that's the important thing, isn't it? How they *treat* me. Mother said I was flawed, but maybe, if they treat me right, it doesn't really matter. You see?"

Yonie understood that to Vedette, this was a profound personal epiphany.

"I'll show you my discovery, if you like," Vedette offered. "But first let's get those wet coats off, shall we?"

Gilbert shot Yonie a glance, and she nodded. Disturbed as Vedette was, Yonie could not resist seeing whatever fantastic jewel-encrusted ornament she might have unearthed.

"*That's* the way," Vedette cooed. "Now, do have a seat, both of you. Oh, and the poor little *kitty*, how did she get so wet?" Vedette leaned down to pet LaRue, but then thought better of it. Now that Yonie could see Vedette in good light, she noticed three fresh pink claw scars running down the woman's cheek.

Vedette bustled around, her muddy clothing a spooky contrast to her cheery domesticity. Yonie ended up next to Gilbert on one side of the kitchen table, her hands still protectively laced around LaRue on her lap. Cups of tea steamed in front of them.

While Vedette was replacing the kettle on the stove, Yonie scooted her chair up close to Gilbert's, and whispered, "Don't drink it."

Gilbert gave her an insulted look.

Vedette turned back to face them. "There we are, then

—all cozy." She gave Yonie a just-between-us-girls smile that said she had noticed the shifted chair.

"I found them in a very peculiar part of the woods. I was trying to dig something out, a type of *tuber* — well, it doesn't matter now. But I pulled one up, and there was a hollow place underneath, as big as a washbasin! And inside were *these*."

She reached behind the stove and dragged out the same tin box in which LaRue had traveled between Gilbert's house and Wicked Ford. The box was now draped with a flowered scarf, which Vedette gently lifted away after setting the box on the table.

Nestled on a dishtowel and some sort of fleecy pillow were half a dozen fist-size rocks, lightly furred with moss.

Yonie and Gilbert exchanged looks, and Vedette chuckled at their expressions. "It's some kind of protective camouflage," she said. "Look what happens when they're disturbed." She reached into the box and removed the fleece-covered object.

"Lambie. My old hot-water bottle," she explained. "It calms them *marvelously*." From the way Vedette was holding the object, it seemed to soothe her as well.

Yonie knew from novels what a hot-water bottle was: a flat rubber bag, filled from the kettle and used for warming a bed at night. She had never had such luxuries (or needed them, since LaRue fulfilled that function). This one had a white fleece cover, stubby black-velvet legs, a head with floppy ears, and enormous embroidered eyes.

"Come to think of it, your kitty might appreciate the warmth," Vedette suggested with unexpected thoughtfulness, handing over Lambie. "Now, take a look at my babies. Just *look!*"

As Yonie settled the hot-water bottle onto her lap under LaRue, she saw that the rocks were emitting some sort of vapor. Then she gasped. They were melting, flowing like candle wax into a new configuration. They extruded tiny legs, pushing up and bumbling around after their lost source of warmth. Some of the more enterprising ones grew small blunt heads and nosed inquiringly at the sides of the box.

"Sunken wrecks," said Gilbert, "they look like puppies, almost." Suddenly Yonie couldn't see them any other way.

"Now you see," Vedette said proudly. She settled into the chair across from Yonie. "You see what they are."

"It's — astonishing," Yonie said. Her hands were finally warming up, and she petted LaRue absently as she spoke. "But what are you planning to do, show them? They'll only be killed if you take them back to Wicked Ford."

Vedette gave her a pitying look. "You *don't* see. You think these are *slybeasts,* shaped by guile." She gestured with her scaly hands. "No. They *are* guile. They are" — she dropped her voice dramatically — "chiridou."

There was a moment of silence.

Gilbert snorted. "Magic? My mama taught me not to believe in that kind o' nonsense. These are strange creatures, all right, but they're flesh and blood like us."

Yonie stopped his hand before he could touch the little animals. His fingers were freezing, and she shifted the hot-water bottle over so he could share it. "You're thinking the ancients kept these animals?" she asked Vedette.

"I think their civilization was *built* around them. You see, these creatures can change more than just *themselves*— they can change the things they touch. That burrow where I found them was bare earth, but it was soft as a pillow. And you see how they've already rounded the corners of this box? These are the tools the ancients used when they built the wonders of Gry and C'thova!"

Vedette looked down fondly at the agitated creatures. "Think of when these little ones are older, and they can be *trained.* I'll set whatever price I like for their labor. And of course I'll use them as breeding stock. What do you think the wealthiest people in the world would pay to have a tame chiridou at their heels? Yes, my future's very bright indeed. It's not *everyone* who gets to change the *world.* I'm almost sorry you two won't witness it."

"What d'you mean by that?" Gilbert asked mildly. "I know you would've liked to go off in the 'ouseboat and strand us 'ere, but that'd be 'ard now we're actually aboard."

Vedette scratched absently at a loose scale on her wrist.

"Yes, it's a pity that didn't work out. I already sank the launch, so there's not much chance you would've survived ashore here, with no drinking water for leagues around.

"Unfortunately, the *Moon Princess refuses* to go for me, the naughty thing. She lets out all her steam, or she disengages her gears, or the door of the stove keeps popping open so the fire dies out. Two years I lived here, and I had no *idea* she was so cunning."

"Thank you," Yonie dreamily told the boat. She burrowed her hands under LaRue to get them closer to the warmth of Lambie.

"Oh, *please,* young lady, do you really think the *Princess likes* you? I maintained her and kept her clean for the past two years. I raised her up out of that nasty river. I even redid her *décor.* I'm sure she'd carry *me* if she weren't held back by some silly legal impediment. I do wish they had held the reading someplace else — wily things can be so *literal.*"

Yonie blinked. "What reading?"

"Aunt Nettie's will, of course. We met right out there in the parlor. I suppose the boat must have been *listening.*" Vedette shuddered. "I'll never forget that day. You can't imagine the sense of *betrayal.* That misshapen old woman, with her strange books and her foreign friends — she thought *Valery* deserved her house? Valery had run away; she wasn't even part of the *family* anymore! And Valery already *had* a house, or a *hut* at least. Not like me, still living with the vultures in that corpse of a mansion, with no hope that a husband would *ever* take me away."

The lulling warmth from the hot-water bottle had soaked into Yonie's thighs and hands and was spreading to the rest of her body. She thought about laying her head down on the table for a nap, but what Vedette had just said caused a little prickle of curiosity.

"Wait. You say Nettie left this houseboat to my mother? But — I'm my mother's heir. Doesn't that mean that the boat belongs to me now?"

Vedette sniffed. "In the purely *legal* sense, yes."

"So that's 'ow come you wanted Yonie dead," Gilbert mused without opening his eyes. He had leaned his head against Yonie's shoulder.

Vedette tugged a claw through her snarled hair. "I will admit, when I read in the *Bugle* that someone was claiming to be Valery's daughter — well, I *cried* myself to sleep, thinking she would come and steal my home away. Of course, that fear turned out to be *entirely* justified." She glanced pointedly around the kitchen.

"But that wasn't the *only* reason. I couldn't have her ruining my business, either. I was so good at it — finding the perfect buyer for each piece. I hadn't had a single unhappy customer until *she* came along.

"All in all, it would have been so much *simpler* and *nicer* if Yonetta here had been home in her bed the night of that fire, instead of out canoodling with some local boy —"

Gilbert muttered in protest.

"Oh, was it *you?* If so, you saved her life. For a while, anyway." Vedette sighed. "It's been pleasant chatting with you, but I can see you're both *very* tired. Drink up your tea, now, and we'll get you to bed."

Yonie imagined sinking down onto the thick mattress upstairs. She slid her hands from under the sleeping LaRue, found the now lukewarm teacup, and lifted it until its smooth rim touched her lip.

Then she hesitated. "You didn't brew it with lakewater, did you?" she asked blurrily. "That wouldn't be healthy." She pushed Gilbert's tea out of his fumbling reach.

"Oh, dear. Are you going to be troublesome? It would be so perfect if you would just drink your tea. Then you'd never cause me trouble again, and you would have done it, not I."

Yonie pondered this groggily. "It would be like shooting holes in the *Dragonfly,* so the water would poison us," she said. "Or leaving us here with no boat, so we'd starve."

Vedette inclined her head. "Though I thank my Elders that neither of those happened, or the boat would *never* have recognized me as its legal owner. This way, it can watch as I become Valery's next of kin."

"So." Yonie closed her eyes contemplatively. "When you locked us down in the hold, with the water rising — it would have been the flood that killed us. Not you."

"Exactly."

"What about when we were attacked in my garret in the middle of the night? Was that you?"

"Of course not! I was somewhere else entirely, with witnesses to prove it."

Yonie nodded vaguely, proud to have grasped her aunt's logic. Soon she would be dreaming, upstairs where it was soft and quiet. She would be asleep already, if not for those last little grains of curiosity itching at her like bread crumbs in the bedsheets.

"The kaleidoscope," she said drowsily. "You arranged for an acquaintance of mine to present it to me?"

Vedette shrugged. "At the time I only had your mailing address at that *dreadful* pub, so my man used someone he met there. But I should point out that you put it to your *own* eye, young lady, not I. I wasn't even there to watch."

That last remark bumbled around in Yonie's mind, raising echoes. She had heard something like it before. Out in the middle of Bonegarden Lake under moonlight, when Vedette had spoken of the fire. That terrible fire that had taken Mama's and Papa's lives.

The peaceful warmth suffusing Yonie's body was flushed away by white-hot anger. She discovered the cup of poison tea still in her hands and swept it off the table to explode against the black iron door of the stove. The baby chiridou cowered and curled themselves tighter. Gilbert's head rolled off her shoulder and landed on the tabletop with a thump.

"I asked you before if you killed my parents," Yonie said in a high, strange voice. "You said no. And I believed you."

She slid sideways off her chair, shifting LaRue's weight and the hot-water bottle down to the seat as she stood. Immediately her mind felt clearer.

"I was telling the truth," Vedette squeaked.

"You believe that, don't you? You might have *hired* the arsonists, but you weren't there yourself, so *you* didn't do it!" Yonie was shouting now. "And it's all right to give poison to Gilbert and me, so long as we drink it ourselves. Even if you use a wily thing to lull us into doing it!"

Yonie scooped LaRue off of Lambie and deposited the cat on Gilbert's lap. Then she snatched up the hot-water bottle and strode to the stove. The tranquilizing effect had spread up as far as her wrist by the time she banged open the stove door and flung the thing onto the coals.

"You *can't!*" Vedette wailed, clutching at Yonie's arm. "I've had Lambie since I was *two!*"

Yonie slammed the stove shut and rounded on Vedette. "What were you going to do if we didn't drink the tea? Wait till we were asleep and stab us? No, too direct. Push us over the rail, maybe? That way it would be the water that killed us, right?"

A hideous smell of scorched wool began to drift through the room. Vedette edged toward the door, but Yonie seized her shoulders. "Be honest with yourself, for once in your life!" she cried. "Did you kill my mama and papa? Did they die screaming because o' *you?*"

"It wasn't *me!*" wept Vedette. "It was Maxime Scarmouche and a couple of his boys. I can get you their names, I promise! I wasn't even *there!*"

Yonie slammed Vedette down onto the table, narrowly missing the chiridou box. She held her pinned with one arm while she reached for Gilbert's untouched tea. Vedette scrabbled at Yonie's arm with her claws.

"If I pry your mouth open and pour this tea in, what will 'ave killed you?" Yonie sobbed. "The *force of gravity?* Or me, Vedette? I want it to be me."

CHAPTER THIRTY-SIX

THE TEACUP wobbled over Vedette's face. The woman's eyes were dribbling tears, and her mouth gaped open in terrified, panting breaths.

Yonie leaned her whole weight on her parents' murderer. It would take good aim to pour the tea just right . . .

Behind Yonie the stove door creaked open, and a gout of black smoke rolled into the room, reeking of burnt rubber. Yonie coughed and blinked. She set the teacup down on the table, feeling ill.

Her aunt made such an unsatisfactory villain, with her snippy voice and her respectable white-trimmed navy dress.

She didn't have a sinister appearance at all — just an abominably low regard for lives other than her own. So this was what a real murderer looked like.

And Yonie had been only moments away from becoming one herself.

"Thank you, Jack," Yonie whispered. She flung the contents of the teacup into the billowing mouth of the stove.

Gilbert lifted his head. "Urgh, what's that stink?"

"It doesn't matter," Yonie said wretchedly. "Help me hold on to Vedette, here. She just confessed to killing my parents."

Yonie took a deep breath, which usually helped her muster her thoughts, but in this case only made her gag from the smoke. "We need to take her back to Wicked Ford," she finally got out. "To be judged. I can't do it myself."

Gilbert secured Vedette to a chair while Yonie opened the windows and back door. The fire had gone out after it burned a hole in the hot-water bottle, causing it to gush its contents, but a vile smell still hung in the air.

Yonie used the poker to hook out the charred mass of Lambie. She took it outside and watched it disappear into the lake. No doubt it had spent years being filled with guile-water from the sunken level of the Bruneau house.

Yonie wiped angrily at her eyes. Killing Vedette would not have brought her parents back. And even if it had, they would have been ashamed of her.

* * *

"This rope is prickly," Vedette said plaintively. "The scarf I put over the chiridou box would be *much* more suitable."

"You killed your own kin for the sake of a boat," Gilbert told her roughly. "You don't get to be comfortable."

"Not a boat, a *house!* A place of my own. Was that so much to ask? And it wasn't me, anyway."

"Listen." Gilbert's voice rasped like a knife being sharpened. "You've caused Yonie and me more grief than I can say. Yonie wants to take you 'ome, where a judge might or might not 'ave enough evidence to send you down the High Road. I admire 'er for it. If I was in 'er place, I don't know if I'd 'ave the courage."

Gilbert touched Vedette lightly on the cheek, and she shrank back. "A convict's brand isn't much, for what you've done. It'll be 'alfway to a scar by the time you walk free on the Coast. If you're willing to work ship's crew, maybe someday you'll even get to a place where they can't read the word *murder* on your face.

"Till then, though, people are going to despise you, and no one more than Yonie and me. Every day on our trip back, we'll 'ave to be guarding you and feeding you and taking you to the privy. It'll be a load o' work, and every moment, we're going to be thinking, is it worth it?" He paused. "Wouldn't it be so much *simpler* and *nicer* if you just 'appened to slip over the side?"

Gilbert's voice had become a growl. "Don't make us think that way, Vedette. I loved my aunt and uncle too."

Vedette's mouth moved as if to say "I won't," but no sound came out.

Yonie felt afraid too, though not of Gilbert. The fear she'd felt earlier in the woods was back, pressing in around her like the air before a storm. On the table, the little animals were trembling in their box.

"Gilbert," Yonie said. She gestured him outside and faced him on the stern deck, cradling LaRue in her arms. "Those puppies, or chiridou, or whatever they are? They're terrified — and they're sharing it with us."

"I can feel it," Gilbert admitted uneasily. "That Lambie thing must've been soothing them down before."

Yonie remembered the moment in the woods earlier that day when the tension suddenly eased. "Yes, I think I even felt the moment Vedette put it in with them. Those men I met felt it too." She paused. "Gilbert, that has to be what they were searching for! These little creatures! That's why they opened my pack. The last C'thovans, looking after the last chiridou!"

"I don't know, Yonie. If the critters are really so useful, why would those men be living out 'ere in the wilderness? They could go live like kings anywhere they pleased."

"That's what Vedette was thinking. But she was wrong. She never could have kept control of them herself — every government on the Continent would be scrabbling to get one. Think what kind of weapons they could be, in the wrong hands. The C'thovans are right to keep them a secret.

If Vedette had taken them out into the world, it could have started the wars of the ancients all over again."

Gilbert was giving Yonie a very peculiar look. "Elders, do you 'ear what you're saying? If you're right — you might 'ave just saved our 'ole civilization."

Yonie looked down at the cat lying unconscious in her arms.

"Sink that," she said fiercely. "I want to save LaRue."

Vedette went first, her hands tied in front of her with a tail of rope leading back to Gilbert. Yonie followed, carrying the little chiridou in the bottom of her knapsack. She hoped the more peaceful impression she was receiving from them meant that they were cozy, not woozy from lack of air.

LaRue was nestled inside her blouse, cradled above her belt. Yonie hadn't carried her that way since she was a kitten, but that was less for reasons of size than of dignity (both Yonie's and LaRue's). The cat still had not woken.

Bringing back stolen chiridou would count as a big favor to the C'thovans, Yonie repeated to herself. It had to.

Vedette led Yonie and Gilbert around the side of the lake that they had not yet explored. She stopped beside two firs tilted together in an upside-down V.

"It was somewhere around here," she announced.

As Yonie ducked between the leaning trees, she got the impression of entering a darkened room. Great shaggy boulders loomed from the earth like squat pillars, and the massive tree trunks were banded with shelf fungus that reminded Yonie of the spiral stairs in the Bellflower library.

"How much farther?" Yonie asked.

"I don't know if I can find their exact *burrow*," Vedette said testily. "Is it really so important?"

"I need to return them to their owners," Yonie snapped. She shouldered past Vedette to take the lead. "Hello?" she called loudly.

Somehow she'd imagined that as soon as they found the right stretch of woods, the C'thovans would reappear, overwhelmed with gratitude, to reclaim the chiridou pups.

Still, she yelped when a burly gray-haired man suddenly stepped out in front of her.

Thank the Elders — it was one of the twins she'd met that morning.

"Good afternoon, sir," Yonie said eagerly. "I'm so glad to have found you. I hope you remember the favor we discussed?"

The man stared at her warily. "I don't know who you are, or what you're talkin' about."

"I brought them back, you see?" Yonie set her knapsack gently on a hummock of moss and let the six rocky lumps spill out. "They're completely unharmed. I know they must be valuable —"

The C'thovan let out an incoherent cry and bent to gather the creatures into his arms. Yonie felt a flash of joy from the pups, which receded into a cloud of comfort and safety.

Then Vedette's voice broke the peace.

"Sir, you have to help me!" she squawked. "These people are thieves and kidnappers! They're keeping me *prisoner!*"

The man clutched the chiridou pups tighter. "Kidnappers?" he hissed. He looked at Yonie. "Is that true? Did you rip these babies out of their nest?"

"Yonie," Gilbert said urgently, coming up beside her. He pointed to a boulder that was smoking like a wet deck in the sun. As Yonie stared, it rocked ponderously and raised itself up onto two rough legs. Around the grove, dozens of blocky forms were stirring. The air filled with the smell of disturbed soil as they shook clods from their feet and stomped toward the gathered humans.

"Wrecks," Gilbert breathed. "I never thought we'd meet the adult chiridou."

"They'll tear us apart!" wailed Vedette. She rounded on the C'thovan man. "You're their master — do something!"

The man's eyes blazed with contempt. "We are our own masters," he spat back.

The advancing chiridou rippled, trailing streamers of mist as they shrugged themselves into more human outlines. The nearest one, Yonie noticed, now closely resembled a man.

A burly, grizzled man, identical to the "twins" Yonie had met in the woods that morning. Just like the man who stood before them now, cradling the chiridou pups in his arms.

Yonie had made a terrible mistake. There were no C'thovans left — no descendants of an ancient people who might give a reward for the return of their lost animals.

There were only these monstrosities who, like the Apple Sharer of Yonie's childhood nightmares, could look like anything — anything at all. And they believed that Yonie had stolen their young.

CHAPTER THIRTY-SEVEN

Mᴏʀᴇ ᴘᴀʟᴇ-sᴋɪɴɴᴇᴅ, bearded figures crowded into the grove. There were woman shapes, too: shrewd-looking ladies with Yonie's coloring and streaks of gray in their brown hair.

The chiridou had taken the shapes of Duncan and Nettie, Yonie realized. Probably those were the only humans they'd ever met before today.

Under other circumstances, Yonie would have treasured this glimpse of her late relatives, but the creatures were shrieking their rage. And as the circle of chiridou tightened, the ground was melting away beneath her feet. They were sinking into the mud, just like the Bruneaus' old rotting house.

"Flooding 'ell, they're trying to bury us," Gilbert shouted. While Vedette screamed and Gilbert cursed, Yonie frantically extricated LaRue from the front of her blouse. If she threw the cat over the wall of chiridou, could LaRue land on her feet and run away?

But the wasted body lay slack in her hands.

Miserably, Yonie accepted that this was all her own fault. She had doomed herself, and Gilbert, and (less regrettably) Vedette, with her far-fetched scheme for saving LaRue's life.

The last thing Yonie heard before the ooze covered her face was Vedette screeching, "It's not fair!"

A seamed face peered down at Yonie, rippled and cloudy as if seen through half a fathom of river water. "You again, granddaughter? I would 'ave thought it'd be scores o' years more before you took my 'ook."

Yonie moved her mouth soundlessly, but the old woman seemed to understand. "Will I be a-dipping you up in my net today, 'long with these others? Don't know as I've decided yet, but one thing's sure. You can't be a-putting their fate onto your own account. You've been honest, and you've done your best. Keep doing that, and be proud o' yourself. That's what one o' my finest little fishes told me."

She was speaking of Papa, Yonie realized.

Granny Pitchers's face wrinkled up into a smile, then blurred and greened as Yonie sank deeper into the water, down until she could see nothing but darkness.

Yonie sputtered and blinked. She was buried waist-deep in a wide subterranean cavern, still holding LaRue in her arms. She struggled to kick free, but the mud held her fast. Greenish-white light from patches on the walls revealed Gilbert and Vedette nearby, similarly immobilized.

"It's not fair," Vedette wailed again.

A Nettie shape stalked toward the humans and confronted Vedette.

"You've asked for justice," it bit out. "We will not deny it, even to such as you. I am chief magistrate, and I will judge — after we have the truth."

Vedette's lips quivered. "How *dare* you question *my* honesty, while you pretend to be my dear Aunt Nettie!"

"Our true form is lost — thanks to your kind," the chiridou said in a voice as thin and sharp as a needle. "Now. Explain to me how you came to hold six of our young captive in your sack."

"We were trying to return them," Yonie blurted. "At least, Gilbert and I were."

"Vedette's the one 'oo took them in the first place," Gilbert put in.

The chiridou swung its gaze to Vedette.

"Why? Were you hunting for food?"

"Gracious, no! I wanted to take them *home* with me. To train them and start a breeding population. I would have been *famous!* I would have changed the *world.*"

The magistrate sighed. "It would have been far better if you had wanted only meat. But you have given us your truth, so we will give you ours." It faced the group.

"The legends say that long ago, fifty of our people were on pilgrimage when something happened. There are hundreds of stories to explain it, but all we know is that the world changed around them and left them in this limbo where we still drift—nebulous, able to touch everything and nothing, unable to find our way home.

"We wandered, lost and bewildered. Our true form slid and warped around us, and not even the earth was firm beneath our feet. By the time your forebears found us, we were malleable in mind as well as body, and the humans made us their dogs. They bred us for shaping skill and mindless loyalty. They forbade us our true form until it was forgotten. As time went on, we shaped their roads and bridges and fortresses and made their soldiers into monstrous things. We were their factories and their war machines, and it was centuries till we got free."

Vedette broke. "You *killed* them!" she shrieked. "There *was* no Speckled Plague, was there? You rose up against the C'thovans and the Gry, and you *slaughtered* them *all!*"

"We did not," the magistrate said harshly. "We *could* not. When our captors bred loyalty into us, they succeeded all too well. In those days, we died of sorrow when our owners died and were buried at the foot of their graves."

Yonie remembered the shorter, submerged tombstones in the lake, and LaRue's fever dream: *an Under Town of dogs.*

All at once, Yonie understood the origin of guile. The strange half-alive substance that permeated the Devil's Foot and changed whatever it touched was the last dissolved particles of those ancient shape-shifting chiridou, still loyally trying to help their human masters.

"When the plague came," the magistrate continued, "it mowed the Breeders down. And though we didn't sicken, most of us died of grief. We here are the descendants of the least loyal, the few who would not die."

It stared at Vedette. "Understand this, you who would be a Breeder," it said forcefully. "We live free now — as wolves, not dogs. We will not see our children tamed again."

The magistrate examined Vedette with cold eyes. "You take for yourself, but offer nothing," it judged. "You are worthless. I see no reason to let you live."

Vedette gave a wordless, gull-like cry.

Yonie's pulse pounded. In the deep corners of her heart, she was glad. Vedette dead! And since they were completely in the chiridou's power, no one could blame Yonie. *She* would not have done it.

Then she shivered. That inner voice had sounded exactly like Vedette.

Yonie opened her mouth, and out came the words "*That's* not true."

Vedette and Gilbert stared.

"Vedette does have some worth," Yonie said stoutly. "She's a gifted artist, for one thing."

"You're questioning my verdict?" the magistrate said disbelievingly. "You, a little earthworm wriggled from the Southern muck?"

Yonie raised her chin. "I'm Yonie Watereye, and I'm from Wicked Ford, the finest city on the Skulk, gateway to the North *and* the South —"

"Enough!"

Yonie closed her mouth. There was silence.

When the magistrate finally spoke, there was great gravity in its voice.

"It is a shame to waste a shaper's talent. But this one would have enslaved our kits and brought invaders to our home." Its eyes closed into slits. "Her spirit is distorted. She's done great harm, and we will not let her do more."

Before Vedette could do more than moan, she sank through the cavern floor and vanished from sight.

The chiridou judge addressed Yonie and Gilbert. "You have committed no crime," it pronounced. "We will not hold you here. We require only that you keep our people and our lake a secret, and that you never return."

The floor oozed slowly upward under Yonie, boosting her toward the ceiling, and she slumped in relief.

Then her hands tightened on a small feline body.

The chiridou were letting them go. Wouldn't it be insane to ask them for more?

But they valued justice. And truth.

"Wait!" Yonie shouted to the judge. "I talked to two of you this morning. They said that if I could ever do your people a favor as big as what Duncan did, you would help with a healing.

"Well, Gilbert and I just rescued six of your children from a Breeder and saved the secret of this lake. That's a pretty big favor, if you ask me. So will you keep your promise?"

The floor stopped moving.

"'As mutable as our bodies, so immutable is our law,'" the magistrate recited after a moment. Yonie guessed that it had sounded better in the original language. "The bargain stands. And it seems that we must also repay your companion." It tipped its head toward Gilbert. "His body seems healthy. Perhaps we must dig deeper?"

Gilbert's hands clawed at his sides. His eyes stared out blindly, as if he were having a terrifying vision.

"Aha," the chiridou told him. "I see a fear that we can remedy. We offer you the freedom of the land, to walk where you will without dread. Do you accept?"

Gilbert looked stunned, and Yonie wished she knew what he had seen. "Aye, I'm no fool," he stammered. "Thank you, ma'am."

The chiridou turned to Yonie, and for a terrible moment, she felt the choking rush of water into her lungs. "You also have a fear we can remove," it observed. "We offer you the freedom of the deep, to swim where you will without dread. Do you accept?"

Yonie imagined slipping into cool water on a steamy summer day. She pictured nights of peaceful sleep, with no nightmares of drowning.

Then she found her voice. "Ma'am, that's a very considerate thought. But there's something I would value more." She leaned forward and laid LaRue's limp body on the cavern floor. "I'm not even sure she's still alive, but if she is, can you heal her? Please, if there's any chance — please."

CHAPTER THIRTY-EIGHT

Yonie opened her eyes slowly. She was lying on the forest floor, sunlight dazzling through the branches above, dead pine needles pricking her cheek.

A few fuzzy minutes later, she felt awake enough to sit up.

Her hands were empty.

Yonie's heart contracted painfully.

Then she heard a scrabbling in the branches overhead and caught a glimpse of a puffy ginger tail.

"LaRue!" she yelled.

The cat slid backwards down the tree trunk, skillfully braking with her claws, and sashayed into Yonie's arms.

Yonie swept LaRue up and held her close, running her hand over and over the cat's back. LaRue was terribly thin, but her breath went smoothly in and out with the pulse of her purr, and her eyes were bright.

"They did it," Yonie said softly. "The chiridou really did heal you. I was so scared. I was sure I'd lost you."

"Chiridou? Yonie, dearest, whatever do you mean?"

Yonie loosened her grip. "They're amazing creatures, LaRue! The ancients kept them as slaves. Or dogs, they said. You know, I bet the old stories about Jack-of-the-Mire and Curly Dog are really folk memories! Think how Curly Dog can change shape, and he's so insanely loyal to Jack —"

LaRue put out a paw to halt the tumble of words. "Merciful waters! You'll have to tell me everything from the beginning, I'm afraid. My recall of events ends shortly after I warned you about Vedette." The cat looked around. "I hope she's nowhere near."

"She's over there," Gilbert said somberly as he approached. "Before we go back to the boat — the decent thing to do —"

Yonie followed his gaze to the mossy hollow where Vedette's body lay, as limp as the rope that still trailed from her bound wrists. Her spirits sank.

"We'll need to go back anyway, for a shovel," Yonie said, trying to keep her voice level. "Should we put up a grave marker?" And if so, she thought emptily, what on earth should the words on it say?

She walked slowly over and stared down at Vedette's face. Without tension pinching it tight, it looked less lined and even more like her sister Valery's.

Yonie remembered the evening she had first met Vedette, and how eager she had been to get to know her aunt. She thought of the delicate, evocative paintings hanging on the wall of the houseboat. She closed her eyes and mourned for what might have been, if Vedette had not been what she was.

"Are you crying?"

Yonie nearly fell over backwards. Vedette had opened her eyes and was regarding Yonie with interest.

"What's your name?" Vedette scrunched up her face. "I can't remember *mine,* but I bet I'll get it pretty soon." She sat up, with absolutely no regard for the modest disposition of her skirt, and looked curiously at the rope around her wrists. "Wow, how did I get these huge knots?" She yawned without covering her mouth. "Are you crying 'cause you're hungry? I'm *so* starving, it's making my tummy hurt."

Yonie couldn't think of what to say. The person before her still looked like a woman in her midthirties, but Yonie had the sense that she was speaking with a small child.

The chiridou hadn't executed Vedette, after all. But neither had they left her whole.

* * *

By the next afternoon, only a few clouds still cast patches of shadow across the plush green surface of Bonegarden Lake. Yonie walked around to the stern deck of the *Jack-of-the-Mire,* where Gilbert was washing wood shavings off of his arms with soap and rainwater, and LaRue was washing for what looked like no reason at all.

Along the side of the house, some two dozen empty crates were stacked for future kindling, as well as a single crate half full of the artifacts that LaRue had declared intriguing enough to be "keepers." Behind the houseboat, dozens of breaks in the duckweed cover showed where Gilbert had jettisoned the wily cargo.

"That's it, right, LaRue?" Gilbert said, giving the cat a wary but respectful glance. His antipathy toward slybeasts was eroding under the barrage of LaRue's charm. He had also been gratified to learn that his first instincts about Yonie's pearly skills had been correct.

"Yes, we're all done, thanks to your help," LaRue purred. "Yonie, how's the boat?"

"The boiler's up and the fire's stoked." She raised her voice slightly. "Jack? Anytime you want!"

The houseboat turned eagerly from its position in the center of the lake, and performed a swift, cocky circle before putt-putting in the direction of the shady outlet that led toward home.

Yonie had been trying not to stare as Gilbert shook the last of the wash-water off of his arms. "Er." She cleared her throat. "So how's that test going? You know, the 'freedom of the land'?"

"Not a trace of a rash," Gilbert reported with almost religious awe. He held out one arm, displaying freshly scrubbed brown skin. "It's been twenty-four hours now, and I rubbed the leaves in pretty 'ard. I think those chiridou did it, Yonie. They made me scourge-oak-proof! 'Oo knows, when I get 'ome, I could be the first person to set foot on Evil Island!"

To one raised in the Sloughs, where scourge oak made much of the land entirely impassable, immunity to it seemed only slightly less magical than the power to fly.

Yonie glanced out over the hidden waters of the lake. The disabling fear that kept her from swimming was intact, but she couldn't find in herself even a sliver of regret for giving up the freedom of the deep. Someday she would conquer that fear herself, and in the meantime, she had LaRue.

"'Ow's Renee doing?" Gilbert inquired. They had all agreed that, given her transformation, Vedette needed a new name.

"I got her set up with an easel on the bow deck. She's doing sketches of the shoreline." Yonie leaned back on the sun-warmed railing. "It's so strange — get her started on art, and she's got more vocabulary than I do. She knows art history, techniques — the chiridou seem to have left her everything they could in that respect. But in other ways, she really is like a child. A child with amnesia."

"She can talk, and dress 'erself, and take care of 'er private matters, which is a blessing," Gilbert said. "I reckon the chiridou were trying to push 'er back to before she started to go sour."

"Before that incident in the bottom of the house, I suppose. Though I notice they left her the claws."

"Makes sense to me. You told them she was an artist. They weren't about to fool with 'er 'ands. 'Ey, I 'ope she doesn't 'ave trouble drawing, now the *Jack*'s underway."

"You sound awfully concerned about her," Yonie said with an edge to her voice. "The same woman who —"

"Nay!" Gilbert shushed her. "She's a 'ole new person, Yonie. You 'ave to believe that."

"I'm trying to." Yonie's feelings toward Renee were more ambivalent than Gilbert's, due (Yonie assumed) to her more suspicious nature. "She's very different, anyway," she allowed. "You should have seen her face light up when I pulled out the art supplies. She even gave me a hug. I'm not looking forward to telling her about her past."

"Then don't," LaRue broke in, switching her tail. "She doesn't need to know a single thing about Vedette Bruneau."

"She has parents —"

"'Oo she did murder to get away from. Seems like the chiridou did 'er a favor taking those memories away."

"I'm just trying to think about her best interests."

"Think about her safety, then," LaRue said darkly. "Vedette had some very unsavory associates. In my opinion, we should alter Renee's appearance as much as we can before we get back to the city."

Yonie thought that with the self-conscious mannerisms gone and her hair pulled back in a simple fox tail, Renee hardly resembled her old self.

"It's a good thing she was in the habit of wearing gloves, so her hands won't give her away," LaRue went on. "Even so, the less contact she has with her old life, the better."

"I guess she could stay at my 'ouse for a while," Gilbert said dubiously.

"Gilbert, darling, it's sweet of you to offer," LaRue told him, "but you must see that would be inappropriate! Obviously she'll stay with Yonie and me."

"I suppose so," Yonie said. "Though there's not much room in the garret."

"My sweet, you're forgetting."

"Oh!" Yonie shot a glance down the length of the boat. She was still not accustomed to regarding the *Jack-of-the-Mire* as her own.

The *Jack* chugged cheerfully south, past the undeciphered monuments and uncharted forests of the Shunned Lands, past the bustling river port of Gabel Town, past the sleepy, peculiar little settlements along the banks of the Skulk.

One day, Yonie promised herself, she would travel northward up the Stride to visit more exotic lands. But for now, it was enough to let the curves of the Skulk and the tensions of the last few months unwind behind her like a coiled spring loosening as she drew closer and closer to her home.

Wicked Ford, full of neighbors and new friends, clients and intriguing strangers and dubious family. Her city, whose odd corners and hidden depths she had only begun to explore.

CHAPTER THIRTY-NINE

I HAVEN'T TAKEN a student for many years, if that's
what you're thinking," August Bassompierre told Yonie.
The kindly old artist's studio was in even greater disarray
than when Yonie had visited to inquire about the locket.
Unwashed dishes stood piled in a basin, and unwashed
laundry overflowed a basket.

"Not a student, sir, an assistant. Someone to help you
keep house, and get your meals, and run errands for you.
Renee could do all that."

Renee's childlike personality, as Yonie had discovered on the trip downriver, coexisted with unimpaired

organizational skills, and Yonie had no doubt that she could greatly improve the artist's day-to-day life.

Renee smiled hopefully up at Bassompierre. She was dressed modestly in a secondhand blouse and a gingham skirt she and Yonie had constructed out of the houseboat's tablecloth. Her brown hair was pulled back in a thick tail tied with pink yarn.

"I'd be happy to clean these dishes for you, sir," she offered. "Where's your water barrel?"

Bassompierre directed Renee up the outside stairs and returned to talk with Yonie. "Your cousin, you said? I can see the resemblance."

"Yes — Renee DelFosse." Yonie had equipped Renee with a surname, the second most common in the Delta, and a nonexistent home village called Five Foxes.

Renee herself now believed all this to be true. She had been highly impressionable in the weeks following her chiridou memory-surgery, and had even picked up an overlay of bayou accent from Gilbert (and from Yonie, who had taken pains to speak bayou around her). Renee now came across as a bayou native trying hard to sound cultured, which Yonie hoped would further protect her from being recognized.

"How long has she been guile-touched?" Bassompierre asked quietly. He had shaken Renee's scaled hand without hesitation, though he seemed bemused by the way her stubby claws were neatly enameled in rose pink.

"Since childhood. But she just lost her parents recently, in the flood," Yonie lied.

Bassompierre shook his head. "Poor soul. Does she remember much about what happened?"

"It seems to be a bit of a blur, thank the Elders. But there's really no village left for her to go back to."

Renee returned with a jug of water and set to scrubbing some crusted plates, humming cheerfully as she worked.

"Doesn't let those hands hold her back, does she?" Bassompierre murmured approvingly.

While Yonie and Bassompierre chatted, Renee finished washing the dishes and went on to expertly clean half a dozen brushes with turpentine, causing Bassompierre to twitch his bristly gray eyebrows.

By the time Renee left the studio, she had a job.

Three days later, Bassompierre took her out sketching.

The week after that, he started introducing her to his friends as "my brilliant new protégée."

"Yonie honey, I missed you!" M'dam Pierpond bustled out from behind her desk and squeezed Yonie somewhat painfully against the large buttons on her rose-colored blouse. "Now, where have you been keeping yourself?" Yonie wondered if the librarian might give the same scolding welcome to an egregiously overdue book upon its return. "You never even told me if you found your grand-aunt."

"Unfortunately, she passed away a couple of years ago,"

Yonie said when she'd gotten her breath back. "But I did find an aunt I'd never met before."

"Oh, I'm so glad I could help — that must have been a real treat."

"It was — er — quite an experience. I ended up taking a long trip on her houseboat."

"I look forward to hearing all about it," Pierpond declared.

"And I look forward to telling you. I'll be seeing you more often from now on." Yonie smiled shyly. "I've been given a scholarship to Bellflower."

In a somewhat embarrassing quiz session, Felix Des-Maray had determined that although Yonie was advanced enough in music and literature for him to secure her admission, she had a lot of catching up to do in mathematics and the sciences (and what he called the social graces, though Yonie was not especially looking forward to that part of the curriculum). He had also suggested diffidently that they meet once a week to discuss her progress.

"That's marvelous, honey!" Pierpond boomed, startling a nearby group of students. "And entirely merited, I must say. Well, well. I daresay your friend Justine will be delighted."

"You mean it?" Justine squealed. Her hair, brushed as black and shining as a well-kept skillet, was braided in a sophisticated fishtail style that suggested her mother had returned from Sinister Bend.

"Yes, from the DesMaray Foundation," Yonie confirmed. "I'll be starting at the beginning of the new term. With a beret and everything."

"I can't wait!" Justine threw her arms around Yonie again, causing the walkway to jounce alarmingly beneath them. "We have so much to catch up on. I'm sure you've been having all sorts of adventures!"

Giving Justine a full account was out of the question. Luckily, Justine was skilled at squeezing every drop of melodrama from the rinds Yonie gave her. She went into raptures over Yonie's summer trip on her aunt's houseboat, without knowing that Yonie had narrowly escaped death at her aunt's hands. She enjoyed hearing about Cousin Gilbert's woodcarving and fishing expertise, without knowing of his attraction to Yonie. And she was entranced by Yonie's descriptions of distant towns like Far Dumpling, Selbyville, and Peppernose, though she never heard about Bonegarden Lake or the chiridou.

"It sounds ever so relaxing," Justine sighed blissfully. "Are you still staying on the houseboat?"

"There isn't much choice — the landlady rented out my garret while I was away."

"Oh, no! What about your things?"

"Taken over by the new tenants. They weren't keen on giving anything back." Yonie hadn't had the heart to force the issue as she stood hunched in that cramped space, deafened by the cries of a tiny baby. "I did manage to trade them a bushel of old newspapers for the rest of my books. They were glad enough—said newspaper would burn a good sight better than the books ever had."

Justine looked horrified.

"There wasn't much to lose," Yonie soothed her, "and I love living aboard the *Jack*. Though I get the feeling Renee's itching to move closer to the studio. She's getting more independent all the time."

Justine's face creased faintly. "That's wonderful, of course." She had nearly wept on hearing Renee's manufactured history. "But, Yonie, if she moves out, will that be quite proper? I mean, Gilbert's still there, isn't he? I know he's your cousin, but he *is* a boy."

"I'm taking him home tomorrow, in any case," Yonie said with a casual shrug.

"Oh. Will you miss him?"

Yonie shrugged again.

Justine, who had absorbed all of Yonie's earlier prevarications without question, gave her a keen-eyed look. "Yonie! Are you blushing?"

"Of course not! Why would I?"

"Is Gilbert good-looking?"

"Justine!"

The other girl giggled. "It's probably a good thing he's leaving, cousin or not," she said.

* * *

Justine was right, Yonie thought as she sat down to dinner across from Gilbert. He had visited a barber that day, and the fresh haircut and sharply outlined goatee made him seem almost like a stranger. It felt highly uncomfortable to wonder whether Justine would consider Gilbert good-looking and whether it was indeed unseemly for them to be sharing the same dwelling.

Thank goodness LaRue was sitting with them, ensconced on the table where Renee's plate normally would be. And tonight, with Renee invited out to a gallery opening, the cat would not have to hold her tongue.

LaRue's coat was thick and glossy. After a few ravenous weeks, she had gained back her lost weight and returned to her usual mealtime daintiness. Once Gilbert had said his usual brief, sincere grace to the Elders, LaRue bent her head to her own plate and took a delicate bite of her fish.

"Ah, Yonie, you've outdone yourself again," the cat proclaimed. "Positively ambrosial! I do appreciate the dill and the squeeze of lemon, though many cats would not."

"Too bad it's store-bought," Gilbert said. Upon their return to Wicked Ford, they had found the *Jack-of-the-Mire*'s previous mooring spot taken and had settled for an open space in the less desirable southern part of Skulkside. Sadly, it was too close to Lake Leery to trust the fish.

"You'll be back in the Sloughs soon enough, Gilbert, dear," LaRue consoled him, "with all the fresh fish you can catch."

"And more fresh game than ever, now I can trap any-where I want," said Gilbert, still awestruck by his resistance to scourge oak.

LaRue bolted down her dinner like a starving stray as Yonie stared in disbelief. "Delicious," the cat pronounced with a hasty paw-swipe at her face. "I hope you'll pardon me if I excuse myself? It's been a tiring day." She dropped smoothly from the table and vanished up the stairs.

"How do you like that?" Yonie exclaimed. "Her first chance in months for some dinner conversation, and she throws it away!"

Gilbert snorted. "Yonie. She's giving us some privacy to say goodbye."

"Oh, for mercy's sake. What more do we have to say to each other?"

"You're back to using your city voice," Gilbert noted regretfully.

"I was only talking bayou for Renee, to help her pick it up."

"If you'd do it for Renee's sake, would you do it for mine?"

There was a pause.

"Aye, I reckon I could this one time, just to make you 'appy," Yonie said grudgingly.

Gilbert gave her an admiring look. "Sink it, but that's fine 'ow you do that. Not that I don't like your 'oity-toity voice, too, Yonie."

"My *what?*"

"I like 'em both just fine," Gilbert said in a rush. "In fact, I like most everything about you, Yonie."

"Gilbert. Please don't."

"I 'ave to! Tomorrow we're going to get in the *Dragonfly* — with LaRue, I ought to mention — and we'll be hours going down to Charwater to see Gustave and Lydie and my mama. And if Lydie's 'ad 'er baby yet, which I reckon she might've by now, there'll be 'oo knows 'ow many other friends and relatives dropping by, and 'ugging you till you bruise, and asking you about the city. We'll 'ave to lie about lots of things, and we won't 'ave any time alone together at all. And I just don't think I can stand it if we don't get things settled between us first."

"What sort 'o things?" Yonie said nervously.

Gilbert reached across the table and laid his hand atop Yonie's. His hard palm rasped against her knuckles, and his fingers felt warm.

"Remember when we were down in the 'old of this boat, thinking we were going to die, and I asked you if you could ever forgive me for 'ow I treated you, growing up? You said 'not yet.' Well, now we've been through things I can 'ardly believe and saved each other's lives I've lost count of 'ow many times, and I'm wondering if your answer's any different."

Yonie found herself unable to draw her hand away.

"I don't think I can ever forgive that spiteful little boy

'oo was so cruel to me," she said in a low voice. "I can never get rid o' those memories." Then she raised her head and met his eyes. "But you're not that boy anymore, Gilbert. Maybe I can learn to think of you as a 'ole different person. If I can do it for Renee, could be I can manage it for you."

"But you're still my cousin, aren't you," he said wistfully.

Yonie looked across at Gilbert, with his firm jaw and broad shoulders and all the strength and steadiness that was part of him. Gilbert, who had against all her expectations become a real friend.

What would happen if she said, "Gilbert, I found out we're not actually blood kin?"

Then she could walk around the table and pull him into an embrace . . .

And then what would happen? Could they court? Could they marry someday? How would Aunt Elisa and the other cousins feel about it? Or would Yonie even be able to call them that anymore?

Why did family have to be so complicated?

Yonie remembered LaRue's voice saying tenderly, "Yonie, my dear, sweet sister . . ."

Yonie had a cat for a sister. That was incontestable. And Papa was obviously her father — not Felix DesMaray, no matter what blood they shared or how well-meaning he might be. Family meant far more than just heredity.

"Yes, Gilbert, I'm your cousin," Yonie affirmed. "And what's more — I'm proud to be."

Gilbert rapidly blinked his eyes, which, Yonie noticed, were the exact same brown as Papa's. "Thank you," he said gruffly.

And that was all.

"Darling, of course I was listening!" LaRue exclaimed, curling up on the bedspread next to Yonie. "You know very well I don't possess that level of self-control. And I thought it was entirely possible that my services as chaperone might have been required."

"LaRue, really!"

"Well, Gilbert's a handsome enough fellow when he's cleaned up, and devoted to you, to boot. But there's more than one fish in the river, as they say, so let me simply repeat: I'm proud of you for making a decision. Now you can get on with your life, and so can he."

Yonie lay back, resting her head on her arms. With LaRue's purr vibrating against her side, she thought about the future. Perhaps she would be one of the (still regrettably few) women admitted to the University. She could follow in the footsteps of the McKnees, as a historian and explorer. Or she could be a confidential investigator, using her research skills and LaRue's more arcane talents. She could be a renowned antique dealer, or even the first scientist to properly study guile.

"How about you, LaRue? What do you want to do? In the future, I mean?"

"My goodness, I should think that would be obvious," LaRue said with a self-assured fluff of her tail. "I'm a cat, after all! I shall continue to indulge my curiosity."

Yonie let out her breath and smiled.

"You and me both, LaRue."